pieces of a story

Kymberle Joseph

ISBN: 978-0-9778698-0-0
           09778698-0-6
copyright: ©2004
website: www.kymberle.com
email: kym@kymberle.com

pieces of a story

Jamual my dearest son, you are the greatest!
Thank you for telling me I can do it, even
when I didn't feel that way. Never stop
dreaming! One day all of your dreams will
come through. Love you more than slice bread.

Mom

Acknowledgements

My dear sisters – Tracy, you have always been my constant source of inspiration. God knew what he was doing when he blessed me with you as a sister. You're a wonderful spirit and worthy of the great blessings coming your way. Love you much! Heather Ann – You are the greatest. Thank you for your constant admiration, support and love. I love you sister! Ieasha – When we met eight years ago, we clicked instantly. We had our ups and downs, but our ups have always prevailed. Thank you for being the best friend a girl can ask for. J.P. – Seventeen years and we are still great friends. Thank you for always being available at just the right time. So what if it's always 7am! Luv ya! Lex – I love you totally. Thank you for stopping everything and listening when I need an ear. And cursing me out, when I need to be put in my place. W4L!!! Susan Mary Malone (my editor) – Thank you for your wisdom and expertise. For believing in my story, as well as believing in me. You took my scattered manuscript and turned it into something. I am forever grateful. Tawana – Thanks for being my driving buddy physically and emotionaly. You are the best! Luv ya! Simone – Thanks for being my proofreader, even if I was a constant pest. Thanks to the "girls". Thank you for all of our Thursday night dinners. Love all of you deeply. To my Verizon family – Marilyn, Delisha, Carmen, Kenny, Carlyn, Duane, Nunci, Mark E., Trudy, A.J. and Adrina (if I forgot anyone I'm truly sorry). Thanks guys for making my eight years at VZ, full of wonderful, wonderful memories. I love all of you guys! Felipe Coronado thanks for the great cover. Verna- Continue to believe in yourself. Your time to shine is coming! Thank you Edwards for putting up with my crap. Luv Ya! Mom and Dad thank you for teaching me to be the best I can be. To my brother I love you. Milanjali – Thank you for helping me become the woman I am today. Through all of my scruffiness you saw a diamond. You made me work meticulously until I saw and believed in that diamond. I am forever grateful and appreciative of all the work you have done.

To those I may have forgotten, understand I love each and everyone of you guys and I am forever grateful for all of your constant support and love. I couldn't have done this without all of you.

8   pieces of a story

His heartbeat was that of the Trinidadian steel band players.

It's thumping was a resonant sound heard on Labor Day, for the West-Indian Caribbean day parade.

His valve like drumsticks, drummed pulsating beats

Steadily drumming slow at first then beating faster more intense.

I imagined the scantily dressed carnival dancers,

Shuffling Afro-Caribbean movements, to his steel pan like heartbeat.

Grooving, swaying hips, side to side to his music.

I wanted to dance to his music, laying there on his chest, listening to the peppery music it was playing.

Rhythmically his heart was talking to me.

His heart was telling me to trust in it, to trust in him.

Together they would never hurt me.

Identical to a garden snake, I slithered my way up his chest.

I stopped when conjoined hearts were created.

It forced us to drum the same beat whether we desired to or not.

We were in harmony at one point in our relationship.

We sang the same melody, harmonizing on key.

His alto picked up where my soprano trailed off.

He never missed a beat in our two-part harmony love song.

Our voices blended together like Tammi and Marvin.

For months we sang the greatest hits.

Then one day I began to sing off key.

Chapter 1

"Does that feel good, baby?" His slender arm reached from behind my tiny little waist rubbing my flat chest.

"I don't like this. Where is my mommy?" I cried.

"Why baby? We're playing. Yuh're Kathy baby doll and I'm her friend Ken. We're playing house."

"I want mommy."

"Yuh have me. We don't need mommy. She doesn't like to play our fun games." Repulsively his tongue licked my neck. My back palm wiped my snot away.

"Move yuh hips. Yuh tease me all day long with your lil nighties. I know yuh have a nice booty move it for me. Make me happy. Make daddy happy."

"I don't want to make daddy happy! I want my mommy! Where's my mommy? Please get my mommy!"

My eyes burst open, focusing on the dust balls taking refugee on the ceiling fan, while absorbing the blare of the busy morning streets. Fighting hard to forget the ugly images I dreamt. A new day in New

York City was beginning.

Below my sixth floor window two-inch heels, rubber soles, leather uppers with man-made soles were scurrying horizontally and vertically to their designated mode of transport. I craved the energy that controlled the streets.

Shaking off my thoughts, I wiggled out of bed and schlepped to the bathroom. A cool breeze from the open window peeking from underneath the bedroom curtain spanked my naked body.

I stayed in the shower longer than usual, not only to allow my tears to intertwine with the water sprayed from the showerhead, but so Dupri could sleep a bit longer.

He was probably as exhausted as I felt. Not once did he budge from his fetal-like position. Searching through my lingerie drawers, I slid into my undergarments, slipped on my slippers and ran downstairs.

I made a quick detour into the den, turned on the morning radio program, before making my way to the kitchen. Still no movement upstairs. Twenty-three minutes extra he's been asleep. It was important to me we have a sit-down breakfast our first day back to work after our vacation and after our fight the night before.

"Dupri," I screamed up the stairs. I walked around the tiled island in the middle of the kitchen, turning on the flame underneath the kettle. It's generally filled from the night before, one less thing for me to do in the morning. I screamed again with a higher pitched voice filled with aggression, "Dupri!" Still no response.

On my tippy toes, I stretched over the stainless-steel sink filled with last nights cocoa mugs, opening the bamboo roaming shades to lure in the morning sun. Reluctantly I over lathered my favorite mug with Palmolive and washed it along with the others. My patience meter was descending lower.

Resting my back against the cold sink with the early morning sun kissing my cheeks, I looked down at my timeworn slippers, trying to make heads or tails of last night's events.

He said everything was cool. But was that his defense mechanism to move past the situation? His eyes told me he was trying but his cracked voice said he was a millisecond away from losing it, taking that ultimate plunge over the edge.

Last night was supposed to be a relaxing dinner at his sister's followed by a romantic evening at home. He envisioned *"Soul Food"*

ending with *"Love and Basketball"* instead he got *"War of the Roses."*
Our connected hearts had begun to divide.

Through the foyer of his sister's place, the pungent aroma of what
was hidden in the pots escorted us to the dining room. His sister, always
generous when we come back from vacation, made us a welcome-
home feast. She constantly loses herself in the jungle of her kitchen.
She cut, peeled, diced, minced and spiced from early in the morning.
Her ice tea was sweetened to perfection. Her plantains were fried right.
The rice was light and fluffy, accompanied with jerk chicken. The
chicken tasted as if it were indeed made in Kingston; sheer perfection.
Not too hot or too mild. And how can I forget, those steamed-to-the-
right-texture of crispiness vegetables. Her *Julia Childs* skill with a
Caribbean twist guaranteed an enjoyable meal every time.

He loved when his sister cooked for him. He explained once that's
how she declares her love for him. He attacked his meal, like most
meals he doesn't eat in a restaurant, with out utensils. Dupri used his
hands, saying he was paying homage to his Ethiopian brothers and
sisters. He showed his sister he loved her cooking by engulfing more
than one plate. Last night was no different. Dupri ate and belched
three times.

Food was Dupri's ecstasy pill. It caused him to act and behave
sexually erratic. In our car ride home along the FDR drive southbound,
I continuously slapped his hand off of me.

"Dupri," I said frustrated.

"What?" he asked with a mischievous grin. I stopped his hand
from moving any further up my inner thighs.

"You know how I get after a good meal," he boasted, placing his
huge hands back in the same position.

"You are going to get us killed if you don't keep both hands on the
steering wheel."

"Relax, woman. I've been a card holder of a NYS driver's license
forever."

"I'm sorry if I can't relax when you a have one hand up my thigh
and the other rubbing my cheek." Using his knee to steady the vehicle.

"I'm just preparing myself for what's about to go down when we
get home. It's been a while." His baritone murmured.

"Yeah," I responded hoping he would decrease his speed. I wasn't

in as much of a hurry, as he was.

The toilet seat slammed open against the tank. "I'm up! I'm up! I'm going into the shower."

Finally, he has risen from the dead. "What do you want for breakfast?" I waited a few for an answer, but none came; instead the shower started and the toilet bowl flushed. I prayed he used the Lysol right next to the toilet bowl. He somehow conveniently never saw it.

I settled on Belgian waffles, turkey bacon, and tea for breakfast. Plugging in the professional waffle maker, my thoughts strayed again. Night just couldn't seem to free my mind.

Salaciously he guided his hand over my body in search of the new world. With directness and skill he massaged my vagina, never once removing his lips from my inner neck. "I love you," He faintly whispered. I attempted to mouth those identical words, but nothing came out. His lips journeyed below my waist.

Dupri widen my legs provocatively with his tongue. His fingers and tongue were dancing in my vagina. One was doing the meringue while the other did a slow salsa. He removed his fingers, leaving his partner to finish the dance solo. He stretched his hand to my mouth and motioned for me to suck my own juices off his fingers.

Wasn't this every woman's dream, to grow up and have a man love us mind, body, and soul? Here I was in bed with a darling of a man, making love to my body hoping it would lead to my heart, and all I wanted to do was scream. I had no desire in wanting to please my man. Forget about what Mama told us about keeping them happy in the bedroom. I wished like hell he'd get up and leave me the fuck alone. If there was ever a time I wanted a sporting event to be on television, it was now. Superbowl, All-Star game, Hockey any damn thing, right about now.

He was still down there working overtime to bring me to complete pleasure. His tongue continued its solo. He'd taken his fingers from my mouth and had since taken pleasure in my breasts.

In the beginning of our sexual adventure, I planned on laying there and faking an orgasm. Through the past couple of months I had become a pro at it. I learned the art of it from watching "When Harry Met Sally" on numerous dateless Saturday nights. But something came over me at that moment; I was tired of faking it. I raised his head from my vagina and removed his hands from my hardened nipples.

"What?" he asked perplexed and annoyed. "Was I too rough?"

"No, No not at all, I am just__."

"Just what?" He rose off the bed.

"I'm just tired from jet lag and stuff."

"And *stuff*?" He barked with his eyebrows in a frown, cracking his knuckles. "I don't know what the fuck and stuff means? What I do know is that I went on vacation with my lady and engaged in no sexual activity. Say it again with me, *no sexual activity.*"

His dismay was a long time coming. I knew better than to answer when he was pissed. His boxer briefs were now on. He started pacing the bedroom floor back and forth, caressing his thick goatee.

"It was jet lag in St. John also. Jet lag the whole fucking trip. You should have that shit tattooed on you, *Jet Lag* along your left breast. The fucked-up shit is, we didn't even go overseas, woman. St. John is a U.S. Virgin islands."

Oops, I fucked that up now didn't I?

"You're using that shit so fucking much, you ain't even sure when is the best time to use it or not. I'm tired of the excuses. It's either you have an headache or your stressed. Shit, I have a fucking headache and I am tired; tired of your ass right about now." He stopped pacing and stared at me until his words made a permanent imprint in my being. I focused on the carpet stains.

"I'm trying, woman. Not sure how much longer my patience is going to hold up. I'm getting the feeling that you don't want to be in this anymore. You don't want *ME* anymore."

His voice was beginning to shake. He was beginning to lose his masculinity. He was fighting hard not to tap into the side many men don't want to reveal exists within. My inconsistencies were causing him to unravel at the seams. I had to help him hold onto the last bit of masculinity he had left. I had never seen him this fragile.

"Don't ever think that, Dupri." Naked and scared I turned his face to mine. His gaze greeted me with desperation. "I love you. I do want to make love to you, but you know how stressed I get right before it's time to go back to work."

"Well, wasn't that the reason for a vacation? To loosen the stress? Huh wasn't it?" My gaze darted around the room running profusely from his. He came closer turning my chin to meet his pleading eyes.

"Look at me. If I knew it wasn't going to work I could have kept my money." He sat on the edge of the bed, popping back up as quickly as he sat down, giving his rant a break.

"Damn woman, your continuously telling me you love me, I believe you love me, but you're not behaving like a woman that loves her man. You and I both have demanding careers. St. John's was a time to pull away from all of that. You were busy working this summer, and then you trekked to Italy with your sister. We barely saw each other. When I come in you run out or go fast to sleep. Woman, what the fuck is going on?" I rubbed my left thumb alongside his chiseled cheek tracing his faint childhood scar.

"I miss you; I need you, all of you," Grabbing my palm from his face, he sweetly kissed its insides.

"You have me, Dupri, all of me."

"Then make me feel like it. Make me feel like you love me. Make me feel like I am your man. Make me feel like I'm not losing the one thing that means the world to me."

Clutching his hand, I guided him back to the bed. Laying him down before slithering my way up to his chest, snuggling the covers all around us. Lightly I stroked his forearm, while he hugged me.

"I'm sorry I've been hurting you. I promise I'll do better by you."

"Woman, I'm trying to be patient, but I lose it at times. I need my woman back. My woman! The woman I fell in love with. Not that imposter that rears her ugly head from time to time. I wanted that woman in St. John's and in the bed just a few moments ago, that's the only woman I want." Dupri seductively allowed his five-o-clock shadow to gently skim my bronzed cheek.

"You have that woman. I'm still that woman."

"No you're not. That woman is somewhere else. I said no matter what I'm going to be by your side so I'm going to stay true to my words. I'll just continue to be patient."

Now his size thirteen feet interrupted my thoughts, making their way down the stairs. Finally out the shower and dressed he was.

Bending down to my level he gave me a good morning kiss. Fragrance sprayed on men as they enter the department stores combined with Dove Moisture seeped through his pores. His scent used to intoxicate me as I came within inches of him. I inhaled his smell, this

morning, smiling at his picture-perfect statuette. He chose black slacks and a tailored wine shirt with a matching tie.

"How are you this morning?" I asked, pausing at the foot of the steps straightening his tie.

"I'm good, just hungry as hell." He pulled out the barstool.

"Then eat." I laughed. When wasn't he hungry?

"Don't forget we have dinner reservations tonight, Miss Lady." He took a bite of his waffle, this time using utensils. I headed up the stairs.

"You didn't forget, did you?"

"No, I didn't forget." I lied. Lawd knows with everything I was dealing with, dinner was the last thing on my mind.

"Be home no later than 6:45pm. Our reservations are for 8pm. The hostess said if we are even five minutes late, she was giving our reservations away to a walk in."

"That's harsh."

"Yeah it is, but that's their policy. We can't change it. All we can do is show up on time. We are going to the upper Westside, so don't be late." He stated wolfing down his breakfast. "What time are you going to be finished with your appointment?"

"I should be done by 6pm."

"That's cutting it close. Do you want me to call the restaurant and push back our reserved time?"

"No!" I screamed pulling on my pantyhose.

"It's okay if you do, I wouldn't get annoyed. I just want to insure we don't lose our spot. Reservations have been tight since they've open."

"Okay, okay, I'll be there on time. Don't worry about it, babe."

"Good, do you want me to wait for you? I'm almost ready to head out the door?"

"No Dupri, I'll drive myself." I bellowed back, having finally gotten on my three quarter-sleeved black knit dress. I pulled out my black knee-high boots with the thin white stripe and matching bag from the closet to complete the outfit.

I heard him place the dishes in the sink and open the cabinet to retrieve his daily vitamins. He probably was drinking ginger ale instead of orange juice. As much bottled water, soymilk, herbal teas, and natural

fruit juices I bought, he always needed his soda.

"Baby, I'm leaving. Have a great day and a good session with the shrink." He chuckled heading out the front door. He knew the shrink terminology drove me insane.

"She's not a shrink. She's my therapist. Get it right, ding bat."

"You can call her a fancy name, but to me she is a shrink!" he yelled back laughing.

Dear Book,

Auntie Cookie said I should name you Dear Diary, but I like book better. You are a book anyway. She said mommy told her I write everywhere. She gave me you, so I'll have someplace else to write. Also so I don't get a beating. I hope I never get another beating again. Last night hurt a lot. I didn't even do nufing. I never do nufing. Mommy listens to him not me. If she did she would know I didn't do nufing. He said I was evedroping. When they were in the liveroom. I was not. They never shut up. Kathy and I were trying to sleep. We have a tea party with Beatrice in the morning. They were so loud. Stop. George go George. I like that George! I wish mommy and George stop so I can sleep.

Bye book

Chapter 2

My past was just that, my past. A bad dream I never wanted to admit existed. I promised myself never to share the intimate details of those nightmarish acts with anyone. However today I was going back on that pledge. My healer would be the first to hear about my haunted past. It was time for the truth to be unveiled.

She sat with her notepad and pen in hand. She poured me a fresh glass of water once I was seated. I gazed into her hazel eyes and knew it was time to share my secrets.

Beatrice, the retarded seventeen-year-old I used to play with, was a distinctive fixture in the corner of the plastic-covered pink tapestry love seat. On most days you could catch her aimlessly staring out the window or at the thirteen-inch television with the foiled hanger antennae. When she stood, her unbalanced frame was an even five-foot nine inches tall. Due to her mental disability she needed assistance when standing. She walked like a toddler taking steps for the first time. Sometimes a walker was needed for support.

Beatrice had big, bright, brown eyes. Her shoulder-length golden locks perfectly matched her caramel complexion, afflicted with mild acne. Even with her disability and her acne, Beatrice was beautiful. She would give any runway model a run for her money. My mother

said once that she was a waste of a beautiful woman.

Her mother tried to make sure she fit in with her sister, often styling their hair alike in two thick ponytails. Though Beatrice couldn't tell the difference, it was important for her mother.

Drooling and weird noises were common whenever Beatrice saw me; that was one of her many ways of greeting me. In her non-speaking state one could feel her smile. We sat in her mother's living room and watched the black-and-white television. They lived upstairs from me. Beatrice's mother was my babysitter while my mom went to work. I didn't mind playing with Beatrice: she was the only one who seemed to enjoy my company.

Beatrice's face would light up like the Christmas tree in Rockefeller Center. Her squeals of hysteria when I entered the room were thrilling. I was her savior and she was mine. On the outside we appeared quite different; on the inside we were very much the same.

Perched at the living room window, I watched my mother and her new husband leave our Brooklyn two-family brick home. In the scorching heat they headed off, hand-in-hand to their prospective jobs. I gazed longingly as they walked down the tree-lined streets until their shadows became a distant memory. They always looked so happy together when I wasn't around. I *hated* seeing them together. Turning quickly, trying to forget the images I saw, I ran up the stairs swiftly. My Beatrice was waiting for me.

The tantalizing aroma of brown sugar, fresh cinnamon and nutmeg filled the air. Mrs. Hawkins' straight from the oven fresh-baked sweet bread always made my tummy growl.

As usual Mrs. Hawkins left the main door to her apartment wide open for me. As I'd done for many mornings prior, I ran straight into the sweet-smelling kitchen, gave Mrs. Hawkins a hug, making sure to say good morning. Staying in the kitchen while Beatrice and I played in the living room, she responded with a resounding, "Good Morning" which was attached to a smile that was as warm as her baked treats.

Mrs. Hawkins was a forty-six-year-old widow with four children: Daniel, Joshua, Shelley, and Beatrice. Beatrice was the eldest and also the only one who had a disability. The doctors never gave Mrs. Hawkins a concrete reason as to why Beatrice was mentally challenged. Many years later, my mother told me that these things happen sometimes. God gave the world extraordinary people she said.

Mr. Hawkins had been dead for five years, leaving behind his wife of twenty years and four children. His death, at forty-two years old, was caused by a massive heart attack on the way to work. His Pillsbury doughboy figure aided to his demise. Mr. Hawkins tried for years to lose weight, but he continued to devour his wife's succulent pastries.

Before the death of her husband, Mrs. Hawkins was a stay-at-home mom; after the death of her husband she continued to be a stay-at-home. Her means of supporting her family were her husband's insurance money and Beatrice's disability checks. Many felt Mrs. Hawkins should have gotten a real job and stopped using the system. But she believed that her children needed her more than any corporation. Her children were her responsibility. Especially Beatrice.

As a proud West Indian woman who resembled Della Reese with a tall prominent stature, thick gray hair, and rare deep gray eyes to match, a mentally retarded child was taboo. Mrs. Hawkins worked in her sleep to shield Beatrice from the world. Before his death, Mr. Hawkins pleaded with his wife to enroll Beatrice in a day-school program for people with special needs. He knew the importance of having Beatrice around others like herself. But Mrs. Hawkins didn't trust anyone; she felt they would harm her unique daughter.

The day of Mr. Hawkins' funeral, Mrs. Hawkins put her pride behind her and honored her husband's request. She gave Beatrice the chance to live since her husband died. She introduced the world to her other daughter. After much research, Beatrice became a student at a reputable day school on the upper east side of Manhattan, months later.

Beatrice's eyes, wild with excitement, were glued to Tom and Jerry as usual when I walked into the living room that day. She had no conceptual idea of what was going on in the television or anything else for that matter. She laughed when I laughed, jumped when I jumped, and clapped when I clapped. That crazy cat and mouse team had us in a fiery frenzy. We loved to watch that cartoon.

During our Tom and Jerry moments, Beatrice and I would play games. She wasn't aware she was playing games or that a game was actually being played. Her seventeen-year-old womanly body had a brain of a four-month-old. Her diminished cognitive abilities allowed me to do any and everything to her.

We didn't play hide and seek, for Beatrice wouldn't be able to understand a game of that magnitude. Operation, Connect Four, Hop

Scotch, and Double Dutch were out of the question also. At the time, I thought they were boring. I wanted to play a more exciting game.

We sat in the brown paneled living room with the singsong chimes singing to us when the only open window invited the wind. I remember the onset of restlessness setting in as the *Toucan Sam* left the television screen, soon followed by a commercial for one of Bruce Lee's Saturday afternoon movies. Mrs. Hawkins was still in the living room. That day, for some odd reason, she kept coming in and checking up on us more than usual.

"Mrs. Hawkins, do you think you can make me something to eat? I'm getting pretty hungry," I asked, hoping she would leave us alone.

"Sure baby, in a minute. Beatrice was not feeling well last night. I just want make sure she is okay." She placed the back of her hand on Beatrice's forehead. "It seems like she feels a little cooler than last night. I'll go make you a peanut butter and jelly sandwich with some apple juice. Would you like that?"

"Yes. Thank you. Can I have some sweet bread also?" I asked in my sweetest voice.

"Of course, love, but go wash your hands first."

My smile covered my tiny little face. Finally Mrs. Hawkins was going to leave us alone so we could play our game. As I walked back toward the bathroom the phone rang. Mrs. Hawkins let out a huge sigh as she rose from the plastic-protected loveseat. "I'm coming!" she shouted to the other party that couldn't hear her. The phone rang at the same time everyday for Mrs. Hawkins; she stayed on it until my mother came home. The ringing of the phone meant Mrs. Hawkins wasn't going to check on us anymore!

I put my then pre-school hands underneath Beatrice's shirt and felt her thick bra. Lifting the bra cups slightly I took out her breasts. I squeezed them firmly, then softly. Beatrice grunted when I touched them. I grunted also, making sure my grunt matched hers while continuing to massage her marshmallowy breasts, similar to the marshmallows in my Nestlé's Quick hot chocolate Mrs. Hawkins served me.

I flicked my fingers back and forth across her chocolate-covered raisin-like nipples. I smiled in triumph when her nipples began to look like my Kathy baby dolls. That excited me more. Beatrice's smile and delightful squeals of hysteria indicated that she liked what I was doing.

I didn't know it at the time, but I was so turned on by her. I longed for those moments.

"Child, I'm home, come downstairs now!" my mother screamed from the bottom of the stairs. Rats! I wasn't quite finished playing with Beatrice. I prepared to leave. Before tucking her breasts back into her cotton polyester blend bra, I stole one more squeeze, and did one more flick against her beloved breasts.

"I love you, Beatrice. We'll finish this tomorrow, okay?" I asked before kissing her cheeks. Making sure not to be rude, I ran into the kitchen and kissed Mrs. Hawkins, who was still on the phone, before running downstairs to my mother.

Tom and Jerry time again. Beatrice was in her usual spot awaiting my arrival. Her lanky frame had already made its usual imprint in the plastic covering. She had probably been sitting there since early in the morning.

I was so excited to see her. It was another scorching day, but as usual Beatrice squealed when she saw me. Sweat beads were on her forehead and under her arms. Mrs. Hawkins didn't have an air conditioner; she tried to keep us cool by placing a big white square fan in the window. It only blew hot air. Staying hot was fine with me. Hearing Beatrice's yelps while running upstairs made me forget all about the heat.

On that day I was going to add a new feature to our game. I was so elated that Beatrice liked our game yesterday. I laid in bed all night long thinking about her. I dreamed of how comforting her breasts felt in my hands. They were warm and soft. Her nipples screamed out to me, begging me to play with them some more, never wanting my hands to leave them.

Longing for the touch of Beatrice's breasts, I grabbed my Kathy baby doll tucked safely under my blankets, and began playing with my doll's plastic breasts. I flicked my fingers back and forth on my doll but got increasingly annoyed. Kathy's breasts refused to react in the same way as Beatrice's. They wouldn't stand at attention. The doll frustrated me so much that I eventually went to sleep.

Kathy baby doll was joining our game. Maybe her breasts would decide to behave like Beatrice's. Content with my decision to get Kathy, I happily ran back downstairs singing and smiling to my apartment. Ever since my daddy gave her to me, we had done everything together.

My pre-school smile turned upside after rushing in to witness my mother and my new father kissing. They were always kissing. My eyes welled with tears. I thought they'd left for work? I stood paralyzed as my mother relished in his kisses. She giggled with schoolgirl delight, as their lips parted like the Red Sea. His tender, feathery love taps on my mommy's lips breathed a new energy into her body.

I longed for that energy. I longed for the love, the passion, and the sweet caresses. She took pleasure in his affection. I needed that affection. My heart was lonely, praying one day they would share that love with me.

They were like only children, selfish, keeping all that love bottled up for each other. Since my new father came to live with us my mother no longer had love for me. It was all for him. She walked for him, dressed for him, and even talked for him. All of her thoughts and energy were for him. She made sure I was in bed at 7 p.m. every night so they could have some alone time. But it was okay, because Beatrice, Kathy, and I've alone time. We didn't need them; they would just ruin our love, like I ruined theirs.

I forgot about my Kathy baby doll and reluctantly turned around to head back upstairs. Beatrice was waiting for me. As I exited the apartment, my eyes met his.

His eyes said it all; tiny eyes hidden behind tortoise-shell brown horn-rimmed glasses, the kind of reading glasses found in Duane Reade drugstores. Hate, malice, and disgust were the color of those infamous eyes. To the world they were as common as Tyra Banks' green eyes, yet to me they mirrored my childhood.

The mirror reflected back darkness, abuse, and pain. I tried often to break the mirror, but it never cracked. He held onto it with the same intensity that was in his eyes.

I never quite fathomed why my stepfather stared at me with those eyes. I was just a little girl and he was my protector. Those eyes, which made me feel nervous, insecure, small, and afraid, signaled his mood. I studied them; I knew how to read them. Those eyes told me when he would strike. They told me when to duck, when to pretend to be sleeping, and when to eat all of my vegetables. Those eyes taught me how to navigate through the fields to keep from being lynched.

Pain wasn't derived from the beatings where he inflicted belts, tiny tree branches, and extension cords on my juvenile body. The pain came from the contempt in his eyes. His stare frightened me, piercing right

through my body, my soul.

If looks could kill, I would have been dead a long time ago. He hated me. And as the years went by I began to hate him as well. I despised my stepfather from the innocent age of five until now. Why did he scrutinize me that way or abuse my body that way? What had I done? What had I not done?

At the tender age of five, I had an enemy. Did I deserve an enemy at that age? Did I deserve those heinous stares, those deathly beatings? Maybe if my skin had been lighter, he would love me. Or maybe if I didn't look so much like Taylor, my dad, he would love me. I tried pointlessly to walk lightly, stay quiet when I played with my dolls, and eat all of my dinner. Everything I did failed; his hate ran deep.

The door slammed loudly, scaring me out of my deep thoughts. Their Siamese kissing images vanished. A river of tears flooded my then frail five-year-old tiny body. They must have slipped out the back door and finally headed off to work. With the tears still swimming down my face, I marched my way back upstairs to my Beatrice. She was waiting for me.

Landing on the top step I walked into the living room to find Jerry running into the mouse hole with Tom hungrily waiting for him on the outside. While Beatrice stared at the old black and white I took a seat next to her. Through her green plaid flannel cowboy shirt, I began to caress her breasts. I really needed her to make me feel better. Keeping one hand on her left breast, making my way to her inner thigh, I kept my eyes glued on the crazy cat and mouse team.

"Beatrice, do you like this? Do you want me to continue?" I asked, knowing her answer would be spit running out the side of her mouth. I took that as a gesture that she liked it. "I'm glad you like it, Beatrice. I like touching you," I whispered as I had seen it done so many times before on the movies my mother and stepfather watched.

Removing my hands from her inner thigh and her covered breasts I changed my position with my lover.

"Beatrice, you're my little spitty whore," I whispered into her neck as I climbed on her lap and proceeded to straddle her. Mother took this position on Mr. George many evenings. As mother rode him, he called her his sweet-tasting whore and smacked her naked bottom. They always assumed I was sleeping, but their heated passion kept me awake.

Moving closer to her vagina, I started using my tongue to lick her now, making circles with my tongue. I wanted to kiss her vagina now. I wanted it real bad. I held my breath, as I got closer to her turned off by her smell. Did Mr. George like Mommy's smell? Determined to continue playing, I stuck out my tongue and licked her more, moving in closer each time. The tip of my tongue finally reached the opening of her vagina. I was about to taste her when she began to shriek.

Her cries were soft at first, but then her wails became offensively louder. Scared and nervous, I worried Mrs. Hawkins would come out the kitchen. If that happened I would've gotten into so much trouble. Mrs. Hawkins wouldn't allow me to come upstairs anymore! Why was Beatrice behaving that way? That didn't happen with Mother and Mr. George, or the ladies and men on the movies they watched.

Mother told him, "Don't stop, right there, right there," when he did those things to her. Why was Beatrice crying? Unaware of the reason for her tears, I cried as well.

Hurriedly I attempted to close up her diaper. I made sure that her plastic panties with the daisies were over her diaper correctly. By the skin of my teeth I got everything straightened when Mrs. Hawkins came in. She looked around, saw that we were fine, and went back to her kitchen.

Didn't Beatrice love me anymore? Or had she become like my mother and new father? I thought if I played this game with her everything would be perfect. I didn't understand. No one loved me; no one wanted to play any games with me. This was supposed to make someone love me, even if it was only Beatrice.

"Child! Child! I'm home! Come down stairs now!" my mother yelled at the top of her lungs in her singsong West Indian voice.

"Coming mommy!" I shouted back. "Mrs. Hawkins, I'm leaving!" I screamed. I wiped the back of my hands across my nose and dried my eyes with my t-shirt.

"Okay darling, I'll see you tomorrow," Mrs. Hawkins replied, walking out to make sure I got down the stairs okay. She waved good evening to my mother.

Before I left I turned around to look at Beatrice. I really looked at her for the first time. Her eyes looked a lot like eyes I'd seen before. They were intense, yet lost, containing pain and sorrow. I'd recognize those eyes anywhere; they were my eyes. I was sorry for what I'd done

to Beatrice. I was just trying to seek out the love my new father gave Mother. I never meant to make her cry.

For some reason, I think my mother knew what happened. The very next day, she took me to preschool. She said I was getting older and needed to be around children my own age. I also didn't go upstairs very often to play. I stayed downstairs, played with my dolls, and worked real hard to avoid my new father.

Chapter 3

"You got to be kidding me. *Move it damn it*!" I belted out the unopened window. The words echoed through my entire being as my consciousness moved closer to my current incarnation. I was getting nearer to the right side of the entrance to the Holland tunnel. Inching steadily to the alleged faster EZ pass lanes. Sometimes they were just as bad as the cash lanes. Filled with folks who acted like they had no idea why their passes weren't working. *Maybe because your payment didn't clear, DAH!!*

"You're not about to get in front of me, I've been sitting in this traffic for far too long," continuing my tirade now directed toward the champagne-colored Camry, trying to cut me off. Before the Camry it was the Jeep Cherokee, then it was the Cadillac I wished they would all just disappear. The owner of the Camry, a white-haired, sixty-something, over-tanned lady, shook her head in disgust at me.

"Get to the back you. ol' biddy." I raised my middle finger and smiled as I watched her fall back into the line of traffic.

Just as I predicted there was EZ-pass drama in front of me. This *would* happen when Dupri was waiting on me. Shit, 6:23 and I still hadn't reached the jaws of the Holland Tunnel.

Stephanie Mills, "Love Like This", came blaring through my car's newly installed stereo system. Giving me permission to forget about the traffic for a split second. I rocked in my seat, singing karaoke style to her music. That song always soothed me.

It started back in the days when Daddy and I were in his dark room, developing pictures from his latest adventure. Pictures we took either at the South Street Seaport, Brooklyn Bridge, or just walking through the angry streets of New York City. Daddy introduced me to Stephanie in the dark room, along with many others. He started my profound love for music.

Daddy carried his camera everywhere he went. He often said that there was always a picture worth taking. That was when things were simple. When Dad came back into my life and loved me. Before he disappeared again. Back when I didn't know who Daddy really was or anyone else for that matter. Now everyone's truth was exposed.

Damn, 6:30. And I still haven't made any real headway. This was going from bad to worse. I eyed the other car next to me. He appeared just as aggravated as I was. This was the worse part, when several lanes merge into one lane entering the tunnel.

"Pay attention, Blondie." I honked at the driver of an old jalopy. She was so engrossed in her cell phone conversation; she didn't realize that the traffic was moving. Maybe if she hung up the damn thing and moved with the traffic, I could make it to Dupri on time.

He specifically said be home no later than 6:45pm, but judging from the time and traffic that was no way possible. This could have very well all been avoided if my session didn't run over.

My new therapy sessions were going well thus far. Today's session was the first session I'd had with any therapist, where I expelled the truth about my childhood. Including Beatrice.

After feeling depleted, emotionally and physically stressed, and removed from my inner strengths, from living with repressed feelings of being abused, I went on a journey to seek some inner solace. A journey I was petrified to take. Being a product of an overbearing Caribbean mother, I was not to see a psychotherapist. I was to tackle my issues by tucking them away safely in the depths of my being. I tried that. It didn't work. In fact it made shit worse. So I went on my journey for guidance.

While taking a lazy walk in the city on a foggy Sunday morning, I

stopped in my favorite expensive coffee shop. I took my overpriced skim vanilla latte to the back to check out the flea market bulletin board. You always found rare finds on the board.

On this particular day I stumbled across a lone black card embellished with gold italic writing, with the name "Sapna" on it. Submerged in a sea of cards that promoted piano lessons, rooms for rent, and yoga classes, her card advertised a form of therapy that was highly effective. Curious by nature, I jotted down the number to contact her later. The card cleverly promised that I wouldn't be in therapy for twenty years. The Lord must have heard my cries. After investing three years in my quest for a great therapist, I was game for anything. Anything had to be better than those quacks I'd come across. They were the main reason why most New Yorkers were on Prozac, Paxil, and Zoloft.

There was Dr. Richard Bergman, who lived on the upper east side of Manhattan in one of those tenement buildings. He was a stocky Jewish man with silver-white hair and a full beard. His yarmulke had a tendency to fall to one side, and he wore his glasses on the tip of his wart-laden nose. I actually thought he wore his yarmulke that way on purpose. He told me once that it was a great conversation piece.

In many of our sessions, Dr. Bergman told me about how much hair he had as a young lad, as he put it. He was always looking for a new hair-growth system. He'd cut out miracle hair-growth ads and ordered tons of hair products off the Internet. The delivery guy had a knack for making deliveries during our sessions.

I should have gotten a clue that Dr. Bergman was a little weird when I walked into his home office for the first time, and lo and behold, there was a bathtub in the middle of the living room floor. As I sat in the brown leather recliner and babbled about my issues, I prayed he wouldn't jump into the tub and ask me to join him.

My second lump of coal was Mr. Junkman. A traveling psychotherapist, he rented office spaces or used a nearby diner to hold his sessions. I believe he obtained his degree from a Cracker Jack box. Mr. Junkman was a whole lot crazier than his patients. His name alone should have clued me in that he was a quack. Instead of Halston, his cologne of choice was hard-boiled eggs; he reeked of them. At times he fell asleep during our sessions. The first time he snored was the last session we had.

I stumbled upon Ms. Cheryl Pierce one day at a church function.

We both stayed after church for fellowship. A mutual parishioner introduced us; he knew I was looking for a good therapist.

Ms. Pierce was a diva who, at sixty years old, didn't look a day over thirty-five. In her youth she'd won several beauty pageants in her home state of Alabama. I found this out during one of our therapy sessions.

She stood a proud 5'10" with Tina Turner legs, Serena Williams's abs, and a weave even Diana Ross would be proud of. From one African-American sister to another, I assumed she would understand my plight. Excessively self-absorbed, we discussed her fabulous body, well-toned legs, her bagless eyes, and envious thirty year olds, during most of our sessions.

Tina, as she preferred to be called, manipulated our sessions with calculation.   No matter what the topic, we ended up talking about her. I stayed with her for about two years and prayed every day that she would become the therapist I so desperately wanted. I'm still waiting for it to happen. Thinking about those crazy folks made me appreciate my new form of self-help. Six-fifty, five minutes past the time I was suppose to meet Dupri. I might as well prepare to pack my shit; I was not going to get out of this one at all. He was going to lose his mind, if he hadn't start losing it already. I should have let him change the reservation time, when he asked. Rush hour was the worse but stupid me said no, when I had the opportunity to say yes.

Thank God, I was finally out of the darn Tunnel, but Broadway was a parking lot. Dupri was trying immensely to reconnect with me however; reconnection wasn't at the top of my to-do list.

"Lord, please help me out with this one." They said a little prayer was all you need. Hopefully they were right.

Chapter 4

𝕵 reached for my latest upgraded Nextel cell phone. Shaking in my black boots, I radioed Pumpkin, as I affectionately called him. I was not looking forward to hearing this man's roar.

"Yes, sexy lady, are you close? I'll start heading downstairs so we can take off." His booming voice was heard after two walkie-talkie chirps.

"No, D. I'm not close, but don't kill me. I'm still in traffic. I should be there in about thirty-five minutes if not sooner."

His Isaac Hayes voice got increasingly deeper. "You're joking right? Tell me you're outside, and this is all a joke. Is this your way at getting back at me for throwing ice water on you the other night, while you were in the shower?" I said nothing.

"Didn't I ask you this morning if you wanted to change our reservations? Huh? Didn't I ask you?" He paused, waiting for my answer. "Answer me, woman!"

"What happened to sexy lady?" I was really fucking with him. "Yes, you asked me, but I didn't think it was necessary. Dag, D. relax. I didn't do it on purpose. Besides I can't control traffic."

"You can't control traffic? You can't control traffic? You fucked up again, yet you have the nerve to talk shit to me. You are fucking unbelievable."

Maybe that wasn't the answer he was looking for.

"If I were you, Mr. Haynes, I would really watch how you're talking to me. You are being a bit rude. Besides, you don't want to raise your blood pressure. You know black men are dropping like flies lately due to hypertension."

"You got to be kidding me." I knew he was pacing the floor. "You are fucking joking around, when I'm pissed the fuck off. I can't believe this shit. You're really losing it. I thought this therapy thing was a joke, but I see your crazy ass needs it for real."

"D. Let me__."

"No don't 'D' me. I'm tired of all of your many excuses. Fucking tired, do you hear me?" I nodded, even though he couldn't see me.

"You're stuck in traffic, the dog ate your homework, and your Jheri curl caught fire while taping a Pepsi commercial. What next, lady? What the fuck next? If it isn't one thing, it's another. We are late for our dinner reservations, that you were aware of a month ago. And might I add, that I reminded you of this morning."

"Pumpkin, let me explain," I coaxed in my sexiest bedroom voice.

"I'm getting increasingly tired of all your explanations. All you do these days is try to explain your way out of shit. Don't do it to yourself. Let yourself in. I'm going to keep our dinner reservation. Lata." The dial tone blared. Well that went over better than I expected.

My introduction to Dupri Harry Haynes, at a parent-teacher conference three spring terms ago, could undoubtedly be compared to a scene out of a Hollywood movie. It was better than when John Cusack and Kate Beckinsale came together in *Serendipity* or when Diana Ross kissed Bill Dee Williams in *Mahogany*. Our meeting was destiny.

In between the parent meeting, I ran next door to Zoe, my fellow teacher colleague, to chitchat about the politics of the public-school system. Zoe and I had been teacher-friends since she started teaching history next door to me, three years ago. I was already a teacher at the school six years prior to Zoe. We had an instant attraction. Our friendship became stronger once we learned we were both NYU alumni's.

Full of energy and always smiling, Zoe brought the sun in every time she entered a room. Her presence was magical. She was the epitome of a person who truly loved life and all it had to offer, the good and the bad.

Unlike myself, Zoe was tall. She had a statuette model-like body, 5'10 with the perfect hourglass shape. She had deep dark eyes protected by rimless glasses. Her tiny waist with a huge booty and large breast was every man's dream. Many saw her as a video vixen. But Zoe was very much a homebody and bookworm. During our hiatus from school, Zoe very rarely traveled the world; she felt there was no place like home. What could one expect? After all she was a Cancer.

She wore her hair in a short-cropped pixie cut, reflective of her fun nature and sex appeal. Zoe's only outwardly imperfection was the sixth finger on her right hand.

Standing in her classroom with a pencil behind my ear, a bottle of Poland Springs water in my hand, ranting and raving like a lunatic, I had no idea Dupri was lurking in the back of the classroom. I was there for ten minutes straight rattling gibberish, not once coming up for air.

I later found out Zoe, who was also his sister, set the whole meeting up. Zoe and I were having lunch in the teacher's cafeteria one day while I went on and on about how screwy my love life had been. Since she had been out of the dating game for four years, she was amused by my stories and the jerks I dated. She was one of the lucky few whom found love on the Internet.

After all of my dreadful stories, she became my personal yenta. She introduced me to decent men, but I always dug until I found an imperfection, whether it was height, locale, or teeth. I stopped any notion of a second date before the first one got fully started.

Out of the corner of my eye I saw Dupri take his last few steps toward me, moseying his sexy self in my direction. He halted right where Zoe and I were speaking. Looking quite stupid with my mouth agape and eyes bulging out of my head, I couldn't help but admire the brother in front of me.

I mean he was just dreamy, like Julius Irving, Morris Chestnut, a bit of class, tons of sex appeal, great energy, and a bright smile all in one standing before me. He had a smile just like his sister's. I had truly died and gone to heaven.

Zoe broke the silence and the smiles by speaking first. Her natural lip coiled slightly as her dark eyes glistened with excitement.

"This is my brother, Dupri Haynes."

Raising my hand to his lips, Dupri kissed the backside of my palm. I started to pull back my hand, but after I adjusted my all of 5'3 frame to meet what I believe was his 6'5 frame, I practically shoved my palm down his throat.

Just when you thought you knew a person. I turned to stare at Zoe. I couldn't believe she had been harboring this Greek God, her brother, all to herself. Zeus had finally risen from the dead.

"Dupri is hanging around until the end of the meeting. We're heading uptown to meet my husband for dinner. You are more than welcomed to join us. How about it?" Zoe asked after clearing her throat.

With my hand still cradled by his, Dupri looked at me with his huge sleepy russet brown eyes. Depending on what light he was standing in they were either deep brown or light brown. At that moment they were somewhere between copper and chocolate. The most gorgeous eyes I have ever seen.

"I really hope you can join us for a few. I love hanging out with my sister and brother-in-law and all, but sometimes the mushiness can be a bit much." He laughed while Zoe punched him in the forearm.

All I kept thinking was that he spoke. The black Adonis spoke. Was Elton John gay? Did I look stupid to this man: of *course* I was going to join them for dinner. Like Lotto, you have to be in it to win it and I was going to be at dinner to win this man. "Sure, I would love to join you guys for dinner. But you have to promise me if I get stuck with a parent, you'll wait for me." I sheepishly answered.

"I'll wait as long as you want me to." He smiled. He had a great big wide smile. His parents surely invested in several years of orthodontic work for him. It paid off.

Zoe put both hands around her neck, pretending to choke herself, behind her brother. I couldn't help but smirk at her.

"All right, all right! Okay, so it's dinner for four later this evening. Now get out of my classroom, before I barf." Zoe laughed clapping her hands as if she was trying to get her students attention.

I smiled at Dupri and he smiled back. His look told me he was

happy at my decision to join them. I sashayed back to my classroom, feeling the heat of Dupri's eyes checking out my obvious curves.

Dupri and I completely lost ourselves in conversation during our cab ride to midtown, forgetting Zoe was with us. I learned that Dupri, who I believed must have been the long-lost identical twin brother of Ty Law from the New England Patriots, was actually Zoe's baby brother. At 6'5 and approximately 227lbs, one would have thought he was her older brother. Dupri was the only boy among three sisters and a self-proclaimed mama's boy. Being a mama's boy wasn't too bad in my eyes; at least he knew how to love a woman.

"So you're a mama's boy, huh?"

"Yes, I am and proud of it may I add." He laughed nervously.

"I've never met a self-proclaimed mama's boy before."

"I read this article once about a brother, struggling to be a father to his unborn son, with a woman who was dealing with serious abandonment issues. Not only did he have to deal with her pain, he also had to deal with the pain of her mother. Since her father left when she was nine months, her mom put all of her energy into her. Making him work harder to prove to this woman, that he was good enough for her daughter. Trying to prove that he was not a man like her ex-husband; he was a man from a long lineage of men who stuck behind their families. The article was so heartfelt and powerful. It made me think about all my prior relationships." He paused giving a nervous laugh.

"In my past relationships, I had to deal with insecure woman. Who were unable to deal with a man like myself. I'm just a dude who believes in the sacrament of marriage and comes from a long line of men who've been married over forty years. My own parents for thirty-nine years and my grandparents made sixty-one years this past January. We had a running family joke that Mom and Dad were our version of Ashford and Simpson. Nanny and Pop-Pop were our Ossie and Ruby Dee." He stroked the wiry hairs of his goatee.

"You know they say, we meet people where we are in life. Do you think you dated insecure woman, because you yourself was insecure?" My gaze penetrated him.

"I never thought about it that way. I don't believe I was insecure. I mean I've got issues, who the fuck doesn't. But it didn't make me do desperate shit. You know how woman can be. Checking your cell,

questioning you and crap."

"We only do that if we have a reason."

"I'm not a saint. In my twenty's I was out there. Who the fuck wasn't? But that was my twenty's in your thirty's shit is different. Some woman can't handle that."

"Okay." Was all I managed to say.

"Look, I play ball, go fishing and check out movies with the men in my family. We go away for father-and-son, third-generation-of-men outings. My mom said that my great grandparents died within months of each other. Long marriages have long since been a part of my family's history." His thick upper lip twitched underneath his defined moustache.

"I just want to be perfect to my mate, you know?" His eyes widened. "I can't do that if she walks with major baggage."

"But doesn't everyone have some sort of demon they are dealing with. Isn't that why we are on this earth?" I crossed and uncrossed my legs, getting more comfortable.

"All I am saying is that I am no longer in the mood to deal with insecure shallow woman. Yeah everyone has his or her cross to bear, but it can't consume our relationship. It can only be the backdrop. Unlike dude in the article I'm not going to fight with any woman, nor her mother to prove how great of a man I am. If they can't see it for themselves, then they need not be a part of my life. I know my rant has nothing to do with being a mama's boy, but it's what was on my mind."

I touched his shoulder as he moved a strand of hair out of my face. "No, your rant was fine. I totally enjoyed it. You let me in. Which is always pretty cool."

"I hope I didn't scare you off?" His russet eyes stared at me intently awaiting the answer.

"Nope, not at all. It made me want to know more." His shoulders relaxed. "Good, so what's your story? Are your parents together, Miss Lady? You don't mind me calling you Miss Lady, do you?"

"Miss Lady is fine, as long as you don't call anyone else that." I eyed him seductively.

"Nope, Miss Lady is all for you. So what's your deal?"

"Unfortunately or fortunately depending on how you look at it, I don't come from a storybook family. My parents divorced before I

was two. From what my mother says, my dad couldn't keep his private in his pants." I shrugged peering out the window. He reached over and turned me around to face him.

"Hey, are you still with me? No peeking out the window in my presence. What, I'm not sexy enough for you?"

"You're alright." I couldn't help but chuckle.

"Damn, crush a brotha's self-esteem why don't you." We laughed in unison.

"My dad stepped out on my mom once." My ears perked up.

"Do you believe that's the reason you love your mom so much?"

"Nah, we were always pretty tight. I guess because I was her only son. But the infidelity crushed Ma. She could have left and I wouldn't have blamed her, but somehow she managed to keep the family together. She had enormous passion for her family and her marriage. She, along with Luther made me believe in the power of marriage and love." We laughed at his one liner. He had a little Eddie Murphy in him.

"It wasn't the Leave it to Beaver house, but it worked." He stopped and rubbed his palms this time he looked outside the cabs window. "My mom had a saying it went, 'we got each other, all poor people have is each other'."

"She ain't never lie, when she said that." He finally turned around. Our eyes made four.

"The infidelity I believe affected Zoe and my other sisters. They all dated jerks at some point or the other. Zoe so far has been the only one that lucked up and found someone decent. I hope the others hurry up and find what they're looking for. My mom hurts for them. Their tears are enough to drive anyone crazy."

"I'm pretty sure someone has cried over you before." I cocked my head to one side twisting my lips.

"If they did, I never knew about it and I'm glad I didn't. That's too much pressure on a brotha. All I'm looking for is a sweet girl, one I can grow with. Not in the mood to be anyone's baby daddy, and booty calls are tired. My mission is to be a decent husband to a deserving woman."

Was he serious? He wanted marriage? No more fuck buddies for me. I hit the jackpot. All of this in the taxi!

Dinner was beyond fabulous. In awe of each other, Dupri and I

forgot Zoe and her husband were at the table. Picking up where we left off in our cab ride, we found we had tons in common. We both enjoyed all forms of music; he confided in me that he owned Charlie Pride's greatest hits. I almost fell out of the chair at that discovery. Who the heck owns Charlie Pride but me? To say I was impressed was an understatement. Both of our dads attended Florida A&M University, the Tazmanian Devil was our favorite cartoon character, and we both felt that the *King of Queens* was an amazing sitcom.

To top off the night Dupri said goodbye to his sister and brother-in-law and took a cab ride back with me from the upper Westside to my Brooklyn brownstone home. Dupri lived in the SoHo section of Manhattan. His scorecard went up one hundred extra points for his gentlemanly action.

In the second episode of our taxicab confession, we picked up right where we left off. Our conversation flowed effortlessly. This time, we discussed our love for food, seafood especially.

He felt he could have done better than the restaurant we just left. He tried to convince the head chef to allow him access to the kitchen to cook up what he called his surprise chicken, but his sister told him to sit his behind down. She said there was no surprise to it. It tasted like shit. We all cracked up. They made me feel so welcomed, as if I were part of their family.

Dupri shared with me that he was a financial advisor at Goldman Sachs and owned his two-bedroom loft in Soho. After college he moved back home with his mom and stayed six months. He saved up enough to purchase his first property and moved out. His first reality purchase was a huge accomplishment for him.

He graduated from Morehouse University with a degree in Finance and a Master's degree in Business Management from Howard University. He was a member of Alpha Phi Alpha Fraternity, Inc., a Big Brother, and volunteered as a basketball coach at a gym in Brooklyn. This man was simply delicious.

Dupri convinced the cab driver to wait for him by handing him a hundred-dollar bill, once we reached my brownstone. With interlocked hands he walked me to my door, where we talked for a few more minutes, neither one of us wanting to say good-bye.

There under the moonlight I studied every inch of Dupri's oval shaped face. His creamy toffee complexion was smooth as a baby's bottom. He didn't suffer from razor bumps as so many other brothers

had. My date's face had a few dark spots leftover from childhood acne and a chin dimple hidden under a jet-black wooly goatee. A faded scar along his temple he got from horseback riding added a bit of character. His heart shaped mole on the tip of his nose was just like the one Zoe had. A family trait, I guess.

His brown eyes crinkled in a smile. "I really enjoyed meeting you and dinner this evening. Usually I don't believe my sister when she says her friends are beautiful, but she wasn't lying this time."

Blushing I responded, "Thank you. You aren't too bad yourself." The moonlight protected us in the background. Both of us stood still not wanting that moment to end. I was getting ready to invite him in when the taxi driver tooted his horn. We church hugged and made plans for our next date over the weekend. If it weren't for the cab driver, Dupri and I would've probably stayed on my porch, talking all night long.

Lately things had changed drastically. I wasn't sure if I loved Dupri these days. Was he just around because of what a great catch he was, as my girlfriends would put it. My heart and mind were going in two different directions. Part of me did love him, but I wasn't sure if I was in love with him. Some would argue they were one in the same, but to me they were quite different. I loved him for the man that he was, but my heart didn't flutter when he walks into the room. Like it used too.

We didn't make love like we used to anymore, which was primarily my fault. After waiting eight months before we gave ourselves to each other, we became like rabbits. If it were up to Dupri, neither one of us would have conventional employment. Our jobs would be missionary to sixty-nine seven days a week.

Dupri enjoyed sex to the highest power. At one point I enjoyed it as much as he did. Now I made it my business to be in the bed before he was. I cringed when he tried to hug or kiss me, or even utter those three famous words. I instantaneously became a student of the Helen Keller School when I heard them and a member of the Catholic Guild for the Blind when those full lips puckered up and those bear arms opened wide. If I'd use those words, I only did it in sheer desperation to get myself out of something, which I more likely started.

I had to go and mess shit up by falling in love. Falling in love during a time when I wasn't ready. I thought I was lonely and tired of fuck buddies, thought I needed a man's love so I stood in the way when Dupri crossed my path. I should have stepped to the side and let

him move on to someone else that was better suited for him. But no, selfish me placed my needs before this man's. It wasn't Dupri's love I was searching for at the time, it was my own I was seeking. I thought he could fill the empty void in my heart. I later realized I was the only one who could do that. By the time that notion was revealed to me, he was sucked in too deep.

It was finally 7:38pm when I made it to D's loft. The semi-confident woman I was anticipated him being there. Prayed he changed his mind and was waiting for me in the den.

"Honey, I'm home," I imagined myself saying.

"I'm in the den, dear, come to Big Poppa," he would have responded back. A girl had the right to dream. However, my logical self knew different.

I threw my keys and purse on the table by the door, pulled off my boots. All was quiet when I stepped in the loft. Like he said, he kept our dinner reservation.

I opened up the fridge and took out last night's dinner of shrimp dumplings and mussaman curry and reheated it. I hadn't realized how hungry I was. I should have really been at dinner right now. Oh, well.

Checking my e-mail messages, I erased all the spam, and forwarded mail as I listened to my voicemail.

October called; her messages were always lengthy. Can my sister ever just leave a thirty-second message? She got such a kick of telling me her life story on my voicemail. When the time was up on the voicemail, she generally called right back and picked right up where she left off.

With my dinner, a box of Kleenex, and *The Joy Luck Club* I prepared for an evening of tears.

The story of these mothers and their daughters was so touching, by far one of my most favorite movies. How interesting that these Chinese-American daughters were fighting their mother's demon similar to myself? When I first saw the movie I was relieved to learn that every culture has these crazy mother-and-daughter dynamics. I stopped the DVD player and replayed An Mei's conversation with her daughter. I knew the lines as if I wrote them myself.

An Mei admits to Rose, her daughter, how her issues became her daughter's issues. Even though she fought very hard for that not to happen to her daughter, it happened. Those words she spoke, that I

knew so well, always made me cry. Words I wished that someday my mom would say to me. My mother was not raised the Chinese way, I was not raised the Chinese way, but it seemed as though our lives were so parallel.

With my eyes filled with water, I stopped the DVD. I loved the movie, and really wanted to indulge in it some more, but my time would be better spent trying to repair my soon-to-be-defunct relationship. I could tell from his voice that Dupri had about enough. *Last night and now tonight.* I was lucky my bags weren't packed when I walked through the door.

He was happy when I started counseling, but had no idea why I did. He just supported my decision. Now he was surely regretting it.

Chapter 5

"**C**rackhead, I know you're there. Answer the damn phone, already." My laugh lines deepened as I listened to October's banter, through the answering machine. This girl is too much. I was just getting ready to slip into something sexy for Dupri, and here she comes a calling.

"I ain't hanging up until you answer the damn phone. You know I would sit here all day and night if I have to. If the tape runs out I'll keep calling back until you answer. You're probably sitting in the living room Indian style with the remote in your hand listening to this." I hate when she does that.

"Come on! Answer already. I don't look good when I'm begging." I doubled over with laughter giving my hair the freedom to swing passionately in my face.

"Besides I have to tell you about the handbag sample sale I attacked today." Shaking my head, I existed the room to dispose of my dishes. My sister would be such a great addition to the Laugh Factory's line-up.

"Since you wouldn't answer I'll tell you anyhow. So, I bought five bags. I know, I know, insane but they were so practically calling my

name. Oh, they were sort of cheap. The bill came to five hundred and eighty-two dollars. I'm not keeping them all though. I'm thinking I could sell them on Ebay or something. When I get the cash from the sale, I'll just pay off my credit card bill." Mother must have dropped this chick on her head at birth.

"Your ass is crazy! What is the point in buying the bags if you are going to sell them, anyway?"

"I knew that would get you to pick up. What's up big sis? They're fierce. I'm only going to sell them if I can't get the boots I've been keeping my eyes on at Nordstrom."

"So you're saying that you can't afford the bags?"

"No I'm saying that there is a possibility I may sell them and get more money than I paid. It's that simple, sheesh. Besides it's the American way." Her deep throat laugh was more boisterous than usual.

"What's up your ass? Have a little fun why don't you?"

"O. you need to be more responsible with your money. You can't go around buying shit and hope you can sell the shit on Ebay. That makes no darn sense."

"Blah, blah, blah." Arggh she can be so freaking irresponsible.

"It's your money."

"That it is. Anyway, I was calling to check on you? I've left you tons of messages and your lazy ass didn't return any. The least you could've done is let your little sister know you landed safely. You're so inconsiderate at times."

"I'm inconsiderate? I'm inconsiderate? You can't even be serious. Look psycho chick, I'm going through something."

"When aren't you going through something? What the fuck happened now?"

"Dupri and I had a fight."

"Oh Lawd!"

"Tell me about it."

"What happened?"

"Not in the mood to discuss it. I'm going to crash now, had a long day."

"No problem, meet me for brunch tomorrow at Café Noir on Thompson. You can vent to me then."

Dear Book,

Tomorrow I'll be able to tell Samantha I saw the Soul Train Music Awards. I was afraid I was going to miss it this year like last year. My track record seeing the show is awful. I always have to sit back while the others gloat about how good the show was and how well the performers were. Not this year however. I swindled my way into seeing it. I managed to stay up past my 8pm curfew.

I told them I'd to watch it for my Music class. I told them Ms. Berkowitz wanted us to write a paper on it and they believed me. Such idiots. Anyhow I wouldn't be left out this year. Book, you have no idea how it feels being left out of everything. Not seeing recent movies and television shows. Since this work this year, I am going to use this excuse every year and with every class. I'll talk to you later.

Bye Book

Chapter 6

The sun unveiled itself to me early the next morning. It radiated vibrantly through the open curtain. I obviously forgot to close it the night before.

My limber body was immersed in our pillow top king-sized bed. Turning my head I smiled at my sleeping beauty not affected by the glimmering light. The last thing I remembered was snuggling in the chaise lounge, awaiting Dupri's arrival.

I lightly stroked his chunky brow while placing a tender kiss on his full pink lips. Peacefully I whispered, "I'm sorry," before jumping up for my sunrise run.

Chaka Khan and I enjoyed jogging in New York's busy streets. In my gray-hooded velour sweat suit, with the wind jitterbugging in my face, I soaked in the scenery and energy around me. The streets were overflowing with people, traffic, and of course, animals.

Dog walkers were out walking their pooches. It never ceased to amaze me how much dog owners and their pooches can pass for twins.

Young African-American, Caribbean, and Hispanic women everywhere pushed strollers filled with overgrown children. The

hilarious part was that the tots belonged to their Caucasian employers. These women cared for these children as if it had been their own legs up in the stirrups.

They cooked for them, took them to the park, helped with homework, and listened to their childhood woes. On rare, but not unheard of occasions, one heard a child call its caregiver mom.

Bike riders and roller bladders went in and out of traffic, almost getting killed by the cars or almost killing pedestrians. They rode those bikes better than the racecars in the Indy 500. Competing against the yellow cabs to get to their finish line.

Lovers of all colors, creeds, and sexual orientations also contributed to the busy streets. Their public display of affection would lead one to believe it was Valentine's Day instead of only the last week of September. Women, who looked like they stepped off the runaway of New York's Fashion Week, openly displayed their love for their same-sex partners. Rejected cast members of *Queer Eye for the Straight Guy* lined the streets as well. These streets were just a microcosm of my city's reality.

Samantha, my redheaded childhood friend, called after me, Chaka and I were fascinated by our surroundings and didn't hear her. She called after taking long strides to catch me, "Gurrl, don't you hear me calling you?" Her brassy yellow complexion glistened with beads of sweat.

I stopped dead in my tracks after feeling her feather-light touch turning around to face her.

"Do you know how long I've been calling you?" her screaming green eyes narrowed a bit pissed.

"Samantha, I'm sorry, but I didn't hear you." I took off my headphones. "Chaka and I were being every woman." I smiled as I gave my friend one of those French styled kisses on her rosy cheeks.

"Do you not check your e-mails anymore? I've e-mailed you and left you a zillion voicemail messages, but you haven't returned any. Is everything okay with you?" Samantha snapped raising her bushy red eyebrows concerned.

"I wish I had a legitimate excuse, but I really don't. It's the beginning of the school year, and I just got back from Italy and St. John. I've been busy, that's all." I knew that Samantha, along with my other friends, was getting real tired of my absence.

"Humph, if you say so, how was Italy? When did you get back

from St. John?"

"It was great; I had a wonderful time as usual. We got back three days ago" I shifted from one foot to the other pulling on my ponytail.

"Look, Sam, I'm sorry__"

"I know you are going through some things. I'll leave you alone so you can get it together." She rubbed the middle of my back. "Call me when you need me. Tell Dupri 'hi.'" This time she gave me one of those French kisses on my cheek, kicked up her New Balances, and continued her run.

Samantha and I had been through the good and bad, so I knew she knew I was lying. She wanted to be there for me as I tackle these issues, but understood I had to do it alone. She knew I felt like shit. My friend knew that talking was not an option right now.

Samantha and I were friends for over twenty years. The only friend I had left from childhood. We did everything together when we were kids.

Staying up all night, talking about how successful we would be, was all too common between us. Not being allowed to play at anyone else's home prohibited, us from having sleepovers, as other pre-teens our age. Due to my cage-like living environment, Samantha and I improvised.

Around nine o'clock every Saturday night, we called each other to begin our makeshift party. Since we both had pictures of each other in our rooms, we used those to feel like we were really together. In our pajamas, with combs and brushes in our hands and MC Lyte's "Paper Thin" blasting from our boom boxes. We jumped up and down on our beds and had our version of a sleepover. On Monday we talked all about it, making our classmates jealous of our time together. If only they knew...

I loved Samantha and her friendship, but we weren't kids anymore. She had always witnessed my drama. Like me, I was pretty sure she was sick of it. I missed her also, but with all that was going on lately, the break was good. Distance makes the friendship grow stronger, I thought after her red hair had long since jogged into the morning.

As the autumn sun shone on my back while I continued jogging on the West Side Highway, my mind began to wander from Samantha to yesterday's counseling session. Thoughts invaded my psyche. Tears filled my eyes. Those events had been buried so deep and for so long.

Exhuming all the emotions wrecked so much havoc on my soul. So many crazy things were happening.

I sniffed the middle finger of my left hand this morning. I could have sworn I smelled Beatrice's womanhood. I could feel her flesh on my fingers as well. The tears fell harder, clouding my vision of the other joggers within my path. I dropped to my knees, right there in the middle of the West Side Highway and began to sob. My cries were deafening and long hurt immensely. How would Dupri love me, once he found out the truth? How could I love me, now realizing the truth? Beatrice was so innocent, hurting like me.

A passerby stopped, after what seemed an eternity, asking if I was okay. I nodded. The man gave me a tissue. I was so glad that my guardian angel appeared to be gay. He could have cared less that I looked like the girl in *The Exorcist* at that moment. I thanked him politely and out of courtesy exchanged business cards with him. I thanked him again and gathered myself to meet October. And Samantha wonders why I was distant. If only she knew...

They say we aren't sisters
Not by blood
Two different daddies
We look different
She's pretty
I'm ugly
They say we aren't sisters
Step — sisters
Half — sisters
Fake — sisters
Same mother
They say we aren't sisters
Picture perfect, made from gold you are
With time, maybe I'll come into my own, they say
I want to be your sister
Do you want to be my sister?
Are we sisters?
They say we aren't sisters
How can we be?
Please let us be!
Please leave us be!

Chapter 7

No way in hell I was going to let October see my bloodshot eyes. It's bad enough I have to confront Dupri with them. I pulled my sunglasses out my miniature knapsack and hid my eyes.

"Took you long enough." October said standing amongst the autumn leaves full of rich color. Her sepia complexion mixed flawlessly with the red, purple, orange and yellow foliage.

"I got caught up in my run. I almost forgot about our date." I lied.

October pulled her sunglasses out of her massive yellow-ocher Shirley temple curls.

"I was about to leave you!" She pushed out her full cup DD's at me. She must have bought Victoria Secrets extra push-up, cleavage bra. Those puppies were practically kissing me.

"Darn it! If only I knew then, what I knew now." I laughed.

"Very funny, chick." She pushed my right shoulder with her perfect French manicure hands.

"Would you ladies like a booth?" The lean Mediterranean with a smoking body asked. October pinched my forearm.

"Why is he so damn sexy? I wonder if he is taken?" She whispered in my ear as we followed him to our booth. My smile widened.

"Pinch his butt before we get to our seat." I laughed and flagged her nonsense away with my hand.

"Is this okay, ladies?" He asked in his ever-present Greek accent.

"It's fine. But I was wondering, are you into black woman?" October asked seductively with her DD's pouring out as she leaned on the table.

My size ten Adidas gave her a good kick in the chin under the table. She didn't flinched. Heat seared my face. I shook my head hidden by my hand. This girl can be so embarrassing.

"I'm into woman, period. I don't discriminate." His dark eyes twinkled with sexual excitement.

"In that case, here is my card. Make sure I hear from you before the day is over." October's deep brown eyes fluttered with sex as she handed him her business card.

"Will do. Enjoy your meal ladies." His stroll held our gaze until he disappeared behind the restaurant kitchen's door.

"You're out of this world. Don't you have a man?"

"Of course I do, but don't car's come with spare tires?" Nodding in the direction of the kitchen door, "Mr. Sexy will be my spare tire." Her dimples deepened as her laughter roared.

"You need the Lord!"

"No I need dick." This time I joined her laughter.

"So Crackhead, what was up your ass last night?" She sipped on her wine awaiting my answer.

"Nothing," I sipped my wine as well.

"I'm only going to ask one time." She had a slippery sexy way of enunciating her words—a cross between Eartha Kitts and Kathleen Turner.

"Nothing is wrong. Let's move on."

Rolling her eyes in the back of her head, "Whatever, chick."

"So you bought bags?" I asked taking a bite out of my seared tuna salad.

"Oh yes, I almost forgot. They're so hot, especially the midnight

blue one. It's sort of ethnic with traces of bronze woven into the midnight fabric. Maybe I'll let you borrow it someday."

"I bought some midnight blue pumps from Nordstrom's the other day. Maybe the bag would work."

"Maybe. Speaking of borrowing, these spicy lamb meatballs are so good." She licked her fingers.

"Would you not do that in public?" I rolled my eyes at her.

"Like I was saying, borrowing." She placed her fork on the table, staring at me attentively. "I need to borrow ten-thousand dollars." Her gaze never left mine.

I spit out my wine. "You need to borrow what? And from whom?" I asked wiping up the mess I made.

Her back was stiff as a board as she spoke. Her silliness escaped her replaced by a seriousness rarely seen in October.

"I got myself in a bit of a problem. I can't really explain. Too much to go into detail now."

My forehead marred into a frown. This chick is crazy. She wants my money but doesn't want to explain what the shit is for. I've heard it all.

October my crazy-ass sister moves from one job to another. In search of who knows what, has always been my constant source of strength. She was a talented oil paint acrylic artist who taught at Pratt University. She has been known to moonlight as a nude model for college art courses, on occasion. A true feminist who loves her body and thought the world should love it also. I always believed it was because she was a Scorpio, and we all know what they say about those freaky Scorpios. From what I heard, quite a few of her students loved her body also.

However free she was with her body, she has always been my right hand. Many felt because we were half-sisters, we shouldn't have been so close. But nothing about us was half. We rarely discussed the fact that we have two different fathers. All we knew was that the same crazy ass mother raised us both, in the same house. Mr. George tried to separate us, through the years, however we remained true to our sisterly love because of it. As woman now, we are not only sisters but also best friends.

We've spent many days and nights trying to figure out why us.

Why were we given the mother we were given? Today we're still searching for that answer. Well I should say me more than October. She has come to the realization that Mother is who she is. I'm still trying to get there.

We both loved astrology, me the flower child; sentimental Pisces got her into it. Together we traveled the world, attacked malls and just plain ol' had a good damn time.

However her craziness drove me insane. Her carefree attitude about serious matters was enough to make anyone scream. She still lives at home, which infuriates me. The thought of having to see my mother and act cordial to my stepfather pisses me off. I've grown accustomed to avoiding them. More often than not, I make her meet me on the corner of the block they live on. I've begged my crazy sister for months to move out. She says she is going to but she hasn't gotten around to it.

"If you want my money, you better get to talking now." All of a sudden I lost my appetite.

"I'm not going to discuss it now."

"How dare you ask to borrow my money, but don't explain what you need it for." I folded my arms under my chest.

"Would you not raise your voice? The other patrons can hear you." She smirked.

"You are fucking mind-boggling. And would you stop tapping your fork on the table? If you want my money, you better tell me what the fuck it's for. Or else you wouldn't get shit." I continued eating my tuna. This chick wasn't going to drive me mad. I had enough going on.

"Damn, I wanted to tell you in a bit more private setting."

"Well, then you should have asked me in a private setting." I took slow deliberate bites.

"I wanted this to be a surprise. But I see that shit isn't going to work. I bought property."

My jaw dropped. "You did what?"

"I bought a house in East New York. The closing is in two weeks and I need ten grand. I was hoping not to ask anyone, but I'm tapped out. So I'm coming to you big sis for help."

"I don't know what to say."

"How about saying you got my back." The left corner of her lip curved into a half smile.

"I'm going to check my finances, but I don't see it being a problem. I'm very proud of you Tober." I gently patted her hand.

"So am I."

I pushed my chair back. "I have to get ready to get out of here. I promised Dupri I wouldn't be out too long. I'll go to the bank tomorrow and I guess we can make plans for me to give you the check after that. How does that sound?"

"Sounds good. Now get the hell out of here. You look like you want to hug or something." She smiled behind her wine glass.

Chapter 8

The goal was to get to the bathroom before Dupri noticed my puffy, vampire red eyes. If he saw that I'd been crying again he would have me committed for sure.

Besides his numerous sports magazines, I could have sworn I saw a brochure of a leading mental institution. He felt my therapist wasn't doing that great of a job if I was crying all over the place.

"Does your insurance company pay for you to see Sapna?" Dupri asked one Tuesday evening on our way back from the movies.

"No, my insurance doesn't pay for it," I sheepishly answered, knowing all too well what was about to come next. "I told you that before. I specifically said, most insurance companies do not pay for alternative medical treatments."

"So you're paying out of your pocket for therapy, alternative therapy that is, which makes you cry more?" He asked without really wanting an answer. "You couldn't go to a regular therapist like the rest of the world. My eclectic girlfriend just had to see an alternative therapist" He scratched his baldhead. "I still don't see what the big difference was; you don't feel any better, still crying all over the damn

place."

"It does make me feel better."

"I don't see that it does, but if you say so, then I guess it does. It's just taking too long for me."

Like most men, Dupri felt that as long as you knew the problem you could fix it. He supported my decision to see a therapist, but wanted to see results yesterday. He wasn't the only one who wanted results. But right now I had to get to that bathroom before he noticed my eyes.

Of course, with my luck, Dupri was sitting in the den watching ESPN. His head jerked once I closed the door behind me. With keys in my hands, I wondered how the heck I was going to get past him without him noticing anything. This was a job for Superman. Too bad this wasn't a comic book but indeed my life.

"Hey, Miss Lady! How was your run?" Dupri shouted over his shoulder, his gaze glued to the television. "Should I call up the Olympic committee and tell them I am living with the next Flo Jo."

"Very funny, Haynes, very funny." I couldn't help but laugh. "It was pretty cool. I'm just tired of competing with the dogs for running space," I shouted back while making a dash for the bathroom.

"The dogs are your friends." He chuckled.

Wow, looked like I had be making it to the bathroom after all, just a few more steps. Damn, here he came for a kiss! I knew it was too good to be true. Dupri cut me off between the den and the first floor bathroom. He moved to embrace me until he noticed my face.

"What the fuck?" Dupri exclaimed. "What happened to your face? Did someone fuck with you?"

I stood there, dumbfounded. I had no idea how to answer him. Dupri's slightly hairy right hand reached out to wipe my face but I ducked and ran into the bathroom. I locked the door behind me.

"Woman, open this door," Dupri demanded. "Why were you crying?" He was yelling loud enough to make me jump. "Were you robbed?" Dupri desperately tried to come to his own conclusion. "Talk to me, woman!" A pause ensued. "Fine, don't say anything. That's all you do lately is cry, and when I question you, you look at me like I'm crazy. I'm not the enemy. I love you." His voice now a whisper.

"Do not shut me out. Show me how to love you? I'm trying to be very patient." Dupri's voice was getting louder again. "You haven't

made love to me in months, you're always late, always crying. When I ask you a question, you act like I am the fucking CIA. I'm sick and tired of your bullshit!"

I stood with my back against the bathroom door, praying for it all to end. I said in a soft voice. "I love you, Dupri."

"Woman, I'm freaking talking to you!" My tears fell faster.

"Don't' you hear me?" He took a breath. "Fine! Stay in the bathroom. I'm out. See you when I see you."

Dear Book,

Can I run away to a secluded island? Some place where no one will ever be able to figure out who I am. I'm sorry to say this book, but even a place you wouldn't know. Well, maybe you would. It hurts too bad, where I am right now. The pain is deep. Every day I think, today is going to be a good day, but it never ends that way. Show me how to have faith. Show me how to release the control. Show me that there is some good in the world. Show me something damn it! Just show me.

Bye Book

Chapter 9

"Ebony Eyes" seeped through the clock radio. I changed my position in bed, bringing my knees closer to my chest, sinking in deeper into the warmth of the bed. I pulled the covers tight to my neck. It was time to open the curtains and let the show begin. The puppet master was trying to pull me off the bed, but I resisted him.

Lying here under the covers listening to Smokey and Rick was so much sweeter. The seduction of Smokey Robinson and Rick James lyrics allowed me to forget how I was hurting Dupri.

I smiled, hidden under the covers and wiggling my toes as I heard Rick's voice. He sang raspy, gritty, lacing each word he sang with sex. Rick paused and Smokey took over. His tremulous falsetto was clean and exotic. Their voices started to play Twister, entangling each note, each verse. My smile grew a little wider and I started moving in the bed. The music was loosening my grip.

As I lifted the covers off, it happened. Their voices, Smokey and Rick, reached its highest peak, somewhere way out on top where funk meets gospel. Their song ended and my smile faded. I turned off the alarm clock.

Dupri wasn't next to me. His side, the left near the door, was empty. His pillow didn't have an indention or its saliva residue. He didn't sleep next to me last night. I thought I hugged him in the middle of the night. I thought his body guarded mine, like it had so many nights before I lost myself.

I hugged myself now, sitting on the edge of the bed, still wearing the same clothes from the day before. When would this all end? Empty bed spaces, unpredictable tears, Dupri's hurting heart, when would I be brave enough to end this madness? I thought about sitting there longer and trying to find the answer but got up and prepared for the Stair Master.

I changed out of my slept-in jeans and t-shirt and quickly pulled on my workout leggings and tank top. I brushed my unruly hair into a ponytail. Looking in the mirror above my vanity, I gasped. My reflection depicted crow's feet by my tired eyes and a strand of gray hair. I made a mental note to add L'Oreal midnight black hair dye and eye cream on today's forever long to-do list. I walked away from the mirror; tears were waiting behind the curtains. I made my way towards the home gym quickly before they made their debut.

Maybe he was in the den. Nope. Still no signs of Dupri. I just knew I was going to trip over him. Instead of making a right and checking the office, I stayed on the path I was heading.

Shit was really fucked up now. I went and sent Dupri over the edge. He always slept with me. We promised not to go to bed mad at each other. All the experts said it's not good, he knew it wasn't good, but we did it anyway. The first time in our relationship, he stayed mad. The first time in our relationship he left me to hug myself at night. Couldn't say that I blamed him, he was being so patient, every woman's dream. Did he see this coming? On our first date, did he know I would leave him to hug himself?

He said he was going to be there at 10am for our first date. He rang my bell at 9:53. As usual I was running around doing last minute things. I didn't make it down the stairs and out the door until 10:13am. I'd him wait twenty whole minutes, but he didn't seem to care. He smiled at me with affection when I opened the door.

"Sorry, I took so long, but you know how it is."

He chuckled. "Yeah, I do. I have three sisters."

I chuckled also. He helped me bring my bike outside. He said our

date was going to be a surprise fun-filled day. I didn't like surprises, but I liked Dupri, so I went along with the date. He asked me if I had a bike, and I did. He told me to dress comfortable and make sure the bike tires were full of air. I bought a bike pump the day after we made plans. I wore a sea-green lightweight with Lycra-hooded sweat suit, a white v-neck t-shirt underneath, and white Nikes. He wore a gray t-shirt with Morehouse sprawled across the front, a matching baseball cap, blue jeans, and a pair of Jordan's.

Standing in front of him I smiled, marveling at his Aries take-charge nature. He hoisted the bike on to his shoulders and carried it down the stairs. Grabbing my hand he somehow managed to open the door to his SUV before attaching my bike with his bike to the back of the truck.

I was overjoyed, a bit giddy, being in the truck with Dupri. I felt like a schoolgirl again, experiencing her first crush. I glanced at him to see if he was just as anxious as I was. He sat behind the wheel tilting to the side scratching the heart mole on the tip of his nose. His relaxed position gave no inkling to his feelings. He just hummed along to Roy Ayers serenading us in the background as he turned on the BQE, heading in the direction of the Long Island Expressway.

"So, are you going to tell me now, where we are going?" I asked playfully, handing him a peppermint, and eating one myself.

"You don't give up? It's a surprise just sit back and enjoy the ride."

"I should call my sister and give her your license plate number, God forbid I don't make it home this evening."

"Very funny, I see you're a regular Roseanne Barr."

"At times I can be."

We moved on from me being a comedienne to the war bombing of the World Trade Center, ending with the season finale of Soul Food. We played who's that artist. I sang a song verse, and he had to guess who the singer was. That was a feat in itself, being that I sing like crap. I talked and talked about my love for Mary J. Blige, Nina Simone, and Oprah.

He listened and listened to my banter. I stopped for a moment to discover we both swam with dolphins, he in the Bahamas and me in Cabo San Lucas, Mexico.

He captivated me as he sat diligently, hanging onto my every word. We engaged in verbal intercourse, which brought me to a mental orgasm

that day in the middle of the Long Island Expressway. My heart told me Mr. Haynes was something special as I watched him check his rearview mirror before exiting the expressway.

Finally we reached our destination, or so I thought. We weren't finished traveling yet. This time we were going by boat. With his muscular arms, he took the bikes down. I grabbed my bag; we raced to the ferry, where we settled into another hour and a half ride, this time to our final destination.

"Now are you going to tell me?" I was getting cranky. He laughed, "We are going to paradise."

I punched him in his leg. "Ouch! That hurt," he lied. "We're going to Block Island."

Our space for the day was a quaint little island between Rhode Island and on the southern end of Long Island. Wild greenery lined the small, lush, and luxuriant island hidden away from the press of city life.

Enchanting shops, multicolored exotic flowers, and romantic seaside restaurants lined the island shores. The sun engulfed the complete island. Not leaving a single spot for shade. It's white sandy beaches and clear ocean water harmoniously coupled at the exact point. Block island was an island, where an invitation for idleness was accepted.

"I like the fitted hat better." I said flipping through the hat racks.

"You do?" he surveyed his image in the mirror.

"I said I did, didn't I?" I walked around the back of him checking out his reflection with him. "This is the hat Dupri, can we go?"

"Not until I find a magnet with my name on it."

Now he knew there was no way in hell, he was going to find a magnet with Dupri on it. However I humored him and rummaged around looking for it with him.

I picked a magnet with my name on it. Dupri was pissed. I couldn't help it if my name was more popular than his. He would never find Dupri on a magnet. He finally settled on a plain ol' "Block Island" magnet. He grabbed the receipt from the cashier before grabbing my hand.

We parked the bikes outside the seafood restaurant, before going in. There was nothing particularly fancy about the eatery he chose.

Captain Hook was outside, protecting the establishment. It had a rustic log cabin feel. A swordfish, trout, and shark decorated the inside wall. A tall brunette with a teased ponytail greeted us when we walked in, her smile taking up her whole face.

"Hi, Dupri," she sang, giving him a wink. "What's up, Leslie? How is it going?" This was crazy!

"Same ol' shit different day. Follow me to the back."

I looked at Dupri with a questioning look. He just stared ahead, ignoring the heat of my eyes on his profile. I followed along to the back of the restaurant, forgetting about Leslie. We were the only patrons. Leslie placed out menus on the table in the back overlooking the water. She patted Dupri on the back and walked away. He finally told me the owner was the father of one of his co-workers at Goldman Sachs. Leslie was his co-workers sister. I felt so dumb at my suspicions.

The view of the sugary sand beach from the restaurant was splendid. The blue-green ocean water glistened. It was close enough to lick but far enough to envy. Melodiously the blue sky embraced the ocean. A thrill seeker sped wildly on a jet ski, through the spirited ocean waves. The sounds of the waves lapping in the shoreline comforted me.

Dupri flashed a friendly smile my way. "I love the water."

"I see. I hope you don't mind, but I'm going to order for you."

I was taken aback however; I relaxed and allowed him to handle everything. I always said I wanted a man to do things for me. When they are placed in my path, I chased them away unconsciously. Not this time. I granted myself the permission to relish in this man's affection.

After dining on stuffed crabs, shrimp and lobster ravioli with white wine we walked and talked to Fred Benson beach, before mounting our bikes. Riding between where the sand ends and the ocean water begins. We rode side-by-side holding hands, at first. Then his competitive nature kicked in and he called a race. At first he allowed me to be in the lead, until he picked up speed. Leaving me in the dust literally. I struggled to ride swiftly to catch him. He laughed at my attempts. We rode through the quaint village until sunset greeted us. I hadn't done this since I was ten, when October and I use to ride in Prospect Park. It was by far the best date ever.

I was silent on our venture home. Dupri was quiet as well. We hummed along to the music from the car radio's cd. No words were

spoken. Our silence was broken as Dupri walked my bike and me to the porch.

Now I was on the Stair Master sweating profusely listening to Nina Simone, not sure of where my man slept last night. I didn't have the energy to search for him either. Today had already started out to be draining. Another week of school, a scheduled two-hour session with Sapna, and let's not forget Dupri. Could I please climb back into bed and listen to Rick and Smokey?

Chapter 10

"Tober it's me, call me back when you get this message."
Because O. is on a tight budget, she seldom answers her
phone during peak time. I leaned against the kitchen wall, with my
arms folded under my small bust.

"One, two, three, four..."

"Rrriiinnnnggg" Ah, there goes the phone. She always calls back
before I reach to five.

"You called madam?" She sang in a mellifluous rhyme.

"You know I did. I went to the bank and I have your money. Well
my money, this is only a loan."

"I know it is, gosh."

I sucked my teeth. "Anyway, I'll be here until six pm. You can
come pick it up before then, or I can mail it to you? Which ever is
easier?"

"You want me to leave Brooklyn and come all the way to the City?"

"Ah, yeah."

"You can't bring it to me? You're the one with the car. My ass has

to take mass transit." Her gruff voice whined.

"Look if you don't come and get it by this evening, I'm going to redeposit it tomorrow." I advised with the same voice I've used on my students.

"Alright, alright I'm on my way." She said defeated.

"Good. If I'm not here, I'll leave it with the doorman."

"Thanks."

"Oh something else, before I forget. I expect my money back in four weeks."

"Four weeks!" She bellowed into the phone. I removed the receiver. All I need is a broken eardrum.

"How the hell am I supposed to do that, shit?"

"That's your issue. Just make it happen, and return my money."

"Okay," her gritty voice was a less than audible whisper. If I don't set a time limit I would never see my money. Even though my time limit doesn't guarantee anything.

"Luv ya." I said laughing to myself.

"

Chapter 11

"Pumpkin did I tell you Tober bought a house?" he gazed at me from behind the Sport's section of the Sunday paper.

"Get out! Miss Thing is stepping up her game. I'm proud of her."

"Yeah, so am I. Pass me your other hand." I was finished clipping the nails on his left hand and was ready to move on.

Generally, this is how we spend our Sundays. Laying in bed with either me reading Oprah's book club latest novel and him with the Sunday paper, cutting each other's nails in between.

Dupri was better at a manicure than Lisa's Nail Salon. Once through with our manicures we put our reading material down and experiment in the kitchen. We'll either swipe a Paula Deen or Pattie Labelle recipe or something either one of us grabbed off the Internet. After dinner we always retreat back to bed to watch Sunday night HBO.

"Where is it?"

"In East New York. You know they are building up the area." I surveyed my work. His nail beds looked ready for a hand commercial.

"Tell me about it. They are doing that all over. My homeboy was

telling me how they are knocking down the projects in Baltimore and building new homes. Shipping all those poor folks further out into the country." He twirled his finger in my wild ebony hair.

I reached up and kissed his cheek. "I think she is doing the right thing. It's about time Miss Thing gets responsible."

"It sure is. But you can't fault her. She always had you to back her." Well. He had a point. "But Miss Lady, why are you always telling me about someone else's shit, instead of yours."

Here we go again, I thought snuggling under his deodorant filled armpit.

"I do tell you things, Pumpkin."

"Somethings! I want to know everything."

"My Mother said never tell a man everything."

"You don't even like your mother." Well, the man does have a point.

"I don't know Dupri. I do want to tell you, but I'm not ready yet. I'm sorry about the other afternoon. One day I'll be the open book you want me to be."

" "Miss Lady it's not about the other afternoon, its *period*. I'm beginning to sound like a broken record. I feel like I'm sleeping with the enemy and shit. A damn intruder in my own damn house." He pulled me closer, planting a wet but sweet one on my forehead.

"I don't know what to tell you Dupri."

"I know that's the problem."

Dear Book,

"

I am so sick and tired of Chris harassing me. The boy has serious mental issues. Why do I have to live next door and let's not forget to mention go to school with a demonic fool? Mom says he has a crush on me. If that's a crush, then I am going to slit my wrist. He is worse than Freddie Kreuger.

Other than stupid Chris, everything is going well. Well as well as expected. Mr. George is still an idiot and mom hasn't filed the divorce papers yet. Gotta go now and get ready for bed. Talk to you tomorrow.

Bye Book.

Chapter 12

My day in the classroom wasn't nearly as exhausting as I'd envisioned. Usually it took a couple of weeks before everyone got settled into the routine of the new school year. So far so good. A few stragglers generally were left registering for class. Thus far, it appeared I had all my children and then some, on my roster, this semester.

Some may find teaching fifteen-and sixteen-year-olds a death sentence. Factor in New York City's Public School system and they probably would want to do the lethal injection themselves. For me it was my life's dream. I was one of those children who always had her hand up when asked, "What do you want to be when you grow up?" The day I passed my teacher's certification and received my school assignment was by far one of the happiest days of my life.

I started out with third graders in an elementary school in Rego Park, Queens. They were like sponges; soaking up everything you taught them. At that age they were still so eager to learn. But I got bored with them. I needed something a bit more challenging. When the opportunity came to work at the school for pregnant teens, I jumped at the chance. There I could have the most impact.

Being a misunderstood teenager, I've always felt that adults didn't "get" teenagers. They some how missed key opportunities to discuss life issues with them, instead harping on all of the negative things that may have plagued a teen.

Some, not all, sort of threw teenagers away similar to the way my mother and stepfather disregarded me. With Mother busy at work all the time, ignoring the issues of the house, and Mr. George taking advantage of her absence and abusing me.

I wasn't a bad seed, just an abandoned one. Lonely and scared I was. It didn't matter whether I got all A's or B's. Either way they never congratulated me. They saw all grades as D's anyway.

Ms. Peru, my journalism teacher, wrote them once. She attached the copy of the school newspaper to the letter she wrote. She expressed to them that I had the ability to be the next Barbara Walters. Joining the school newspaper would aid in making that dream a reality, which would require me staying after school. They never acknowledged the letter or the newspaper article. They did, however, acknowledge her comment that I can be a little chatty at times. Chatty at school I was, only because I was muted at home.

"All right everyone, I want you too pass up last night's paper on Aphrodite. I hope everyone wrote the recommended four pages." I stated eyeing the thirty something plus students, in my classroom.

"And suppose you didn't write the recommended four pages? What's the repercussion?" Amanda asked sluggishly doodling in her chair.

Amanda, a student in my English Literature class, was far from being muted. In only the first month of school she had made an impression on me, with her quick wit and explosive tongue. If you said one thing she said another. That girl had an answer for everything.

"Well, Amanda, the repercussion would be that you would have to write it again, this time adding ten more pages. Along with being responsible for an oral report due this Friday. So I sincerely hope you were just asking that question, just to be asking and that you did indeed do all of what I required of you."

She quickly nodded and sunk down lower in her seat.

Some may have seen her as rude, but not me. She was a sassy, smart mouthed, free spirit with a pretty cocoa-bean chocolate complexion. She was just reaching out to anyone who would hear her.

She reminded me of why I used to dream of chocolate.

My high school crush, which was also my neighbor, Chris, started my dreams of chocolate. In the hallways of our school or his porch, he taunted me by calling me ghastly names. He juggled back and forth from calling me either "Midnight" or "Charcoal." "What's up, Midnight? Don't stay out in the sun too long, you'll get blacker." He sneered as I walked through the halls of our schools. His words broke my heart.

Back on our block, he continued educating me on my complexion. "You, hey you over there, I know you can hear me calling you." I was listening, but pretended to be absorbed by my book. "Women your color love chocolate men, but chocolate men would never take a woman like you home to meet their mother. You ain't capable of pretty babies." He said laughing like a king.

Still acting as though I was lost in my book, I never once let him see how his words affected me. Not once showing him, my tears.

"If we were back in slavery you would be a field slave. Your kind is not good enough for the house. If the slave master did let you into his domain, he would jerk off in your face. Your pussy is two black for his white dick. Shit, you're too black for any dick." He snickered sinisterly. My porch lessons always ended the same. I threw my book, which shielded my tears, at him and ran into my mother.

"Love, don't worry, boys will be boys. He is only doing this because he has a crush on you." My mother tried to reassure me.

"A crush, Ma, that's a crush? If that's the case, then my midnight ass would be celibate." She was disgusted by my choice of words but knew my pain ran deep. She refrained from chastising me.

Mother did take notice, however, when Chris's mother began to join him. My mother approached her. She felt they could have a mother–to–mother heart-to-heart. Boy was she wrong.

"Make sure she marries a white man, so you could see your grandchildren."

My mother closed her eyes, said a prayer to the Lord, asking for forgiveness for what she was about to do. She let the Caribbean out and assaulted Chris's mother with a barrage of insults and curse words. Mother reasoned that ignorant people raise ignorant children.

Chris and Mr. George could have been father and son. Mr. George was also in my chocolate dreams. Telling me I should wear bright

colors. He called me "blackbird" as a term of endearment.

Their harsh words propelled me to wear baby powder to bed. Hoping when I woke I would be twelve shades lighter. I used every skin-lightening cream on the market. Determined to be more like my lighter-skinned eighth-grade classmates, I longed to wear pink and red lip-glosses as they did. Instead I gravitated toward the earth tones.

I thought everyone viewed me as they did, dark and ugly. The compliments I received from strangers or friends meant nothing. They were surely drunk and blind.

Not until Samantha showed me a picture of supermodel Roshumba. I thought she was the most gorgeous woman ever. Prettier than my Mother. She was a friend in my head, slowly changing my obscure opinion about my color. In time I began to embrace my chocolate complexion. Taking compliments became a tad easier. I received them with a pinch more grace. Having Amanda in my class made me see it was still okay to dream of chocolate.

Through the years, I often wondered what happened to Chris. Why did he really insult me so? The strange part of it all was Chris was darker than I. He was as black as the night is dark. Chris saw me as black or 'midnight,' as he liked to tell it. Our white counterparts saw us plain ol' black people. Not light brown, medium brown or dark brown, but black people. Only Chris saw my color, I guess because he was too afraid to see his own.

Chapter 13

"Babe, you expecting anyone?" His voice roared up the stairs in an Isaac Hayes timbre.

"No, Pumpkin." I shouted down the stairs tighten the belt around my robe. I checked my reflection wiping my naptime crust out the corner of my eye. Sleep still lingered in me.

A burnt orange radiance sparkled through the skylight window. I woke up just in time to catch the sunset. The full moon illuminated the entire top floor.

"Who is it Dupri?" he shivered as my breath whispered over his ear. The quintessential alpha man squeezed my thigh as I walked in front of him. "I have no idea. I don't hear anyone." He shrugged scratching his goatee.

"Something tells me its Tober."

"Who is it?" I bellowed.

"Open the door, Crackhead." I shook my head. What the heck does she want?

"Took you guys long enough." She whisked in as though someone

was chasing her.

"Hey Dupri." She beamed giving him a bear hug.

"So what brings one of my special ladies by this evening?"

"Yeah, why is your ass here." I snickered with my hands on my hips.

"I see we woke up on the wrong side of the bed. Relax chick, I am not staying long. I only came by to share my good news in person." She moved a strand of hair out her eye.

"What's the news, October?" Dupri responded handing her a cold Corona before taking his place in his chair.

Better him than me to be enthusiastic about her damn news. I can careless. She always had a way of popping up unexpectedly. Being totally oblivious to how it infuriates me. But when approached she would say, "What did I do?"

As kids she was ignorant to everything. She often left the fridge door open, after pouring herself a cup of juice. Then of course because she never- did anything wrong, I would get in trouble. Don't let her father be home, it would really be hell to pay then.

She looked into her oversized chocolate pocket book, shaking a set of keys savagely in the air.

"I'm a home owner, I'm a home owner." She danced frantically in the middle of the living room.

"You go October." Dupri popped up to join her. Making synchronized movements. I couldn't help but smile with them.

Finally she was making a move in the right direction. Now I would no longer have to wait for her on the street corner, when I picked her up for one of our outings. I could finally call her and not worry that one of *them* may answer.

My hand fell from my hips as my lips curled with excitement. My baby sister was finally growing up. I was scared shitless she would use my ten grand for some other crap.

"This calls for a celebration. I say we all go out to eat." I said taking off my robe heading upstairs.

"I'm going to get eaten alright, just not with you guys. My Korean lover and I are going out to celebrate. We are having sushi." Her gritty voice filled with laughter. Heat seared through Dupri turning him beet

red.

"On that note, I'm out." He said making a mad dash for the den.

"Do you always have to be so disgusting?" My eyes touched the top of my eyelids.

"What? Its just sex." She smirked. "Seriously, I would love to do dinner with you guys, but maybe later on in the week. My future baby daddy is waiting downstairs for me."

"Why didn't you bring him up?"

"Because I had no intention of staying long. And like I said we have plans. I just wanted to come by and share my excitement. Also to request your presence at my party next week."

My eyebrows united. "October, didn't your ass just move in? How the hell are you going to have a party already? Let's start being responsible, damn." I walked over to the door and opened it. I needed her to leave.

"You have no fucking faith in me. It can be so annoying sometimes. How about saying "Congrats Tober" instead of judging me?" She snatched her bag.

"For your information, Miss Perfect, it wasn't your average party. I was having a paint party. I wanted you guys to come by and help me paint the freaking place. Don't bother to RSVP."

Chapter 14

Realizing that I had approximately thirteen minutes before my appointment with Sapna, I parked. The day of our first session, Sapna made it a point to advise me that a time would come when I would try to avoid sessions. Today was one of those times. I could, at this very moment, stay in my car, turn around, and go home.

These feelings just came out of nowhere. I was having a great day, the students were fine, but now I was feeling a bit sucky. Despite my sudden mood change I decided to stay and face the music. No other therapeutic method had been so revealing, so eye opening, and so very honest.

When I learned Sapna was a drama therapist I investigated this style of healing thoroughly. I spent hours online and in the library, learning the history of this particular therapeutic method. I was shocked to see that it was fairly new but was becoming more popular. Through the use of theatrical, dramatic, and physical integration the therapist sought to assist the client with personal growth. Because I thought I should have played Cleopatra instead of Liz Taylor, this form of therapy seemed right up my alley.

Surprisingly enough, it helped me rejuvenate my overworked system

and to reconnect with my inner wisdom. We hadn't begun to play yet; she was still taking me history. I looked forward to getting to that point. Dupri thought because I was crying like a newborn, it wasn't working. But my core was telling me change was taking place.

I thought it would be a walk in the park, but that was not the case. Some sessions were better than others. Some sessions I cried and some I didn't cry at all. Tapping into that side of you that is so ugly was the scariest shit ever. I had not even gotten to my core yet. If I did there would a celebration bigger than Dick Clark's *New Year's Rocking Eve*.

"Hey, Sapna, how are you?" I asked. A lone white candle burned from her desk. Her olive skin glowed under the dim light.

"I'm doing well," Sapna responded in a concerned tone, "but the question is how you are? A lot of things came up for you during your last session. How was your processing this week?"

"It wasn't easy. I can't digest that I molested a retarded girl, Dupri hates me, I collapsed on the Westside Highway, and I still haven't spoken to my mother. And oh by the way, I lent my sister ten thousand dollars, but I'm worried as hell she may never pay me back. Other than that, things are great. I can't complain." I exhaled.

"Take a deep breath. I can understand how all those things can become overwhelming, but it has to get hard and painful before it gets better," Sapna explained. "What you are experiencing doesn't look or feel good. I know it's a lot, but trust me it will all pay off."

"Okay," I said, drained already.

"Now, let's begin."

Veronica Clarke, my mother, was eighteen years old when she came to New York City. She spent the first eighteen years in her birthplace of Barbados West Indies. She came over with her younger sister, Vivian. Aunt V, as I affectionately called her, was four years younger than my Mother. My granddad lived in the United States for five years before he sent for his two eldest daughters. He was a widower.

Veronica finished her education in the States. She attended high school during the day. She spent her nights partying with her sister and other young West Indian immigrants. Though she enjoyed her youth, Veronica so desperately wanted to get married and have children of her own. She longed to be the mother that was taken from her at a young age.

At one of those infamous parties that Veronica met Taylor. Taylor

Harper, was a dynamic, charismatic gentleman who frequented the party scene. He was 6'2" with chocolate brown skin, full lips, and a neat Afro. With dashing good looks, he was full of life and very vibrant. He wasn't from Barbados. That was a problem for Veronica; she wanted to stay true to her West Indian heritage.

Taylor was born and raised in Jackson, Mississippi. Despite this problem Veronica found Taylor quite intriguing. Taylor's confidence and ability to charm the pants off the Pope, won her over. He had no problem getting what and whom he wanted. He was use to having things handed to him. He loved the challenge of actually working for something.

Veronica was the challenge that the other women never gave Taylor. She made Taylor work for her affection.

Working feverishly to win Veronica's love, Taylor came out of himself. They took carriage rides through the city. There were spontaneous picnics in Central Park. A brown-uniformed deliveryman would shower my mother with a dozen roses at least twice a week, courtesy of Taylor. Some mornings she would step outside to find tiny jewelry boxes on her front porch.

Kissing Veronica was not allowed. The only place his lips landed were on her cheeks and hands. Veronica wanted to save that special moment, of their first kiss, for their wedding day. After six months of dating, Taylor went to her father, who was rather strict, and asked for her hand in marriage. Roland Clarke looked at Taylor and said, "I would be honored to have you as my son-in-law." Taylor had even won over Roland's heart.

The wedding bliss was over before it started. After being together for four-and-a-half years, Veronica still hadn't given birth. "Are you really a woman?" he would often say, making her feel less than a woman. He even went so far as to call her a disgrace to the female population.

Taylor began to see other women. Veronica came home, once to find another woman's underwear on her bed. She cried into the panties, which were on her bed. She felt like such a failure. But she never told a soul, for she was a very private and proud person. She allowed her family to think her life was perfect.

In the spring of that year, Veronica got the news she had always dreamed of. She was pregnant! After four long years, she would finally be a woman and give her husband what he so desperately wanted. A

baby! She was going to have a baby! Veronica called all of her friends and family and began preparing for her new bundle of joy. When she told Taylor, he was so happy. She'd never seen him that thrilled.

That night, he made love to her as he never made love to her before. He even went as far as to reenact their honeymoon. He also made a solemn promise to stop seeing other women. Veronica couldn't have dreamed of a more beautiful night.

Taylor started to love his wife again. They took long walks in the park. He came home every night as promised. They made love regularly. The delivery guy in the brown suit began to pay Veronica regular visits once again. It was just like the beginning.

On February 27, 1970 Veronica gave birth to a healthy, eight pounds three ounces baby girl in Brooklyn New York. She was just perfect, with cocoa-brown skin and full lips just like her daddy's. The baby's eyes were slanted and quite intense. I, Anna Story Harper, was born. My mother felt my eyes told a story, hence my name.

Regrettably, on the day of my birth my dad, the infamous Taylor was nowhere to be found. He had gone back to his old tricks. Everyone asked for him, but even in the state my mother was in, Veronica was able to come up with a truthful lie.

In those days there were no cell phones or pagers, so of course there was no real way to contact him. He thought his excuse was legitimate: he supposedly got stuck on a major project at work that needed his immediate attention. But everyone saw through it. Taylor even went so far as to get his boss to cover for him. His actions were ignored. Instead, they celebrated my birth.

Taylor walked in with flowers for Mother and a teddy bear for me, the very next day. Aunt V. shook her head in disgust when he asked, "What did she have?" Though pissed Aunt V. and Grandpa Roland kept their emotions to themselves. They weren't going to spoil Veronica's happiness. Though my mother never shared with her family about his infidelities or abuse, they knew he was hurting her. They knew her pain. They played along with her and kept mum. The family knew Veronica would come home when she was ready.

Taylor tried real hard to be a great dad to me. He loved me immensely but the streets were his first love. He would run in and run back out. He stayed only long enough to physically abuse my mother and take her money. Taylor never hurt me, though. He treated me like a goddess. I made him smile. Veronica tried desperately to keep her family together. She ignored the calls from the other women and the

dwindling bank accounts. When Veronica came home from work she would change soiled sheets. It became as common as putting out the garbage. Seeing other women's panties in the bathroom or bed became a part of her life.

Veronica's desperate need to have a family allowed her to persevere. She allowed very few to know her turmoil. She shared her pain with my babysitter, Mrs. Hawkins, and would leave her check with her on payday.

Taylor had a habit of stealing her money. He would be so infuriated when she only came in with twenty dollars to her name. Veronica had to come up with a good excuse as to why she didn't have any money on her payday.

If the excuse wasn't good enough a battle followed. Taylor fought Veronica with the same dedication that Muhammad Ali fought Sonny Liston. On payday he forgot that Veronica was five feet tall and one hundred and thirteen pounds. Instead, he saw her as a punching bag. Taylor was so caught up in his own needs and them being met that he forgot he was a husband, a father, a friend, a lover, a confidant. He had succumbed to his anger, his violence.

Her desperate need to have a "normal" family, due to the death of her own mother from pneumonia, clouded Veronica's vision. She figured that, Taylor's behavior would soon pass. He would realize that the streets had nothing for him and come home to his family. She was anxious to give her daughter the family she never had.

Taylor was getting ready to go out, as usual. Veronica hugged his waist begging him to stay. She promised to be a better wife, never to complain. He ignored her. Trying to free himself of her grip.

She gave up falling to her knees sobbing. She pleaded with him to feel sorry for their family and do right by his wife and daughter. Instead Taylor ran down the stairs, out the door, and into the night.

Veronica laid on the floor in a fetal position as I waddled to the steps of the second floor. My toddler self wanted so badly to be with my daddy. In my attempts to be with him, I fell down the flight of stairs; my dad forgot to lock the safety gate. My mom jumped up, forgot about her tears, and came to my rescue before she began to cry again. This time she cried for herself, she cried for me, and she cried for her marriage that she knew was over. Veronica Harper would soon become Veronica Clarke again.

After the divorce my mom swore to give me a family again. She

felt every child needed one, especially little girls. We went to live with my grandfather for about two years. Granddad did everything for me becoming my dad.

On the way to work one morning, Veronica was greeted by Taylor sitting on Roland's porch, "Aye, what are you doing out here?" she said, shocked to see him first thing in the morning.

"I want to talk to you," He begged.

"Talk." Veronica whispered with her heart still hurting from the pain he caused.

"I want to be a man, and come back to my family. I want us to be a family again. You, Anna, and me. I'll go seek help like you wanted me to. Just don't leave me. Veronica please, don't walk out on me."

Veronica looked at Taylor and smiled. She didn't want him to see that this was paining her also. "Taylor you walked out on me. Now excuse me I've got to go to work." She walked down the steps and never looked back.

Taylor became a distant memory once the divorce became final. The only memory my Mother and I had of him was me. I was his spitting image.

Veronica soon decided to take a trip back to her native island of Barbados. As she held me tightly in her arms, she smiled as she looked out the window and watched the planes descend into Grantley Adams International Airport. It was one point five miles from the capital, Bridgetown. She hadn't been back since she came to the states at eighteen. Veronica hoped to rekindle a relationship with her old flame, George. She thought this would be the opportunity to give me that family she thought I should have.

"Okay, Anna, we are finished for today," Sapna said. I slowly opened my eyes. "You really shared a lot today. How do you feel?"

"Relieved, I've never told anyone about my childhood."

"All right then, we will continue next week."

"No! Is there anyway you can fit me in sooner?" I pleaded.

Sapna's tone was dubious. "Are you sure?"

"Yes."

"Okay. Well, then, tomorrow at 6."

I took the appointment card from Sapna and headed into the night, relieved. An extra week would have given me time to think about not coming back...

Chapter 15

"October the stripes on the walls are hot." Zoe's perfectly painted cherry red lips curled into a full smile. "I was scared when we opened the paint can. Who the hell paints their living-room walls lime green?"

"I think even I was scared." October sang walking out into the living-room to serve her guests a tray of crab wontons.

"Zoe is right Tober. The stripes are fabulous." I chimed in as she walked back in. You heard her gold chunky bangles before you actually saw her.

"Of course they are. No thanks, to you, that is." O. scoffed rolling her eyes dramatically.

"Do you have to go there?" I leaned against the side of the kitchen wall, my full lips in a pout.

"Yes I do." She shouted over her shoulder as her permed straight hair trailed behind her. Zoe nudged my side with her elbow. "Can you two cut it out? Can we all just get along?" She chuckled lightly.

"I don't see what's so freaking funny. Besides she started." I whined.

"That may be the case, however you are older. So you need to show more discipline. You two are out of control."

"Whatever, if it weren't for me, she wouldn't even have this fucking place."

"What the hell has gotten in to you? She's your sister and you chose to help her. How the heck are you going to complain after the fact?" Zoe adjusted her knee length dark skirt.

"I can complain when ever the heck I want. That's how she gets by in life. Everyone always comes to aid poor dear October, don't anyone ever come to my freaking aid. It would only make sense that we are here basking in the glory of October's new home, that someone helped her to purchase. Her dependent ass couldn't have done this shit on her own." I stood there proudly.

"Right now you're behaving like someone I've never seen before." She shook her head sliding her hand over her cropped hair. "You're acting like a child. If you were going to be nasty about the money, why lend it to her? If you're going to give, then give from the heart."

"I gave her the money to prove to everyone that she isn't all that perfect. Little Miss Educated October, living in her parents home and having the whole fucking world at her disposal."

"Hold up! Hold up! Ain't your ass college educated also? You are scaring me. Before this thing gets ugly, I advise you to go home and sleep your attitude off. You obviously had too much to drink."

"I don't have an ounce of anything in my system." My slanted eyes smiled.

"How dare you turn my night of celebration into your Goddamn pity party! You are always complaining about some shit. I see you truly need that fucking shrink. Tonight is my night chick and I'm not going to stand by and have you ruin it."

Zoe stood in the corner by the stove, her sleeveless arms wrapped around her, as tears bit by bit escaped her eyes. I looked at her first and then at October, praying hard like hell, that my own tears wouldn't follow suit.

I snatched my teal leather clutch off the table before practically knocking down the guests, in pursuit of the front door.

Chapter 16

"What the hell got into you?" He lifted his heather gray turtleneck sweater. "You can't go around snapping and biting at folks, because you've got issues."

Pulling off my wedge boots, I rolled my eyes at his banter, wishing like hell he'd shut the fuck up.

"There is a time and place for everything." In his boxers he pulled a beer out the mini fridge in the corner of the bedroom. "You had to go and ruin your sister's night." He put the bottle to his head. "Oh and let's not forget how much of a jackass you looked like trying to get out of the frying pans heat."

"Can we not discuss it? I am tired." I pulled on my nightgown.

"You need to start discussing something. These unnecessary outbursts are getting old."

"Why do you care so much? Are you and her fucking?" I raised my naked eyebrow at him. He slammed the beer bottle down on the dresser. Sending a deafening blare out into the air. "Your smile lights up a million times when she is your presence. I was waiting for a good time to mention it, and there is no time like the present."

His face muscles tightened as he scratched his neatly trimmed beard. His temple bulged. He opened his mouth, but nothing escaped it. He stood motionless clenching the beer bottle. I never took my eyes off the bottle, fairing it would end up my way. Maybe they would leave me the fuck alone.

Chapter 17

"Class starts at 7:50 in the morning. With just my luck Crystal my '89 Corvette, decided not to start. I'm pretty sure she had been telling me for weeks that she didn't feel well; I just chose to ignore her. I did what I do best: put the key in the ignition and drive.

"Hey luv, Crystal is acting up again. Can you help me?"

"I'm on my way down," Dupri replied.

My poor baby never started. We ended up leaving her parked and Dupri drove me to work. He promised to take her over to his uncle's shop, so he could take a look at her.

It was moments like this that I appreciated him. With my raunchy behavior lately, I would have left me to fend for myself. Not Dupri, he was there for me no matter what. Lately he had become feisty, but I pushed him there.

There was a time when I would kill for a man to love me. Shit, I needed a man to love me. They were one of the many masks that I've grown so accustomed to wearing.

One fellow for whom I begged to love me the worse was Paz. With Paz, I was the female version of Richard Ramirez, the serial night

stalker. Paz was a Puerto Rican bad boy I met in the airport worked at the security checkpoint station. I was so excited, all I kept thinking about was those possibly wonderful surprise dates to the Caribbean.

I figured everyone who worked for an airline got discounts on airfare. He was sure to get free, if not half-priced airline tickets. I hit the jackpot. I just knew we would soon visit many tropical islands such as St. Martin, Aruba, Grenada, along with many others. My checkpoint lover was going to use his bargain flights with me.

What a joke: the closes we came to the Caribbean were stewed chicken, rice and peas, and plantains with a kola champagne from the Golden Krust restaurant and bakery.

The evening of our first date, I picked Paz up in my two–door, cherry-red Corvette. Paz, my knight in shining armor, couldn't pick me up like most gentlemen would have because he didn't own a car nor did he have a license. That was a huge problem, but I chose to ignore it. All I kept thinking was how incredibly sexy he was and a possible free trip to the Caribbean. I knew if I worked hard enough I would be eventually lying on the beautiful black beaches of Grenada.

That night Paz and I went to a club in the city, where we danced the night away. We did everything from salsa and slow dancing to some every intense bumping and grinding. Our seductive movements were passionate, warm, and romantic. Paz held me, overpowering me with his physical affection. My silhouette melted into his muscular frame with his magnetic aura making its way into my body. With his eyes interlocked with mine, our hips gyrating in synchronized movements. My Paz brought me to ecstasy in the middle of the dance floor.

Lost in our own trance, I marveled at what had just taken place; no one had ever brought that much passion out of me. Passion experienced with our clothes fully on, in the most obscure of places.

From that night on, everything about Paz was perfect in my eyes. He was confident, cocky, and sexy as hell. Paz would call me at 2 in the morning for sex. I was always much too happy to oblige. After dressing in a hurry I would speed over to his house, breaking every traffic rule known. He would always get into the car and greet me with his roller-coaster cinnamon-flavored kisses. He was a fanatic for cinnamon flavored tic tacs.

We were so impassioned when we saw each other; we had sex in the car. Paz once preformed oral sex on me while I was driving. He

somehow got his big head underneath the steering wheel and up my skirt. With his lizard-like tongue he indulged himself in my womanhood. The intensity of his lovemaking with his tongue made it impossible to control the car. Somehow I managed to keep it under control, even as I reached the point of ecstasy.

I later found out that there were other women who felt "our" passion. I called his mother's home one day and she spilled the beans. In her broken English she told me that I was a sweet girl, but so were the other ten women that called Paz on the regular. She went on to explain that Paz had a main girlfriend who lived out in Astoria. It seemed that every time Paz and his girlfriend got into an argument, he would leave her, go back to live with his mother, and indulge in other women to keep him busy.

Crushed and devastated, I screamed at the top of my lungs after replacing the phone receiver in its cradle. Cursing, crying, hugging my heart, I couldn't believe my true love was a complete jerk. I gave him sex whenever he wanted and however he wanted; my aim was to please. I did what I had to do to satisfy my Paz.

Did he not recall our first date? Why would he ever do this to me? When I confronted Paz about it, he shut me up by shoving his tongue down my throat. I wanted to love him again so badly, I eagerly accepted his kiss and all was forgiven.

After some time I grew tired of Paz's infidelity. As quickly as I fell into lust is as quickly I fell out. Paz became a distant memory.

We got to school in about twenty minutes. I kissed Dupri and thanked him for the ride. He promised to pick me up after school and take me to Sapna. *Thank God Paz was a jerk.* I thought to myself relieved.

"Did I just see my brother pull off?" Zoe asked as I walked into the school building.

"Hey, Zo, yep, that was your brother. My car was acting up this morning so he drove me in." I waited for her in the entryway, so she could catch up to me.

"He left me a message saying he had something important to ask me, but I didn't get a chance to get back to him. Do you by any chance know what he wanted?"

"Nope, he said nothing to me. I'm pretty sure he'll get back to you."

"Do you want to go for a cup of coffee after school today? I have some things I wanted to ask you." Her eyes widen behind her glasses.

"No, Zoe, I'm sorry but I have an important appointment this evening. Can I get a rain check?"

Chapter 18

My body was introduced to the tiny tree branch at six years old. I remember that pain as if it were yesterday. October, six years my junior finally made her arrival after she and Mother spent several days in hospital. Auntie Vivian came to stay with us. Mother figured Mr. George could use the help.

About five days after they returned home, I was longing for my Mother. She had a Caesarean section and was stuck in bed so I couldn't see or hug her much. Mr. George felt I should stay out of her hair.

"Mek sure yuh stay out of yuh motha's way, yuh hear? Yuh're are a pain in de ass and will just git in her way. I don't want to hear a peep out of yuh, or else." He threatened from behind the tightly shut wooden bedroom door.

My need for my mother was larger than his threats. I stayed outside the bedroom door and cried. My tears were endless. I screamed so hard and loud that October began to join me. It soon became a choir of cries in the house.

Mr. George slammed the bedroom door open, nearly removing it from its hinges. He held a puny but long tree branch. "Didn't I tell yuh

to shut yuh mout? Huh, didn't I? I told yuh keep it down. You can't listen. But that is alright. Those that can't hear shall feel." He commanded in his English laced African-Creole singsong bajan accent.

"Yuh is hardears. She has yuh pun a pointless pedestal. I'm gonna knock yuh blackbird backside off it, hear." he barked. Motionless, I looked up and stared straight into his hateful eyes at the very moment he allowed the tree branch to leave his side and say hello to my behind. I shrieked with horror.

The tree branch, with Mr. George's assistance, struck me over and over again. My body buckled right there outside the bedroom door with my mother peeking out and Auntie Vivian hiding in the living room. He beat me until every place on my body was covered with his lashes.

"Now, don't lemme hear another God damn sound from yuh. Or yuh would git more than what yuh were given," he bellowed not pronouncing any vowels. Confident, imposing, and arrogant he sauntered back into the bedroom. Before closing the door behind him, our eyes made contact for what seemed like forever.

"Now git yuh backside up, and git in your bed." He kicked my battered body in the behind, then went back to tend to my mother.

My abused body found the last bit of energy and crawled into the other room.

"I told you to be quiet," Auntie Vivian whispered.

Crawling into a corner, I grabbed my Kathy baby doll and cried my eyes out. Remembering the torture I had just undergone I made sure to stay very still.

Why did he do that to me? All I wanted was to see my mommy and October. Why didn't Mommy come out and rescue me? She said she would never let anyone hurt me. "Anna, I will always protect you from evil, you wouldn't ever need Wonder Woman you have me, your mother. I love you." She repeated that verse several times. I guess her lasso wasn't working that evening or several other evenings, days, and nights.

Through teary eyes I looked at Sapna and took a swig of water.

"Wow," was all she uttered. "Do you want to stop, or can you continue? We have twenty-five more minutes." Nodding, I took a deep breath and continued. This time reciting an event that took place when I was twelve years old.

Mother worked overtime on most evenings and the weekends. In her absence Mr. George was the caretaker for October and I. I never enjoyed those moments. I stayed in my room with a book, to protect myself from him. Sometimes it worked and other times...

One particular morning we were summoned to breakfast. The menu consisted of scrambled eggs, orange juice, and fiber cereal with two-percent milk. I longed for the day when Lucky Charms or Froot Loops with whole milk would be present at the breakfast table. I guessed I would've to eat at a different restaurant for that.

Being a member of the clean-plate club, everything was devoured except the eggs. The smell of them made me queasy.

Mr. George walked into the kitchen as I was disposing of the yellow substance into the garbage can.

"Aye, wat yuh doing wit those eggs?" Mr. George asked looking from the garbage to my plate.

I stuttered, "Throwing them away."

His hand smacked me directly in my mouth. Blood shortly replaced the saliva.

"Sit yuh rass down an finish those eggs!" he ordered.

I made an about face and marched back to the kitchen table. Lieutenant Mr. George stood behind my chair and waited. I raised my fork and placed the now ice-cold eggs in my mouth. As soon as they went down my throat I began to gag. His nostrils flared. Steam escaped them. He knocked me on the back of my head with his fist. He kept pounding and pounding; my head became a human punching bag.

"If yuh bring up those eggs, it will be yuh and me this mawning. Yuh hear?" Mr. George warned. "I swear I'll mek yuh lick up de bile."

I nodded and tried to keep the eggs down. But without fail, they spewed from my lips. Creating a whole new tablecloth on the kitchen table.

And promised, I was made to eat the filthy yellow bile, every drop of it. Embarrassment, and shame rested within. One by one my tears dropped. If I'd a nine-millimeter gun, I would have shot Mr. George dead, with not one ounce of regret. Living my life behind bars would have been paradise, compared to my shit box, called home.

Mr. George smiled with satisfaction, after I swallowed the last drop. His smile vanished when the eggs came up again. Enraged, he dragged

me out of my chair and threw me against the wall. He looked at me with those wicked eyes and spat, "Yuh a piece of shit, do yuh hear me? Yuh a wortless piece of shit, noting but shit. Those eggs cost a dolla twenty-nine a carton. Yuh'll neva have another meal in dis house, if I have anything to do wit it."

I stood there with my eyes tightly shut and inhaled his hot breath. I prayed, "Dear God, please get this man with his nasty breath out of my face. Thank you. Amen." My God, being the effective listener that He was, granted me my wish. Mr. George released me, but not before he smacked me across my face and stormed out of the kitchen.

When he loosened his grip I fell to floor, hugging my war-torn body and covered my blood-soaked mouth. On all fours, like an infant, I crawled to the bathroom locking the door behind me. Leaning over the toilet bowl, I stuck my finger down my throat to bring up what was left of the eggs. I cried uncontrollably, remaining in the bathroom for hours. I wanted to take refugee in the bathroom for the rest of the day or for the next six years; nevertheless I had to face the music and Mr. George.

Opening the bathroom door slowly I listened for his breathing. Silence. I tiptoed out of the lavatory. All was quiet in the house. Mr. George must have taken October to the park without me. There must indeed be a God.

I picked up the rotary wall phone and dialed my mom's job number. "Duncan, Smith and Woods?" she sang verbalizing her company's name.

"Mommy, I need you to come home, Mr. George has gone crazy," I said, choking on tears. Blow by blow and play-by-play, I updated her on the morning events and made sure not to forget any integral detail. I stood there in triumph, knowing she was about to tell me to pack my bags, she was on her way home to get us the heck out of this hellhole. The lasso was finally going to be put to good use.

"Anna, I know things are a bit rough now, but things will get better. He didn't mean anything by it. You know with the price of eggs going up, it pained him to see them go to waste. All those commercials with those starving children, is enough to push anyone a bit. They are over there suffering and you're wasting food," My mother whispered. "Next time just eat everything to avoid any confrontations."

Was I hearing things? Did she not hear a word of what I just said? I'd seen an ear specialist in the past, but he said nothing about me

being partially deaf. I shook my head as my tears returned. I bowed my head and prayed for a miracle while listening to my mother's theory.

"Look, Anna, Mr. George pays the bills, he's October's father, and I need one of my girls to have their father in their life. This won't be forever; you'll be eighteen in six years and this will all be a distant memory. Now, I have to get back to work. Is there anything else?" Not waiting for an answer, she continued, "Good. I will see you when I get home. I love you."

Sapna and I made eye contact; I spoke before she did. "Next Monday, same time, same place?"

"Yes, Anna that will be fine. Are you okay? Do you want to stay a moment and process? That was a lot of information covered. We went from six years to twelve years quickly."

I shook my head.

"Okay, we have covered a lot of ground. We'll do a couple more sessions of delving into your childhood and then we will begin some exercises that'll allow you to process this better. We can't stay in this place for too much longer. I usually like to get as much history before we start playing. I think we are almost there."

I nodded again.

"I would like to begin healing those old wounds. They have remained open and exposed for far too long." Sapna paused, gauging my reaction. "So yes, next Monday same time, same place, have a stress less week."

Dear Book,

Is there really a fucking happily ever after? Do you really go off into the sunset and live a beautiful life? I guess that only happens to those who are not married with children. Once you add children to the equation you might as well kiss the dream goodbye. I am never getting married. Unless maybe Levar Burton, James Worthy or if Kojack are in to black girls. Marriage is out of the question. What's the point? Get married later, get divorced, marry a jackass and have them abuse your child. Sike! That shit is not happening to me. I rather be an old maid for that crap.

It's weird how most of my friends are from divorced parents. Not one lives with both their parents. Not one I tell you. Book, were your parents together? Or were you like the rest of us? Something tells me, your family is a lot like mine. Fucking lunatics!

I am going to go now and get some rest. Besides he may soon take his nightly walk to see if we are sleeping. All he needs to do is catch me up this time of night. He will break my fingers and we will never be able to talk again. This is the only time I feel relaxed. Good night my friend. I'll be back tomorrow to unleash more of my thoughts.

Bye Book

Chapter 19

I walked toward Dupri, who was waiting for me on the corner of Hudson and Third Street. During my thirty-second stroll toward him, I couldn't help but notice the half-naked trees that lined the street. They lost their leaves in the fall but come back vibrant and colorful every spring. My leaves had been gone longer than a season. Lord, could you please work on bringing those leaves back? My poor branches were freezing.

I climbed into Dupri's royal blue SUV and gave him an affectionate kiss. For some odd reason I was happy to see him tonight and wanted him to know it. Maybe tonight the Cold War would come to an end and I'd feel his warmth inside of me. I glanced over at his profile and reconnected with the reason I love him.

"You seem like you're in a good mood," Dupri smiled. He reached over and rubbed my inner thigh. "I take it you had a decent session?"

"It was revealing." I locked the car door. "What did the mechanic say about my car?"

"I didn't get a chance to call him back. I'll page him tomorrow."

"Oh, okay."

"That's good, you had a good session. Listen, I was thinking, since

we are already in Hoboken we could drive over to Washington Street and grab a bite to eat." His sleepy deep eyes swam from corner to corner of my heart-shaped face.

"Sure." I giggled. "Dupri, I'm sorry about last night."

"Don't worry about it Anna." He raised the volume a bit. There was calm over us that evening. We drove over to Washington Street, humming together Lisa Fischer's "How Can I Ease the Pain." I think we were both asking ourselves that very question.

Washington Square, also known as "*Mile Square City,*" was similar to Dupri's Soho neighborhood. It had trendy restaurants and cool little shops. Just fifteen to twenty minutes outside of New York City. We'd eaten dinner in this quaint neighborhood several times. It was our way of getting out of the city, but still feeling like you were in the city. Our home away from home.

We decided on *Augustino's,* an Italian eatery with incredible mouth-watering entrees. D. ordered on the *veal chops* while I had *shrimp fettuccine alfredo.*

It was much like our first date to Block Island. Like then, this evening I talked and talked. Through bites of his chops, Dupri laughed at my silly jokes, on cue. I told him about my students this semester, about October's fifty-six-year-old Korean storeowner boyfriend.

"Anna, I have something to share with you," he began. I rested my fork on the table. "I'm going to hand in my resignation letter to Goldman Sachs this week."

My jaw dropped as my eyes exploded. "Excuse me, you are going to do what?"

His full mouth arched upwards. "I haven't been feeling very productive sitting behind a desk lately," Dupri explained, "And there has been a huge void in my life. I make six figures, drive a nice car, own a beautiful loft in a brilliant area, and have a very large nest egg, but I need and want more with my life." He took a deep breath and said, "I'm going to take my savings, purchase property, and open a jazz café. You know I love me some Thelonius Monk," he smirked. My mouth opened even wider at the sound of his plans. Not missing a beat he continued, "It will be a place where live musicians can come and showcase their works, probably have a poetry night where poets will have a voice. You know a place where creative people would have an outlet." He took a bite of his chops.

"Maybe I'll do my own Def Poetry Jam. I have no idea what I would call it, but I'm sure you can see what I'm getting at." He took a swig of his vodka and orange juice. "I don't want to grow old and have any woulda, coulda, shouldas, nagging at me. You feel me?"

I eased my chair back and leaned across the table to plant my glossy lips on his. His light mustache tickled my nose. He tasted of alcohol but I didn't care. The family in the booth in front of us smiled at my public display of affection.

"Yes I feel you. I'm so proud of you! You have my support all the way," My pouty, full lips expanded into a broad smile.

"Thanks, babe, it is very important for me to have your support. I couldn't do this alone. I hope you know I am doing this for our future, our children." A slow sexy smile smoothed his upper lip touching the ridge of his teeth.

For the rest of dinner we brainstormed together, coming up with ideas for Dupri's big new venture. We laughed and talked and really enjoyed each other. After paying the bill and leaving the more than recommended eighteen percent gratuities, he pulled out the chair for me and grabbed my hand. We walked hand in hand toward the car.

As we drove, with my head nestled on Dupri's shoulder, I was lost in my own thoughts. I felt ashamed for not paying attention to Dupri. Leaving such a prestigious company took great balls and though Dupri had it in him, he proved it again to me this evening. He was making a fantastic move and deserved a fantastic woman at his side. I was determined to be that woman for him tonight and every night thereafter.

Dupri let me out in front of the loft while he parked. I ran upstairs and began to prepare for our long-awaited night together. I dashed to my love drawer, and removed what I needed for the night's festivities.

Dupri arrived fifteen minutes later and was greeted by the O'Jay's "Lovin' You" and the scent of vanilla candles. Rose petals from the roses he sent me earlier in the week were scattered from the front door, up the winding stairs, to the bedroom. When he entered I was dressed in thigh high four-inch black boots, a black corset, which gave the impression of a size 26 waist, and a glass of bubbly in my right hand. I took my hair out of its usual bun, and allowed it to flow. It hung seductively over my face exposing only my left eye. A satisfied smile curled his lips.

He grabbed me seductively with his mammoth right arm pulling

me closer to him. Not once did the bubbly spill. He took the glass and drank most of it in one gulp. Spilling the remainder down my cleavage. His chameleon extended tongue lapped up every drop. Not breaking his gaze from mine he glided me over to the chaise lounge, where we began to make love under the stars, exposed through the opened curtains.

His loving kisses adorned my sex-starved body. Inch by inch, using only his probing lips and devilish tongue, he seduced my throbbing sexual desire while he massaged my neglected B cups.

"You taste so good," he said through heavy breaths.

My sexual squeals and squirming with orgasmic delight was the only way I knew how to answer him.

Dupri licked my love juices from his lips as he prepared to enter my love haven. His throbbing manhood entered me slowly, passionately. His lovemaking was enchanting, magically beautiful.

"Ah, Anna, I love you. You're so beautiful," he whispered sweetly while making love to me. "Do you love me, baby? I need you to love me, tell me you love me."

"I love you, also Dupri," I responded in a shaky voice.

My eyes began to water as emotion overtook me. I was beginning to crumble again. I tried to fight the tears but they wanted to be set free. Within seconds those light tears became Hurricane Gloria as I began to sob.

"What's wrong, baby? Did I hurt you?" Dupri asked.

Struggling for an answer I sobbed, "No, Pumpkin, you did everything right. You are magical; the problem is with me. The problem will always be me."

Dupri cradled me like an infant in his strong arms as he rubbed my lower back. I nestled in his clean-shaven chest and cried myself to sleep.

The taste of his sweet nectar on my neck.
Oh how I used to long for his kisses, now I run from his kisses.
A kiss I've decided to throw away.
The taste of his perspiration after he plays ball
A kiss of death
The kisses that after a time are no longer pleasurable
Nothing was pleasurable
I no longer wanted to please my man
I no longer wanted my man to please me
Beat me! Slap me!
Give me a reason to leave
You can't do this to a good man
He must be bad for me to neglect him
I'm bad, bad for wanting out
What kind of woman am I?
Every woman wants a good man
The taste, the taste of direction
The taste of someday being free of my indecisiveness
The taste of victory
The taste of structure
The taste of agony
The taste of winning
I will win and I would taste
One day I will taste that sweet nectar again

Chapter 20

"Hey October, what's up lil sis?" I asked after she answered on the first ring. Knowing my sister, she was probably sitting on the telephone waiting for her Korean love interest to call. I was nervous about calling her after our last encounter.

"What's up, big sis? What do I owe the pleasure of this call on this here Sunday afternoon? Isn't Sunday the day you and Dupri call your "date day" Don't you guys lose yourself in each other, at least that's what you told me in the past." She giggled using her private eye voice. She spoke like everything was normal again. I didn't mention anything and neither did she.

"No, Dupri went to watch the game with his brother-in-law." I lied. "So I figured, since I'm all alone today, why not call my loving sister and spend some much needed quality time with her."

October chuckled. "So you are using me, is that what it is?"

"No, not at all, we can go uptown and hang out. What do you think?" I knew she was going to agree to go out. She can never resist the opportunity to hit the streets.

"You are so lucky I have nothing to do. What time are you picking

me up?"

My sister was so predictable. She would bitch and moan, but there was never a time we didn't have fun together that she was bound to say yes. As long as I'm not cursing her out that is.

I turned down the radio as I pulled up to my sister's place. Half of the siding was off and the front door was changed. The dingy wooden fence was knocked down, replaced by a white picket fence. The remodeling was coming along nicely.

My sassy sister was waiting patiently on the porch. I was shocked to say the least, for she was rarely on time.

As I got closer I noticed her outfit. October's aesthetic eye always searches for clothing that entertains the masses. Today she had her dirty brown hair with Sunkist blond highlights pulled back in a tight ponytail, which reached the middle of her back, with a perfect high school bang. She changed the color, again. She wore gold, army green and tan wedge boots, an army green pencil skirt, and a cream cardigan with a cami underneath topped off by a tweed brown blazer. She looked cute and chic. Of course her boobs were bouncing along with every step she took. Those things are her prized possession. I turned down the radio as she entered the car adjusting the olive scarf around her neck.

"Hey, butthead," October said after slamming my car door.

"Woman, how many times do I have to tell you not to slam the door? This isn't Sal's junkyard special!" I exclaimed. "This may look like a '89 Corvette, but it has a spirit of a Mercedes, so treat it as such or else."

"Whatever! I see someone is on the rag." October changed the radio station. I guess Faith Hill wasn't doing it for her.

"Where are we off to? I heard that there is a very good foreign film at the Angelica Theater. My co-workers went to see it and said it was good. What do you think?"

"Sounds cool to me, then we can grab a bite to eat at this new Thai spot I found in Soho." With our plans set, we headed off to the city for our day of togetherness.

Being out with October is just what I needed to help me forget Dupri and the crying incident that took place. He has tried everyday to reassure me that things were okay, but I pulled away from him. I knew he was losing it sitting at home; being that Sunday was generally

our day. I just couldn't face him.

The crying episode left me feeling ashamed and more insecure. Everything about that night was wonderful until I somehow ruined things with my tears. I saw in his eyes that he was hurting for himself and for me. I had a gnawing suspicion that my avoidance of him would soon come to an abrupt end.

"Did I tell you that Cho and I are taking a trip to Miami? He said we're leaving sometime next week; the actual day is a complete surprise. I think he is going to pop the question," October invaded my thoughts with idle chatter, not realizing I was in deep thought. "I decided that if he does, I'm not going to accept, so he would have no choice but to ask me again. Maybe the second time around, he'll take me to Paris." October checked her reflection in the passenger side mirror. Her caramel complexion was luminous.

"You and your crazy ideas, just be happy he may propose to your crazy ass. But if you do go, make sure you bring me something back," I said laughing quietly, but wishing she would shut up.

"Okay that was not your usual boisterous laugh, what is up your ass? What is the real reason you dragged me out of the house today?" She finally realized from my unfamiliar laugh that something was bugging me.

"Nothing's wrong. I just have a lot on my mind."

"If you say so, but I know my sister. I'm going to make you spill your guts at dinner," she commanded as we pulled into the Manhattan parking garage.

The foreign film was what I needed. I lost myself in the story depicted on the movie screen. The subtitles added to the movie-watching experience. Instead of going straight to dinner, October and I decided to do some mindless makeup shopping. There was nothing like a new lip-gloss to make a girl smile.

We followed the host to our table as we toted our miniature shopping bags filled with new makeup. We placed our orders, making sure to add a strong Mojito, and got into the nitty gritty of our day.

"So Bighead, what did you do to upset my soon to be brother-in-law? That man is the epitome of perfection, so I know it had to be you that caused the friction."

"For the record, Dupri does fuck up at times, like leaving a trail of his clothes all over the place. However this time you are right. It was

my fault why I'm out with you and not spending my usual Sunday afternoon with my man." I chuckled nervously as I lifted my water glass for a sip. On the defensive, I explained the pathetic events of how our wonderful evening was destroyed by one of my now-famous crying fits.

October's expression was incredulous. "Wait, wait, let me get this crap right. Your man gave you some good loving and you cried because it was great, then you ran from him. Is that correct?" She probed like she was a defense attorney.

"Well, something like that," I hedged.

"It's official, your behind is crazy as shit! Bighead what is wrong with you? You are going to lose that man. But it's okay, because I've got someone all lined up for him, when he dumps your pathetic ass." October paused as the waiters placed our *Pad Thai* in front of us. As soon as they were out of the way I threw a little piece of tissue at her for her snide remark.

"You can throw whatever at me, but you are going to go too far until you lose him. Is that what you want?" She asked stuffing her face.

"I don't feel like I deserve him, October," I confessed. "I think he is too good for me, know what I mean? I think my life would be better if I was still dealing with the Paz's of the world. At least with them I can't expect much. What you see is what you get with men like that. With Dupri, you have to be worthy, he deserves that, but I don't feel worthy of his love. Can you believe after all of this time that we have been together, I've never told him the truth?" I felt ashamed as I searched my sister's face for a reaction.

"Tell him the truth about what?" She asked after taking a sip from her Mojito.

"I never told him about the abuse and our crazy childhood, among other things. He just thinks mother and I aren't that cool, because I'm hotheaded and stubborn."

"That man sure does know you. Hotheaded and stubborn ain't all you are. I could add a bit more adjective's but we'll leave it with those two." She snickered.

"O., would you listen to me and stop playing around. I'm dying over here woman, sheesh." I was getting a little annoyed she wasn't taking this as serious as I would like.

"Look, I don't think you deserve him neither," October joked again. "But I do know Dupri is a good man and he loves you. Everything is going to be alright. Just be frank and honest with him. Go home and tell him your fears and see how receptive he is going to be. I'm sure he would understand. And like Mom says, and Lawd knows she doesn't say too many profound things. *What is for you, you shall have.*"

We eased up on our conversation about my love life. There was no need to inundate out sister time with my madness. October was right; everything is going to be fine.

We polished off our meal as we discussed the new shades of lip-gloss and eye shadow we bought. My sister surprised me by paying for dinner and parking. I guess her relationship with the Korean Store owner was going to benefit me after all.

On the way home we rode in silence, to the early sultry sounds of Chante Moore, both of us in our own thoughts, but still content being in each other's company. At the corner of my sister's block, I turned giving her a huge hug and thanking her for spending the day with me. And of course she had to slam my car door.

Chapter 21

"Anna, please leave the lights off. I don't want to look at you while I tell you what has been bothering me for sometime." Dupri's usually opaque husky graphite voice filled with richness began to fall, leaving just a rasp of a whisper.

My knees got weak at his words. The key was still in the lock. I held onto the doorknob for support preparing myself for what he was about to say. I had an ailing feeling that it was not going to be "Will you marry me?"

"I've tried everything, short of taking my own life, in order to love you. I give you time when asked, space for you to grow. I gave you my heart, my home. I gave you me, but that doesn't seem good enough. I've been pacing up and down, banging my head against the wall lately, trying to figure out how the fuck can I make this right, and I realize now I can't. You are in great pain, Anna; I see it every time I look in your pretty little face. I figured if I moved according to your clock, you would shortly overcome your challenges." Dupri sighed deeply.

"I love you, Anna, and I want to help but I'm hindering you instead." He hesitated. "I-I want you to move back into your own place."

My legs caved in and I collapsed to the floor, letting go of the

doorknob. This was not happening. I was not in the doorway of the loft listening to Dupri give me the boot. This was actually part of the foreign film I just saw. Any minute now the director was going to shout, "CUT!" I'll go to my trailer skipping happily and Dupri will be waiting outside with a dozen long stem roses. He would give me a big sloppy, wet, kiss and tell me how wonderful I was and that I should be nominated for an Academy Award. Why hadn't I heard "CUT" yet? Oh shit, don't tell me this crap was MY movie? Don't tell me the man who had cared for me for two years, was giving up on me, giving up on us? Please say "CUT" Dupri, please say it and make love to me. I was ready to make love now.

Dupri kept his composure. Never once flinching or noticing that I was now on the floor. He never did utter "CUT." He spoke again, this time his voice fridge, sending an answering shill up my spine.

"Don't stay here tonight, get your stuff and leave. I'm going to my mother's; please be gone when I return."

The wooden legs of the armchair scratched the parquet floors as he pushed it back, leaving two long streaks behind. Dupri grabbed his jacket and walked out the front door. He never looked down in my direction but merely stepped over my collapsed body on his way out.

With a heavy heart I peeled myself off the floor and closed the front door behind Dupri. I placed my purse on the maplewood coffee table before sitting in the chair Dupri recently occupied. I hugged myself tightly pulling my knees close to my chin, rocking back and forth as I replayed the fifteen-minute trailer that had just taken place. Move out? Did he really tell me to pack my stuff and leave? I had been distant and not the greatest girlfriend lately, but he made a vow to me. He promised to be there for me. They weren't marriage vows, but they were words he said he would never go back on.

After replaying the trailer a zillion times in my head I finally made my way to the bedroom. I grabbed the duffel bag we usually used for weekend getaways and started packing my things.

I always dreamed that this day would happen, us moving into our five-bedroom house in the Catskills, not me moving back into my lonely Clinton Hill Brownstone. This shit was sick. How the heck did I go from a warm body in a king-sized bed to an empty bed surrounded by stuff animals? Grabbing the last of my things that fit in the duffel bag, I walked out of the loft.

Speckles of rain began to melodically hit my front window. I turned

the windshield wipers on low. With drops of mascara stained cheeks, I identified with the rain driving toward my home. I drove through the maze of yellow cab drivers, over the keeled scale of Brooklyn Bridge. I strained my dark eyes to take in the view offered by the bridge. I drove past the Verizon building on my left, the vacant lot where the Twin Towers once stood on my right, and the huge clock on the Watchtower building in front of me.

I made a right at Cadman Plaza West toward my barley lived-in place. The reality of having to stay by myself left me feeling worn-out. I'd become use to living with Dupri. Since the fourth month we'd been dating we'd lived together. Our instant connection compelled me to stay with him, not to mention that he begged me to.

I dropped my bags by my Crate and Barrel entertainment center. Turning on every light in the place so as not to feel alone. I checked the bathroom to make sure that I had no unwanted guests and securely locked the front door.

I walked around, getting reacquainted with my home again. The living room was still beautiful and warm. The walls were painted yellow, with beautiful art on the far right wall. Art pieces I'd collected from my"travels to various places. Brazilian carnival masks and a painting from David Wilson a Jamaican artist were just a few that lined my walls. Next to my expensive paintings was also a portrait of October and I, my prized treasure. October herself painted the piece. It was a picture of us in Barbados when I was eleven years old and she was five.

My Build-A-Bear, Gorgeous Giggles, was still on the same spot of my bright orange leather sofa, safely hidden amongst all of the velvet throw pillows.

I walked toward the unused kitchen to discover an old grocery list still on the fridge. Inside sat an old carton of milk and leftover food that must have been in there for months. I threw them away, pinching my nose.

The bedroom mirrored a hotel room checked into for the first night. The sheets we're crisp off-white 350-thread-count sateen; the linen was tucked and folded with precision. Not one wrinkle was on the champagne-colored Moroccan inspired quilt.

I flopped onto the bed with my street clothes still on. As had become oh-so-familiar, I cried myself to sleep.

Chapter 22

How I made it through school the next day was remarkable. My students did some independent studying in class and were dismissed ten minutes early. Amanda must have sensed something was wrong; she was on her best behavior. Not once did she question any of my instructions. Thank God.

One wrong word from her and they would have walked me out of the building in handcuffs, with Eyewitness News asking me what made me do it. Kill my student that is.

During those extra minutes I replayed the events from the day before. Did I really wake up in my brownstone this morning? Did Dupri really tell me to get out? Like Taylor, Mr. George, and every other man I'd come into contact with, Dupri had failed me. We made a pact to be there for each other. Tonight's session with Sapna promised to be a long one.

Sapna answered the doorbell after two rings. With bouncy jet-black hair in a pageboy cut and sparking hazel eyes, she greeted me with a huge smile. "Come on in, Anna. How are things going?"

"Things have gotten a bit crazy. How long is our session today?" I

plopped onto the plush loveseat sinking into the deep cushions.

"Well, it's one hour. I know that you are aware of that, but today my patient after you has cancelled, so if you need it we can run a little over. Let's begin."

I sat there for what seemed to be time without end. Semi-centered, I opened my mouth, babbling more events to my healer.

It always amazed me that my mom stayed married to Mr. George. My prayers were always the same: "Dear God, take October, Mommy, and me out of this house. Give Mommy lots of money so she can buy all three of us a huge house on the lake. Oh, can we also please have our own rooms. October snores real loud. I'll promise to be real good and I'll make sure October is perfect also. Thank you. Amen."

God must have had his headphones turned up real loud because my mother never left. When asked why, she would simply tell me, "When you and October get older you'll leave me and I would have no one, so I'm going to hold onto Mr. George, no matter how bleak things look now." To this day I didn't fully understand that concept. I always believed I would be there for her. I was supposed to be there; she was my mother, but obviously she felt differently.

Loving my mother and having her love me back with no interruptions was a dream of mine. Mrs. Brady and the three girls on *The Brady Bunch*; Claire Huxtable and her girls on *The Cosby Show*; even Samantha and Endora on *Bewitched* had loving relationships. Those girls didn't know how lucky they were.

Mr. George made sure I did all the chores around the house. I was not allowed to watch television on the weekdays and I had to ask his permission to visit Taylor, my father. Mommy, for some odd reason, found nothing wrong with any of his actions. When I would share my discomfort with her she repeated her famous line, "This will soon pass and become a distant memory." I would look at her with pleading eyes, begging her to do something but knowing in my heart she couldn't. I took that familiar long walk back to my room with my tail between my legs.

Early one Wednesday morning during the second week of my sophomore year of high school, Mr. George and I had one of our all-too-common altercations.

I was in the bathroom, taking forever as most teenage girls did. I just couldn't get my eyeliner to give me a straight line above my eyes.

October knocked on the door, yelling. "Anna, Anna! I've got to go to the bathroom."

I swore she scheduled her piss sessions to coincide with my teenage girly stuff. "Go away," I told her, forgetting about my eyes and concentrating on my hair.

"No, I'm serious; I've got to go to the bathroom."

If this girl didn't shut up... "Like I said before, go away. No, in fact, go piss outside on the porch."

I heard her jumping up and down outside the bathroom, this time banging the door a little louder. "I'm not playing; I really got to pee-pee. Do you want me to go on myself?"

"No, I want you to go outside. I'm not opening the door. You do this crap all the time."

Mr. George must have gotten wind of what was happening, for next thing I knew he was the one pounding at the bathroom door. He bellowed and pounded at the same time, "Git your bakside out of de bathroom. Yuh've bin in there long enough. Don't mek me come in there after yuh." He bellowed in his coyly naughty patios

I got balls from somewhere that morning and pounded back. "I'm not finished. So I guess that means you would have to come in after me, muthafucka."

"*What* did you *say*?"

"Clean the wax, bitch. I'll repeat myself again; make sure you listen this time. When I'm done, then she can use the bathroom. Now leave me the fuck alone." I smiled to myself; I couldn't believe that I just answered him back. All of those pent-up emotions from being beaten with belts, tree branches, and extension cords flooded through me.

In the tiny bathroom I stood in my newfound confidence. A smile curled my lips. I really showed that fool.

A thunderous pounding at the bathroom door changed the direction of my smile. It didn't sound like Mr. George's fist. The jackass was using my softball bat! I trembled with fear as I looked around for something to protect myself with. I grabbed the plunger and wielded it in both hands, prepared for battle.

The doorknob fell to the ground from the blows. Mr. George entered the bathroom. His diminutive eyes caught my gaze. My palms involuntary began to sweat, while I pissed on myself dropping the

plunger. As he lunged for my neck, I ducked. Mr. George tripped over the plunger and landed in the bathtub. Without thinking I snatched the plunger and cracked the wooden handle over his head with the same intensity he used on me in the past. I cursed and cried as I abused his head, his back, his legs, and his groin with all the strength I had.

"You stupid son-of-a-bitch, I'm tired of you fucking with me. What have I done to you? Huh? Didn't you see I was busy? October could have waited. All I wanted to do was comb my hair. But, no, you had to come and bang on the door."

My breathing was heavy. "You are always, I mean *always* fucking with me. From the time I was a baby. You beat me something awful over stupid shit. Whether it is reading to loud, or laughing hearty at a cartoon. I'm not a baby no more and I refused to have you fuck with me any longer." Not once did I stop using the plunger, I was trying to kill him.

I was determined that this son of a bitch was going to feel every ounce of pain that he had given me. All my hate and malice toward this man, who was to protect and serve me, came pouring out that morning. I paused with the plunger in mid–air as I looked at him. For the first time, I noticed how little Mr. George was. His 5'10", 170-lb body lay in the tub with blood on his forehead. No longer did he terrify me. In fact, I felt increasingly empowered. I gave him one last hard look before dropping the plunger again and stormed out of the bathroom.

In a zombie-like state I packed my knapsack. Placing my music, books, journal, a few pairs of underwear, the only picture I had from my mom's and dad's wedding, and lastly, a picture of October and me in it. For the last time I surveyed the room I'd shared with my sister for the past eight years before walking out. I knew at that exact moment that I was never going to return to that place again. I inhaled the scent of the room, touched my bed one last time. I held my head high as I walked to the front door. I never once glanced over at the bathroom, where Mr. George still remained.

As I opened the front door, October's youthful voice begged. "Anna, don't leave me! I will never hurt you." She cried and cried. I ran back and hugged her tightly. I kissed her forehead. "I know you wouldn't hurt me, but it's time for me to go."

"Can I go with you?"

"I would love if you could come with me, but you can't, October.

You have to stay here, but remember I love you today, tomorrow, and forever."

I ran out of the house and never looked back. I ran and ran until I couldn't run anymore. I ran all the way to my best friend Samantha's house, where I sought solace. After I cried and recounted the morning's events to her, Samantha persuaded me to call my mom so that I could explain my side of the story. We both knew that if Mr. George got to her first, he would paint me to be the bad guy.

"Mom," I said to her. "He was going to kill me with the bat! You should've heard the way he was beating on the door." I *knew* this time she was going to say she was leaving work, and we were going to put this to an end.

In her calmest tone my mother said, "You will not ruin the relationship I have with my husband. I lost one husband and I will be damned if I lose another. Do not, I repeat, do not come back to my house. All locks will be changed." She hung up the phone.

I wiped my tears away. Hardly looking at Sapna I asked, "Why did she tell me to leave, Sapna? She said I was the daughter she always wanted. Why would she then turn around and ask me to leave?" I asked the question but didn't really want an answer. But before Sapna could answer, I began to rattle on again.

Being out on my own was painful. All of my family members felt I deserved it since Mr. George was a blessing in their eyes. They refused to believe he was a nightmare.

I got a full-time job at a local department store and attended night school in order to graduate on time. I was able to rent a room for sixty dollars a month. I decorated the walls with posters of my favorite singers, my poems, and the picture of October and me in Prospect Park. The ten by twelve picture-decorated room became my new home.

"Anna, it's time to stop now," Sapna interrupted. "We can continue but I feel it's best if we conclude here for today."

"It's okay," I said in a half-hearted tone. "I have papers to grade and if I leave now, there shouldn't be too much traffic."

Sapna reached for her date book. "Okay, so next week, Monday, same time, I'll see you then."

"Sapna, Dupri kicked me out of the loft," I blurted out.

Sapna turned to face me. "Anna, I'm so sorry to hear that, but

forgive me when I say this. I think that is a good thing. You need to be by yourself, to reconnect with the true essence of Anna. You can't achieve that by hiding behind Dupri." She paused. "This may seem tough to comprehend now, but trust me; it's for the best. You need to heal."

"I love him, Sapna. We can fix this." I hoped she would tell me to go home and call him, but no such luck.

Sapna looked me straight in the eye. "How can you love him if you don't even love Anna?" She passed me a tissue. "Go home; take this time to start loving Anna. Learn to embrace your outer and inner beauty. You have been through a lot. You need space also to start the healing process. Try a tai chi class, start writing again, do something productive that is for Anna. The session after next we will start the exercises, like I said in our last session." Sapna gave me a hug. "You're doing well."

The touch, your touch, my touch, our bodies touching

Inhaling, exhaling, your scent, my scent our scent of love

I am longing for you

I am longing for me

I am longing for us

The kiss, sweet tender affection filled with passion laced with sex

The hug, firm strong embrace, emerging our two bodies making
one

I am longing for you

I am longing for me

I am longing for us

Together

With passion, with love our souls will stop longing, stop craving
for

We will, someday soon, will kiss; again, we will touch again

Together

I will look into your eyes and you will look into mine.

Our hearts will make love to each other, losing ourselves in ecstasy

Until then

I am longing for you, I am longing for me, I am longing for
us

Chapter 23

"October you have a minute?" I sipped on my cinnamon tea.

"I have a few minutes. I have a class tonight." I heard her moving around on the other end of the phone.

"Don't try to catch me at D.'s anymore, I'm back home." I exhaled loudly placing the mug on the coffee table.

"Why are you back home?"

"Dupri felt it was time for us to move on." I held back my head to avoid those pesky tears.

"Are you fucking serious? Did you not go home and be honest with that man like I told you too? Oh Lawd have mercy. This means you are going to be a royal pain in my ass now."

"Tober, this is not the time."

"Sorry."

"I didn't have a chance to apologize to him or be honest. As soon as I walked in Sunday night, he said he wanted to talk. In a nutshell he said he needed his space, he couldn't do this anymore."

"In his defense I don't blame him. Anna you are not yourself lately.

You're biting and jumping down everyone's throat. Who the fuck wants to deal with that? Anyone else, or should I say everyone else would say fuck you. Look around woman, Samantha, nor the others, fuck with you. Shit after the other night, I need to join them also. I only tolerate it because I'm your sister and I love you. Sometimes. But he's a man, and his patience is not like ours. Give him a minute, I'm sure he'll come around."

"You think?" I needed more reassurance.

"Look woman, I'm not Ms. Cleo, damn! But I do know that you guys had something special. Which made me want to barf most of the time. Relax everything will fall where it needs to fall."

"Thanks." I blew my nose.

"This conversation is depressing me. There is a wine tasting Thursday night, meet me there. It's on the Upper Westside."

I pulled the belt on my robe tighter sitting up straight in my sofa. "Did you say wine? Woman I'll be there with bells on."

Her Kathleen Turner husky voice laughed. "Now that's my sister. Whew, that depressed chick before was annoying me." We dissolved into breathless giggles.

"Alright, so it's on Amsterdam and eighty fourth street."

"Thanks October." My voice dropped.

"No thanks to wine tasting."

Chapter 24

"Drop by drop tears scurried down my face; I wondered what the fuck I was going to do with myself now that Dupri was gone. Being his woman fed a hunger to be loved by someone or something.

My four lonely walls enhanced my nervousness. Like a maniac I turned on all the lights in the house and locked all of the windows. I made a mad dash to the kitchen and grabbed one of the chairs, which I propped underneath the front doorknob. I felt proud of myself; I was keeping all the bad guys out. The funny thing was that Dupri used to keep the bad guys out. He made sure that I was always taken care of.

I picked up the phone and decided to dial my protector, hoping that I could fix this mess that I made. I knew October said chill, but I couldn't help it. The love we had for each other was supposed to last forever; this was nothing but a minor setback. His love for me couldn't have possibly changed that quickly.

After about four rings Dupri finally answered. The phone went to voicemail on the fifth ring.

"Hello?" His deep voice was so comforting to me. "Hello?" he

asked again, before I could muster up the courage.

"Hey D., it's me, Anna."

"I know who it is. I figured you would eventually call. What's up?"

His cocky attitude almost pissed me off. I was damn near three seconds from hanging up the phone, but instead persisted with what I wanted to tell him.

"I was thinking that I'm really sorry for everything that I've put you through. I see where I went wrong in our relationship, and I'm willing to work at it. I asked Sapna and she gave me a name for a really good couple's therapist. I figure maybe we should give it a try. What do you think?" There, I said it. I laid everything on the line. If this were a Harlequin romance novel, my dashing boyfriend would be waiting for me outside my door on a beautiful white horse. But since this is only my misguided life, I was pretty sure that he was going to tell me what I didn't want to hear.

"I know it must have taken a lot for you to call me. Like I said, I knew you would be calling soon, but I believe that things are best this way," he stated.

Things are not best this way, Mr. Haynes. "I know you don't feel that way, but I do. Hear me out first before you say anything." Dupri paused. Reluctantly I encouraged him to proceed.

"With you, Anna, I felt like a king. No other woman ever made me feel that way. From the moment I saw you in Zoe's classroom I knew you were the woman for me. I made it my business to prove to you that I was the man for you. I was ready, willing, and able to satisfy you in every way imaginable. The beginning was beautiful; we talked, laughed, cried, danced, and traveled the world." He paused his rapid-fire soliloquy. "But you found a way to shut me out of your life. I don't mean to toot my own horn, but woman; I'm a damn good catch. I took the time and energy to do things right because I wanted you."

"I love you, Anna. There was not a time when I pressured you. I stood by your side, doing all of the things a real man should do. Woman, love is not a game to me. When I love, I love hard and strong, and I love you with all I have." His voice became laced with regret. "I'm not the man for you; I can't be. There is no way I could possibly be the man for you." He finally came up for air.

I sat on the other end of the line and tried to rescue myself from

the blow. *Dupri, you are the man for me, you're the only man for me.* Nothing at that moment wanted to escape from my lips. Dupri really wanted to move on. He really wanted this to be over, but I was not about to go out like that.

"Couldn't our love heal the pain of the past? Couldn't we try again and rewrite our story? Are you going to give up without fighting for me? If you love me like you say you do, you would fight for me, Dupri. Fight for me, fool, fight for me," I begged.

"I did fight, Anna, but I was fighting by myself."

"Listen, let me speak. I gave you the floor, now listen," I went on, not giving him a chance to answer.

"We can make this better. Either you come here or I come to your house, and we can cry together. Just hold each other tightly, making love like we never made love before, with all of our emotions poured in our tears. Dupri, I love you and I need you, you can't leave me now!" I sniffled throughout my speech.

Dupri's voice was weary. "Baby, I didn't leave you, you left me. You stopped communicating, you stopped sharing, and you stopped sleeping with me. Sweetie, your body was here, but your mind was on the other side of town. Just like the O'Jay's song. Shit, baby, this is hard for me also. I don't want us to end; we were supposed to get married. Yet we need this; like I said, this is for the best. It makes no sense for us to torture ourselves with this conversation. I love you, Anna." He hung up.

An automated voice came on the line, saying, "A receiver is off the hook." It woke me from my trance and I hung up the phone. Through tear-soaked eyes, I tried to rationalize what I just heard. This was so hard; how do you go from being totally in love to being totally left alone? My heart was in so much pain. I never meant for things to get this bad. I was just trying to figure out stuff.

As the tears poured from my eyes I toppled into bed and sobbed, my chest heaving in and out. I replayed the conversation over and over again in my head. I really fucked things up now. I couldn't possibly go through this without Dupri. "I love you, Dupri!" I screamed at the top of my lungs. "I love you, dammit!"

Dejected, I rummaged through my almost-extinct tape collection. In my time of comfort I turn to music. Placing Ma Rainey in the tape recorder, I took a seat on the living room floor yoga-style, and lost

myself in her profound lyrics. They were intended for women who have been beaten, laughed at, and made to suffer due to a man. Just what the doctor ordered. I medicated my inner pain as Ma Rainey sang, from her poignant classic "Sweet Rough Man." Who needed Tylenol when you had Ma Rainey, Queen of the Blues? How relevant her words were though they were written so long ago.

My thoughts shifted to Sapna and her advice to get back to my writing. It had been so long since I picked up a pen and paper and wrote.

Ms. Peru, my high school journalism teacher, always told me I had a knack for telling a story but Mother thought it was safer to be a doctor or teacher. It's amazing the aspirations our parents had for us when half the time they had common jobs such as secretaries, janitors, and bus drivers. But being that all I ever wanted to do was please my Mother, I went ahead and became a teacher. She was lucky that I was wishy-washy and had my eyes on both professions. In her book I did as exactly as she would have liked.

As Ma Rainey continued the blues, I searched for my unused journal. I untangled myself from my yoga position and walked over to my hallway closet. I removed the plastic tubs from the back of the top shelf and laughed. So many unused journals! To my surprise, there were seventeen journals that had been started but not finished. As I flipped through them I couldn't help but notice the different styles and textures, all bought within a two-year period. This was probably when I was in my excessive-shopping state.

I chose a fluorescent-green one with a pink dandelion on the cover. I changed the tape to the jazz great Charlie Parker cd, *Evening at Home with the Bird*. I loved music, especially when hurting inside, but the richness of the jazz horns soothed me right to the core. Dupri was the only other man I knew, besides Taylor, who would bask in the glory of those magical horns. But Dupri was gone now. He made that clear.

I entered the kitchen to make lemon ginger tea. I cried realizing that I'd made a grave mistake. Dupri was the best thing that had ever happened to me. This couldn't possibly be the end.

Sitting the tea and biscuits on the nightstand, I laid on the bed, engrossed by Charlie, and prepared my thoughts to land on paper:

Jazz

Me

Jazz

Me

Elements of Ragtime, marching in the band and playing
the blues

Improvisational art, making it up as we go along

Scattered harmony scales

Like the country that gave us birth

Jazz and Me, Me and Jazz

Forever changing, but nearly always rooted in the blues

Trying to find a place in Western Music

With our rewarded individual expression, but demanding

Selfless collaboration

The song a starting point

Me, me, me

Taking terrible risk

Losing everything and finding love

Jazz, jazz, jazz

Making things simple and dressing to the nines

Enjoyed by huge popularity, trying to survive hard times

Increased difficulty yet dynamite music

A complex minx

Lady of ill repute

Me

Me

Me

Only one true music

My rhythm of life

My survival

My life expression

Jazz and Me, Me and Jazz

Chapter 25

The very next morning I paid careful attention to what I wore. Samantha always said if you look good on the outside, you feel great on the inside. I hoped like fuck, she was right.

I removed my black Donna Karan pants suit from its dry cleaners bag and added a hot-pink camisole for a splash of color. My Charles David black pumps with the brightly colored pink heels completed the outfit. I surveyed myself in the mirror, and was proud of what I saw. If I did say so myself, I looked damn good. A half smile pierced my lips.

Traffic was a breeze, not once did I have to curse the yellow cabs. I always said I was going to take the train, but I just loved driving. It was such leisure to be able to jump in your car after a long day in the classroom. Maybe one day, I would hop the train. For now, I would drive and curse the cabbies when needed.

As I headed into the main office to get my mail and sign in, I prayed I wouldn't run into Zoe. I was able to escape her last week, but it wouldn't last too long. Out of the four siblings, Zoe and Dupri were the closest, so he certainly told her about our treacherous ending. Zoe was such a doll; I was looking forward to one day being her sister-in-law but that crap wouldn't be happening. Hopefully she wouldn't think

I was awful to her brother and we could still have our colleague-friendship.

Just as I was about to walk out of the office, in walked Zoe with her usual chipper self. She noticed me right away and smiled.

"Anna girl, wait for me a minute. We can walk to class together. I have something important to tell you." She ran into the main office.

"I'm waiting." I smiled back. Just as I thought, I had to face the older sister. I waited outside the office, tapping my heels, until Zoe was ready.

"Hey, how are you?" Zoe asked as she gave me a huge bear hug. Before I could answer she continued, "You look great! I never saw that suit before."

"Thank you. I decided to try something new, and I'm doing well."

"Good. I'm glad to hear and see that." Zoe raised her recently waxed right eyebrow. "Listen, Anna, of course you know that Dupri told me what happened, and I'm extremely sorry." She paused biting her lower lip.

"I love you guys together, and I know Dupri loves you. You were and still are the only woman my brother ever brought to meet my parents. That boy was in love! He was always a bit quiet, but you brought out the best in him." Zoe paused for a moment, broadly beaming deepening her chin dimple. "He became a complete chatter box after he met you. Between you and me, he is hurting, hurting deeply, but he is too proud to admit it. Instead he comes to my house and eats me out of house and home." I couldn't help but laugh.

"I know my brother. He needs time, Anna. I think after some space you guys will get back together. His last day at work was last Friday. You should drop him a card and wish him well; he would like that." Zoe looked at me again and took a deep breath. "Even though you may not be my sister-in-law any longer, you are still the best English teacher I know, along with being the worst karaoke singer out there," she said with an impish smile.

"I love you, Anna, and I don't want this little setback to put a wedge in our friendship." Zoe grabbed my hand.

We stopped walking in the middle of the hallway. Despite my mascara tears and the girls beginning to file into my classroom, I gave Zoe an affectionate hug. I whispered in a low tone, "Thank you for that."

Chapter 26

$\mathfrak{I}$ took the PATH train to Sapna that evening. October picked up my car and promised to meet me after my appointment this evening. Didn't feel like messing with the assholes on the road. I wanted to sit back read the paper, gather my thoughts, and reevaluate my life. Getting tired of the therapists, even though Sapna was the best thus far, I just want to put these demons to rest.

"So, Anna how was your week?" Sapna quizzed as I made myself comfortable in my chair.

"The week sucked, it was frustrating, lonesome, and morbid."

"Tell me about it. What was so frustrating? Was it Dupri?" Of course it was Dupri, what else could it be? "Yeah, Dupri, I'm lonely in my place. I've nothing and no one to do anything with. All my girlfriends are off living their lives, my sister is trying to get one started, and my mother is psycho, so where does that leave me? Let's say it together...*alone!* Fucking alone, Sapna, so damn alone, it's not even funny!"

Before Sapna could butt in, I continued with a half smile. "I did,

however, start writing again like you suggested."

Sapna smiled in return. "Oh Anna, I'm glad to hear that. You'll see that journaling will be one of the key things that will get you through. Just keep it up, keep writing. Now, where would you like to begin today?"

"Anywhere, I don't really give a shit." I began to speak even though I wasn't sure of what to share today. I hoped it made sense to Sapna, because none of this shit made sense to me.

While working at the department store I started dating one of the stock guys, Gianni Contandino. Gianni came by every night at the same time to collect the hangers from the stock room. One evening he took it upon himself to interrupt a conversation I was having with a co-worker.

"Excuse me, can I ask you a question?" he asked with a sly smile.

"You can ask whatever you like, that doesn't mean I have to answer it," I retorted with my hand on my hip.

"I'll try my luck then. I was eavesdropping on what you were saying regarding Karl Malone. Do you really think he's a great ball player because he has talent or because he wears those basketball shorts?" This time not only did he have a sly smile, but also a glimmer in his green eyes.

To say I was taken back was an understatement, but I wasn't about to let him see me sweat. "He has very good stats," I answered as though I knew his stats.

"What are they?" Gianni asked, knowing darn well I didn't know shit.

"I forgot at this moment. Now I hope we are finished with the question and answers, I have a customer that needs my attention." I rudely walked away, while he laughed at my silliness.

To add insult to injury I saw Gianni that same evening in my night-school class. He smiled when he walked in and saw me sitting at the front of the classroom. After class I tried to duck out, but he caught up to me. He told me he thought I was cute and was wondering if we could speak about Karl Malone amongst other things outside of work and school. I couldn't help but say yes. From that night on we became inseparable.

Gianni's father was Italian and his mother was from the island of Belize. He had the prettiest complexion, the warmest smile and lashes

that would put fake ones out of business. I used to buy loads of mascara to keep up with him, but it never worked. I often thought about burning them off, but loved him too much to actually go through with it.

Gianni and I fell madly in love. He stayed with me most nights. After class we would buy a bottle of cheap wine, head back to my cubicle of a room, and make soothing endless love for hours. Our lovemaking wasn't as passionate as I later experienced with Dupri, but it was more calming. With each stroke Gianni reassured me that things would be okay, that I was beautiful and deserving of his love.

Chris was wrong. A lighter-skinned man did take an interest in me. My color couldn't have been as bad as he said. If we had kids they would indeed pass the test; the paper bag test that is.

Unlike many others that I knew, Gianni's parents were still together. He would often share with me that he wanted a love like theirs. He just wanted it without all of the prejudices that they had to endure. Even his paternal grandparents had a turbulent time dealing with their love affair. However, his parents managed to keep it together, build a life for themselves, and raise Gianni and his sisters

Gianni hated the fact that my parents weren't together. He also didn't understand how my Mother could allow her husband to abuse me. He always said my Mother was worse than my stepfather.

"Yo, Anna, this may sound kind of crazy, but your stepfather is a whole lot better than your moms. He put it all out there. He let you know from jump what kind of person he was. She, on the other hand, tried to act like everything was all-good. Think about it."

I did think about it. He was right, but I never wanted to own that reality. Gianni promised to love me forever and never to hurt me like they have done.

Like clockwork Gianni came by to pick up the hangers at the same time. We snuck away on most occasions for a five-minute love fest each time. One special evening instead of puckering up to accept his kisses I puckered up to tell him the latest news.

"Gianni, something happened."

"What happened? You spoke with your moms?"

"No, I wish it were that. I'm pregnant."

"Pregnant? Pregnant? How can you be *pregnant*?" Reaching for my waist, his mouth dropped, sea green eyes expanded.

"Well the way it works, the man puts his penis in the woman's vagina, bust a nut, and poof a baby is created." I laughed.

But Gianni saw the truth, he saw I was scared as shit. His grip got tighter. "Very funny, smart ass, what are we going to do?"

My lower lip quivered as my teardrops took turns falling. "I don't know, Gianni, I really don't know. I'm scared as shit."

"I'm scared also, but you're not having an abortion. We'll get through this. I promise you I'm not going anywhere. I love you, crazy lady."

Being young and dumb, we never wore protection; we thought it couldn't happen to us. I thought he would want me to have an abortion. Thank God he didn't. I wanted to have our baby. I'd finally found someone who loved me.

Gianni came with me to all my prenatal appointments and Lamaze classes. He interrogated the midwives and doctors and never allowed my prenatal vitamins to run low. He did 3 a.m. runs for my cravings of ice cream, pickles, and McDonald's cheeseburgers. He soaked my swollen feet, rubbed my back, and adored me throughout my pregnancy. Gianni was absolutely a breath of fresh air for me. Even with the extra twenty pounds I gained during pregnancy, he made love to me as if he were making love to my prior one hundred twenty-one pound frame. Gianni also worked more hours and got a second job in his father's accounting office. He wanted to move out of the cubicle and into a one-bedroom apartment. He wanted our baby to come home to a warm space.

To our amazement, Gianni's parents and grandparents handled the news favorably. They were thrilled that a new addition was about to be added to their already exploding family. My mom, on the other hand, was disgusted. October stopped by the store one day with the bad news. October did say that my mom did, however, want to see me, which puzzled me. But that was my mother for you: puzzling. October gave me an envelope from mother with fifty dollars in it and a note that read: "Just a little something to help you out."

Resealing the envelope, I told my little sister that I would come by early the next morning.

Standing on that old familiar red porch brought back ugly memories, such as the day I vowed never to return.

But that was in the past. Today I was going to walk in there and

hear what my mother had to say. My shaking finger didn't seem to want to connect with the doorbell. I should've taken Gianni up on his offer to come with me. He didn't get paid for his days off, and I figured we needed as much money as possible. In hindsight, that was a foolish idea.

Seconds after finally ringing the doorbell I heard October's piercing scream, "Who is it?"

I screamed back in the same piercing tone, "It's me, idiot! Who else is going to be ringing the bell at 7:30am in the morning?"

October opened the door and mushed me in the head.

I walked down the long, dark, familiar hallway. Nothing had changed during the year I had been gone. My mother was awaiting my arrival in the living room.

It had been a while since I last saw her, which did not prepare me. Her healthy glowing mocha skin had now wrinkled. Her face had sunken in and aged seven years. She looked lifeless and scared. Gone were the days of my mother's dancing eyes and twinkling smile and a singing heart.

She sprung off the sofa and gave me the most earnest motherly hug ever. With tears streaming down her cheeks she kissed me full on the mouth. "I love you," she whispered.

I hugged her back. "I love you too, Mommy," I cried. How much I loved and missed my Mother! I was happy to be in her arms again. I had waited a long time for that moment.

In the middle of our mother-and-daughter reunion, keys rattle in the main door. Mr. George must have forgotten something and was returning to collect it. I looked at my Mother to see if, for the first time in her life, she was going to stick up for me and tell him where the fuck to go. My Mother shoved me into October's room and told me to stay very still in her walk-in closet.

"You forgot something, George," I heard my Mother say.

"October dear, go fetch my gym bag for me," he instructed his only child, ignoring my Mother.

October walked out of the room with her father's gym bag in tow. She pulled her door shut.

There I was, nine months pregnant, ducked down amongst Guess? and Levi's jeans, platform shoes, and her furry teddy bear. I couldn't

believe that this shit was happening again. The one time she had the opportunity to stand up for me, for herself, for October, for us, she shoved me in a fucking closest. This woman was crazy! Gianni was right, she was worse than Mr. George; at least he didn't hide his assholeness.

I listened for him to leave. Hearing Veronica's voice speak to him almost made me barf. After all of this time she was still catering to this fool, kissing his ass. She still hadn't gotten a fucking backbone.

When the coast was clear Veronica came to rescue me from the closet. She tried to apologize for her actions, but by that time I had had enough. I looked at her pathetic soul, kissed her on the forehead, and walked out the front door. This time I was definitely not going to return. That was not a threat but, indeed, a promise.

I used the pay phone outside our one-room home and dialed Gianni's dad's office. When Gianni came on the line I rattled off the events of the morning through my tear-thickened voice. I told him how my Mother kept me captive in the closet like I was a stowaway or something. How embarrassed and ashamed I felt, how lifeless...

Chapter 27

*G*ianni arrived home to find me sitting in a pool of liquid; my water had broken. Since we couldn't afford a phone we didn't have one. The closest phone was on the corner. My only option was to sit there and cry and hope Gianni showed up quickly.

Gianni ran in and back out. He went to the pay phone and called 911 and his mother. He came back in, picked up the bag we packed a head of time, and waited.

At the hospital, they couldn't get me in the delivery room fast enough. As soon as my feet were placed in the stirrups the baby's head started crowning. I cried and screamed. Scared beyond belief, I felt something ripping out my insides. Gianni was by my side, holding my hand. He tried to get me to use the Lamaze exercises, but that was a lost cost. Three minutes later the baby was born June 22nd, five days before my high school graduation, I gave birth to a six pounds, eight ounces, nineteen inches beautiful baby girl. We named her Giovanni Spirit Contadino.

I lifted my head from staring at the soiled spot on the carpet while I relived those events. Sapna usually gave the occasional "Okay," "Continue," "How do you feel about that?" when I shared my stories

with her, but I could have sworn I heard her gasp when I gave the details of the birth of my daughter. I searched her eyes for any emotion.

Liked the trained professional she was, there was none. All I got was, "Would you like to continue?" I told her yes. She nodded, repositioning her notepad on her lap as she waited for me to begin again.

We called her Spirit. She was the prettiest little thing. Gianni was so proud of her, he brought all of his friends to see her in the nursery. His family came everyday, swamping me with tons of gifts and affection. My mother never showed up but October did everyday.

The day Spirit came home was just as exciting as the day she was born. The whole Contadino family was waiting in out new one-bedroom apartment, compliments of Mr.Contadino. He got us our new apartment while I was in the hospital. He wanted the best for his first-born grandchild.

I was pleasantly surprised to find my mother there as well. When she laid eyes on Spirit, she beamed with grandmotherly pride. She took her from Gianni's arms and held onto her all night long. Spirit came home to a grand reception: she was a loved baby.

The day after we brought Spirit home we prepared for my high school graduation. Everyone from Gianni to his parents, to my mom, October, and little Spirit, made an appearance on that very special day. My mom and Mrs. Contadino objected to her appearance on the red carpet, my graduation. But I needed her there. Their West-Indian superstitious beliefs stated she needed to be on lock down until she was baptized. I thought other wise.

When they called my name, Anna Story Harper, vigorous applause was heard. If you asked me, even little Spirit was clapping.

After Gianni and I left my graduation dinner at his parents' home, we noticed that the baby was low on diapers. Gianni ran across the street to get his precious Spirit her supply.

I heard gunshots. I ran outside in a frantic leaving Spirit wailing in her crib. Instinctively, I knew that my sweet, sweet Gianni had been hurt. So desperate to get to him, I didn't knock on my neighbors' door to ask them to watch her. I rushed past the already formed crowd.

Just as my heart had predicted, there lay my blood-stricken Gianni. I collapsed in the street next to him. I held him close to my heart, while his eyes blinked constantly, fighting to stay open. His body shook

hysterically while blood discharged from his mouth.

"Please baby, hold on, hold on Gianni. Remember you told me you were going to start to teach me how to drive this weekend. You kept complaining about having to take me to the supermarket when the game was on. We are too broke to pay some dumb auto school. Besides, only you can tolerate my mouth, they probably would kick me out of their car. Oh, and don't forget we have to take Spirit to get her ears pierced before she is christened." I pleaded with him, rocking his head close to my chest. "I'm begging you, Gianni, hold on, baby, hold on."

"*Where is the fucking ambulance?*" I screamed in the air.

I started to undo his pants and took mine off as well. I wanted to make love to him at that moment, one last time before he left me. I needed that reassuring stroke to let me know things were going to be okay. I started to stroke his penis in hopes it would get erect. It grew just a little enough for me to climb on him and insert him in me. Once I felt him inside me I started to cry harder. I shoved my tongue down his throat, hoping his would twine in harmony with mine.

Someone tried to pull me off him, but I shrugged off the grip. I glared at the stranger with murderous eyes and screamed, "*Get off me, you stupid bastard!* Can't you see I'm making love to my man? He can't leave me he just can't leave me! We have Spirit to raise and a life to live. He can't leave me." I paused to swallow, "Not even God himself can take him from me."

People in the crowd started to cry and pray for me. I faintly heard a Hispanic lady rattle her rosemary beads and say the "Hail Mary" in the background.

I gyrated my hips on top of him hoping Gianni would begin to move. As my tears hit his face and the bystanders looked on in shock, I rode Gianni until I had an orgasm. I fell on top of him, shuddering and holding him in my arms. "I love you Gianni."

Far in the distance ambulance sirens dimly blared. They got louder as they grew near. It took three ambulance technicians to pull me off Gianni.

"Miss, miss, please calm down. We are here to help." I kicked and screamed for them to leave me alone, not allowing them to cover my baby's face.

"Calm down, calm down! The love of my life is lying in the middle

of the street dead and you want me to calm down. *You* fucking calm down." I screamed getting up.

With my emotions going wild I continued, "Instead of telling me to calm down, tell me why it took you ten hours to get here? Tell me how I'm going to raise our newborn baby with out him." I pointed to his body.

"Tell me how I'm going to live without him. But don't you fucking tell me to calm down." I pounded the burly EMS worker chest. I cried and pounded, pounded and cried. Eventually he grabbed a hold of me, letting me cry in his arms. His partner was about to cover Gianni, when I snatched it from her. I bent down over Gianni and kissed him over his entire face. I smoothed his eyebrows and made sure his lashes were straight. I affixed his pants and whispered, "We love you," covering his face for his final sleep.

I walked back across the street, drenched in blood, in a daze, while the ambulance drove off. I felt the gazes of the spectators bore into my back. Many were still praying for my loss.

Inside our new apartment I took comfort in Spirit. I cradled her tightly in my arms while I dialed Gianni's parents.

As expected his parents lost it. Gianni was there only son keeping the Contadino name alive. They invited Spirit and me to come and stay with them permanently. I packed my and Spirit's things and moved in with Gianni's parents.

Gianni looked so peaceful at the funeral. The funeral director did a good job of making sure Gianni looked like Gianni. They even curled his lashes. His mother was so stricken with grief that she did not attend the funeral. She didn't want the sight of him lying in a coffin to be the last memory she had of her only son. Instead she stayed home with Spirit.

As Gianni's casket was lowered into the ground my soul wanted to jump in with him, but my logical self told me to stay put. I had to live. Gianni would be disappointed in me if I stopped living. I had to be strong for me and Spirit. Instead I threw in the picture of us in the hospital, the day Spirit was born.

Shortly after the funeral, a bunch of college acceptance letters arrived, which I had totally forgotten about. I placed them on my dresser, never to look at them again.

College was out of the question since I had a daughter to raise.

Until one day when the Contadino's brought up the subject of Spirit and my education.

"Anna dear, you know Gianni was our only son," Mrs. C. said while I was feeding Spirit late one evening.

"I'm aware."

"Well, there is nothing left here in the states for us anymore. I've already handed in my resignation letter and my husband is closing up his office."

What about Spirit and me? Where were we going to live?

"Spirit is all we have left of Gianni, and we were wondering, my husband and I. This is hard for me to say, if you would allow us to raise her in Italy."

I had heard it all. These people were fucking nuts. That was all they had of Gianni, what about me? They had nineteen years with him. I only had one. They had more memories than I did. Now they want to take the only thing I have left. I wanted a drink.

"Hear me out," she continued. She must have seen the look of disbelief on my face. "I saw all of your college acceptance letters. You are a smart girl, Anna, and you shouldn't let your talent go to waste. Mr.Contadino and I have decided to use the money we would have spent on Gianni's education on you. We would also allow you to stay in the house, if you continue your education in New York. Of course, if you decided to go out of state, we will pay your room and board."

Was I really hearing right? This was unbelievable.

"You can come see Spirit whenever you want. I would never deprive you of that. To show we are honest, we will go to a lawyer and have papers drawn up. I already spoke to your mother, and she thinks it's for the best also."

Of course, my crazy-ass mother would think, "it's for the best." Didn't she throw me away? This crap was right up her alley.

"When she gets older, if she decides to be with her mother, we would not stop her. We just really want to hold on to a piece of Gianni."

"Mrs. C., I don't mean to be rude, but what about me? Spirit is my daughter. I also want a piece of Gianni."

"You'll have a piece, you'll be staying in the house, and you can see Spirit whenever you want. Think about it. Don't race to a hasty decision. You'll see in the end it is the best for everyone involved."

With that she walked out of the room.

After about a week or so of deliberation, I agreed. They were right. I really wasn't in the right state of mind to raise a baby, much less alone. What could I really offer her? I was eighteen and alone in the world. They had more to offer her at the time. I also figured she would have the richness of the Italian culture and would be open to so much more in life than being raised in Brooklyn.

They were elated, to say the least. We had papers drawn up to make sure that everyone had a clear understanding of what was to happen. Right before the New Year, the Contadino's and Spirit left for Italy and I prepared myself for college as a student at New York University. I threw myself into my schoolwork, men, and shopping to ease the constant pain...

"So Sapna, you have heard my story in a nutshell," I explained. "Do you now see why I was so distant with Dupri? Not only was I abused, I also pimped my daughter for a free education. Shit, I'm no better than Veronica." I sighed. "At least she rejected me for something easily attainable, like a man. I did it for a piece of paper. This makes me a smarter rejecter, whoop dee fucking doo." I exhaled.

"Don't beat yourself up, Anna," Sapna cautioned. "You and your mother both did what you had to do. They weren't bad decisions or good decisions, but just decisions," she said patting my knee. "In life, you have to make a decision, good or bad, and deal with it. You can't change the past, so you learn to deal with it." Sapna's tone was firm but sweet. "Did you keep in touch with Spirit? Does she know who her mother is?"

"Yes." I exhaled. "I talk to her at least once a week. I send money to her all the time, and I visit her a couple times a year. She is such a beautiful girl, and looks exactly like Gianni," I said pushing out my chest.

"The Contadino's did a lovely job raising her. Spirit is sixteen now and wants to come live with me in the States. I want her to come also. I'm ready for her now."

"I think that would be nice if she comes. She needs her mother now, and with all of your wisdom, you have a lot to offer her."

"Yeah, through all this crazy crap, I do feel ready. I'm thirty-four now, how much more ready am I supposed to get? Know what I mean?" I wasn't looking for a real answer, but got one anyway.

"Before we began your therapy you said you were alone. You are not alone, Anna, you have tons of company. You have your writing and most importantly, you have Spirit. Concentrate on those things and all will be well." Sapna smiled before continuing, "I would like to go back to something you said earlier in the session." Sapna asked with a concerned psychoanalytical voice, "Can you sit a minute?"

"Sure, what did I say?" I searched my brain for all comments I made within the last forty-five minutes. None of them stood out more than the other.

"Who is Chris?" Sapna asked fusing her gaze with mine.

"I mentioned Chris: I can't remember mentioning his name. Did I really mention his name?" I asked in bewilderment.

"Yes Anna, you did." I exhaled deeply before responding. "Umm, he was my neighbor as a child." I reluctantly allowed the truth of his existence to free its self from my lips and my spirit.

"What was his significance in your life? Why did you mention him, Anna?"

I started shaking my knee, while guppies went upstream and downstream in the pit of my fishbowl stomach.

Reflecting back on my prior sessions, this would have to be the first session with Sapna, I felt emotionally exposed. How do I sincerely explain that I hated myself because of the color of my skin? How do I admit to hating what other's say is beautiful. "Chris use to tease me when we were kids." I hoped she didn't ask any more questions, but I knew better.

"What were you teased about, Anna."

Oh gosh, shut up Sapna. I had no desire to answer questions concerning Chris. Why didn't I tell this woman that I had to rush home? My big-ass mouth, and me, I still didn't know when to shut up.

I told her his teasing in a whisper as if I were sitting back on that porch at fourteen years old. Picking my voice up I continued, "But that was in the past, I got over that. He is a thing of the past." Lawd, where was she going with all of this? My thoughts ran rampant. Could she stop all this questioning and hand me my appointment card? I was not in the mood to dredge up Chris.

"Did you really? Is Chris really a thing of the past?" She raised her penciled in eyebrow peering over her glasses. "If that was indeed the

case, why did you mention him?"

"I don't know why I mentioned him, Sapna." I answered a bit annoyed. Why did I mention him?

"I think subconsciously you are still plagued by Chris's ignorance."

"Not at all. Maybe before, however that is not the case. Chris's teasing use to really fuck with my psyche, but not any longer, and that is the truth. I worked day and night in combating that issue. Besides, Dupri isn't real light or anything, for goodness sake. He is lighter than me, but nothing of major significance."

"But you are still your complexion, Anna." That irritated the hell out of me, but I didn't have an opportunity to ponder for too long.

Sapna continued. "I was planning on starting our play sessions next week. We have built enough history to really work with. But in light of your comment earlier, I think we can do a short but intense play session."

I glanced at her with my right eyebrow raised. I truly wasn't prepared for this at all.

"You can stay a bit longer, correct?" She asked again, preparing to leave her seat, but she paused sitting on the edge.

"I can hang around a few." I said one thing but me size seven and half feet wanted to run the fuck out of there.

"Good." On cue she left her seat and headed over to the wall closet in the back of the room. She rummaged around for a few minutes and then walked back to her seat with two masks, one in each hand.

One was a plain stark white mask, similar to a mime. The plastic covered the entire face. The other mask was beautified with dazzling colors. The base was black with crimson, orange, hot pink with subtle trademarks of violet streaks. A mask the woman, who gives up their beads at Mardi Gras, could probably be seen wearing. The pretty mask was a full-face one as well.

"In a normal session where we will explore with the masks, I generally have my patients make their own. But because this was impromptu, we'll work with a couple I already have. I want you to wear each mask, individually of course." She let out a little giggle at her last comment and I followed suit.

She walked over to her drawer and took out a white soft disposable mask and handed it to me. "You'll put this on first and then put the

other mask over it. The masks have been worn before. I want you to wear the disposable one first for sanitary reasons.

I nodded. I put on the disposable mask on first, then reached for the white mask off of her desk.

Sapna stopped me. "Just a minute, Anna, I want to explain what exactly it is that we are going to be doing today."

"Okay."

"Once you have the mask on, I want you to speak from it. Tell me how you feel with each mask on. These masks are the faces that you have lived with all of your life. Allow the mask to be your true face. Speak earnestly from that face. Do not hold back whatever comes forth. Whatever comes out is complete relevance; so don't be nervous about saying anything. Do you understand?"

"Yes, I do." I sighed, reaching up to secure the first one. The mask was a bit uncomfortable; I had to adjust it properly to my face. Awkwardness swept over me when the mask was securely fastened on my face. This was not Halloween and I wasn't wearing my Wonder Woman costume. She wanted me to say something, I could feel it, but what I really wanted to say was trick or treat. If I allowed those words to fall from my lips, Sapna would have me committed for sure.

Sapna chose her words carefully. "How does the mask make you feel?"

I got a sense that she felt my uneasiness. I didn't really care. I was just happy as fuck that she broke the ice first.

I thought carefully making sure that I didn't come off like a nut, before answering, "I'm not sure how I feel, this is sort of weird. I feel like its Halloween or something and I'm playing dress up. And then a part of me feels really emotional, like I'm on the brink of tears or something."

"Anna, this exercise will not be a walk in the park. The beauty of drama/play therapy is all the emotion that is felt and that is brought up during a session. You are sitting there confused, trying to come up with the right words. All I can say, Anna, is let it all flow. What ever you are feeling or want to say, say it. Allow all the emotions to take over you like they want to and go with those feelings. Play with it, Anna, play with it." Sapna reached across and grabbed my hand, patting the back of it gently. She looked into my spirit to see if her words had penetrated me. They had. In what form, I'm not sure, but I

knew I wanted to make the most of my first session at drama therapy.

Sitting back she began to question me again. "So Anna, after my little speech." She giggled and I smiled out of nervousness. "Are you now ready to continue with the session? Can you begin to answer my questions?"

I nodded lightly as Sapna sat back in her seat.

"Anna, how do you feel sitting before me with the mask on your face?" She repeated.

I gave careful thought this time as to how to respond to Sapna and how to respond to myself. "Walking through the streets of Brooklyn would be a breeze with this mask as my true face. I'm a beauty queen. All heads will turn. Boys would want me and girls will be envious of me. They would be so green with envy that they would long to be my friend. This mask would open all doors for me. I would be the captain of the cheerleading team and date the sexiest, most popular boy in high school." I began to smile behind the mask. I believe that Sapna felt my smile. She smiled back.

"You know that pretty girl in school that everyone wanted to be? That's me, Sapna, that's me right now. I'm that pretty girl. The chick that in her yearbook everyone writes is most likely to succeed and is named prom queen. The girl that Chris told me I would never be." I paused to come up for air.

"Do you understand what I mean, Sapna?" I asked her rhetorically. "Mr. George would have no real reason to mistreat me. Why would he? I would be perfect. Perfect people do not get abused. They get loved." I started to sniffle, trying hard like shit to hold back the tears.

Barely audible I continued, "With this face, I would have been treated like a delicate porcelain doll." I exhaled waiting for Sapna to continue, I had no more in me.

"Anna, if you had to choose a name for yourself, what would that name be?"

I pursed my lips. I had no idea what the heck I would name myself. It sure wouldn't be Anna. "I'm not sure, Sapna, can we just move on?"

"We can if you wish, but don't you think it would be nice to put a name to that face you are wearing now? What would all the people who envy you, call you?" A frown creased under her dark bang. She continued, "I know this is a little different, out of the ordinary, but I

really need you to think outside of yourself. Try to have an out-of-body experience and don't be Anna for a minute. Imagine that you lived your life with that mask you are wearing at the moment. Imagine going to the supermarket, school, work, and so forth. The world saw you with this face, not the one you are used to. What would *your* name be?" This chick was good. She really knew how to get me. What would I name myself?

"Sapna, I would name myself something pretty and exotic, maybe something like Tiffany or Ashley. Pretty girls always have one of those names."

"Which one will you choose? You can only choose one."

"Ummm, I guess if I had to choose one it would be Tiffany Pure."

Sapna smiled. "Good but why Tiffany Pure?"

Lawd, I thought this chick was done with the questioning. Didn't I give her a name like she asked for? I looked at her from behind the plastic mask, wiggling my nose for room. The mask made a crackling noise. Sapna patiently sat there eyeing my masked face with her pen and pad in tow, her rimless glasses waiting for me to answer.

"Tiffany Pure just sounds like an unaffected name, a name safe from turmoil."

She smiled. "Okay Tiffany, take off the mask and let's try the same exercise with you wearing the other one." I took it out of Sapna's outstretched arm. For some reason I wanted to but the mime one back on. I felt exposed, once it was removed. The colorful one couldn't go on quick enough to prevent the weirdness that was happening within me.

With the Mardi Gras mask on, something happened. Tears flowed instantaneously. One by one they began to trickle down my face from behind the disguise. I reached up to remove it, but Sapna stopped me.

"Don't! Just let it all out. It needs to come out." She sat back in her chair while I cried like a baby. I wept for what seemed like an eternity. Sapna waited until my eyes were dry before she began with the questioning again.

"What are you feeling, Anna? Why are you crying? What is this mask bringing up for you?"

Through my tears I spoke. "I feel really stupid and vulnerable. I feel like I'm sitting back on the porch with Chris again. I can hear him

loud and clear, Sapna. But it's not just him. It's everyone. The whole world is pointing and judging me. I feel foolish with all of this color and attention that is coming my way with this stupid face. I'd rather wear the other mask again."

"Why do you want the other mask, Anna? This mask is nicer."

"No, it isn't. This mask makes me feel angry and scared. I'm so pissed, Sapna. Why am I so ugly? Why this face? Why? Of all faces, did I have to be given this one? Do you know how much pain this face has caused me? Do you? From Daddy leaving, Mr. George, and Chris, and let's not forget Gianni and Dupri. I'm so tired. I don't know how much more I can take. I wish I could hurt all those muthafuckas, the same damn way they hurt me. Every last one of them needs to pay, Sapna." Pain laced my every word.

"Pay for hurting you, Anna? You want all those people you mentioned to pay for hurting you?" She paused a second. "But Gianni didn't hurt you Ann, Gianni got killed."

"Oh yes that bitch hurt me. He didn't have to leave me. I begged him to get up, Sapna, but he didn't. He didn't listen. None of them listened. None of them heard my cries, my pain." I exhaled. "They must pay for everyday of my childhood I missed. Pay for me not going to sleepovers, sleeping with baby powder on my face in hopes that I would wake up lighter. Pay for not telling me that I'm beautiful and that I'm going to be somebody. Pay for not instilling self-confidence in me and letting me go searching for it in dick." My chest was heaving in and out.

"Are you finished? Is there anything else that you want to say?"

"There is so much more I want to say, Sapna, so much pain within me. It hurts badly, Sapna." Them wretched tears just wouldn't leave.

"You can take the mask off, Anna, so we can begin to process what you are feeling." I gave the mask to Sapna and she gave me a tissue. She waited a minute before she spoke. "How are you feeling? Are you still angry?"

"No."

"Good, for starters, I must say you did a wonderful job. However, let's close our eyes before we begin the processing part. Close your eyes and inhale."

I did as I was told.

"Exhale, again, inhale slowly." She paused before beginning again, "Now exhale, again, inhale slowly." She paused. "Now, exhale it all out very slowly." She did the breathing technique with me also between her instructions. "One last time, Anna, inhale." I followed her directions for the last time. "Now, open your eyes and let's move forward in processing what you just experienced." She nodded and smiled. I nodded back.

"For starters, you did a fabulous job, wearing the masks are hard. So many emotions come up, as you have experienced." I nodded, trying to understand what just took place. "Most mask exercises I have my patients act out improvisational scenes with the mask on. But since this was our first time, I figured it would be safer to have you seated and see what happens as you wear each mask." She tucked her cascading locks behind her left ear, sipping her water, revealing a jade earring.

"The first one, Anna, was safe for you. Being that you were tortured about your skin color, it was safer for you to be colorless. Hence, the white mask. Is that a true assessment?"

"Yes, it is," I answered, blowing my nose. "I thought I was over that. I thought I worked through that pain."

"Sometimes the pain is so dreadful we bury it deep within us. We assume it's over, not realizing it's nesting, waiting on the perfect time to reveal its self. Today you saw that pain out from hiding."

"Tell me about it. You couldn't tell me that I hadn't gotten over that. I just mentioned Chris, just because, not for any particular reason. I'm disappointed I didn't have a normal family I longed for, but I never realized how angry it made me. I stay away from my parents to avoid the pain. Who knew it would cause more pain? Who knew I would still feel pain from Gianni's death?" I shook my head in bewilderment. "I still can't believe the mention of Chris's name is what sparked all of this. Color is no longer an issue for me. Dupri isn't light. Sapna, I'm drained."

"Of course you are drained. You have suffered for many, many years. You've lived with this festering hate. Everyday it was slowly killing your spirit."

"Tell me about it." I breathed disdain.

"It'll get better." Sapna, reached over touching my hand. "Everything we mention is for a reason, that's why we mention things.

It's not about Dupri and his color, Anna. It's about *you* and *your* color. Chris was just the catalyst we needed to bring these emotions to the forefront."

"I understand."

"The colorful mask sparked many emotions. Most abuse victims, such as you, generally paint bright colors on their masks. Bright red and orange are just a few of the colors they may use. Those colors represent their anger." She breathed. "That's why you got exceptionally angry when you were wearing the colorful mask. All of those years of deep anger and pain came flooding back. You can't hide, with the mask on. Everyone sees you with the mask on. Your pain, your hurt, your prettiness, your colors, everything is visible. We want you to get you to the point where masks aren't needed."

"Where I can stop dreaming of chocolate." I sighed.

"Chocolate?" Sapna questioned removing her glasses and chewing one end.

"That's how I referred to Chris. I always said he made me dream of chocolate."

"Yes, where you don't have to dream about it any longer. We are working to get you to a place where you can actually live with it. How does that sound? Does that make sense?"

"Yes, it makes tons of sense." I gathered my purse.

"Next week is going to be an exciting session. We are going to continue some more playing. It will get more intense than what we experienced today. This was just a little something to get the juices flowing."

"If today is any indication of what is to come, I'm nervous."

"No need to be nervous, though it is understandable. I will be right by your side throughout the whole process. If it gets to be too much for you, we can stop at any time. I want to make sure you feel safe when we are doing these exercises. How does that sound?"

"It sounds doable."

"Good, you gave us a perfect opportunity when you mentioned Chris. Today was good," she smiled. "Go home and call your daughter, write about this session and what it brought up for you. Let it all come out. If that should happen again, do not stop it. The pain has to be ripe to deal with it. You are doing well, Anna, real well."

I smirked.

"We are going to start really moving that energy around and get us healed," she said one last time handing me my next appointment card and sending me on my way.

Dear Book,

How the hell do you become a decent mother if yours is crazy as shit? Oprah doesn't have any kids so you can't model after her. I longed to follow Carol Brady but her husband was gay. What is that magic potion needed? They have every sort of book and DVD out there that teaches you how to become good at something. From how to lose weight, live a better life, belly dance, pleasure your man in bed to how to build a good fence. Why the hell they haven't come up with how to prevent growing up without your mother's behavior haunting your every Gosh darn fucking move you make? The way I look at it that shit would be a NY Times best seller.

Bye Book

Chapter 28

With it being mid-term season, I managed to keep myself busy with grading papers and handing out unnecessary reports. Zoe made several attempts for us to hang out but I always managed to get out of it. I loved the woman, but I was not ready. Seeing her would make me want to call Dupri again, and I was *not* doing that. She would, however, be happy to know that I sent Dupri a card as she suggested. I was pretty sure he told her; Lawd knew he told her everything.

Everyday got a little easier being without him. Between writing and throwing myself into my students, I don't dwell on how bad it hurts without him. For some odd reason the loss of Dupri was equal to the pain I felt when I lost my Gianni. I thought I would never experience that intense pain again, with just my luck I did. I think my mother and father made a horrible mistake when naming me. They should've just named me Anna Intense Everything That Can Fucking Happen Harper. That had a whole lot truer meaning than Anna Story Harper.

Later that night, after correcting papers, I ate dinner alone. Well, not exactly alone, the evening edition of Dr. Phil joined me. I decided

to give Spirit a call. She had been in France for the past two weeks with her friends, so I was unable to speak with her. I needed to hear her voice now. I got comfortable on my bright orange leather sofa.

"Hey, baby, how are you? I've missed talking to you. It's been so long. Well, not that long, two weeks but you know what I mean? How was Paris with your friends?"

"Mommy! How are you? I miss you too. I was going to call you tonight, also. But I'm glad you beat me to it. Paris was great! We had a good time. Grandpa gave me tons of money, so that made it even better." Spirit's voice was filled with excitement. "We went to the Eiffel Tower, the Dapper Museum, and the Montparnasse, where many African-American artists lived and worked," she said with pride. "Oh, oh, Mom, guess what? We also walked the Champs Elysee, where Josephine Baker worked. You know I was so excited! I'm a *lot* like Ms. Baker, you know." She said the last part in a mock haughty voice.

"Yes, love, I know you were Ms. Baker in another life." We laughed.

"You know I could have given Lynn Whitfield a run for her money. They should've cast me instead." As usual, Spirit was so full of energy.

"I'm pretty sure you would have been dynamite. How is school going so far?"

"It's going well. I'm doing well as usual." She paused. "The only problem I'm having is with math. I don't understand why I have to know why x-y=z? That is so annoying, Ma. I'm not going to use any of that in the real world, so why do I have to get graded on that."

If this kid wasn't mine then I didn't know to whom she belonged to. I wasn't a fan of math, either, but I sure as heck wasn't going to tell her to throw the damn book out the window, as I wanted too.

"Spirit, math is very important. It's going to help you with your money, logic, amongst other things. Just give it the best you have and sign up for extra tutoring if you have to. I'm glad to hear that you are doing well otherwise in school." I paused, storing up my courage before asking. "Spirit babe, I want to know, do you still want to come back to the States?"

"Of course I want to come back, are you kidding me! I miss you, Mom. Should I start packing now? I love Grandpa and Grandma C., but I want to live with you and hear the stories of how fabulous my daddy was over and over again." Spirit rushed it all out, barely coming up for air.

How much she was like me even though she hadn't been raised by me.

"I'm not going to front, Mom, I'm nervous. We only spent summers and holidays together. It's going to be too wild being with you all the time and being in New York for more than three months. But I've dreamed of being in the States with you for as long as I can remember."

"You said it perfect. It will be hard. We don't really know each other's living habits. I have to get to really know you and you have to get to really know me. It's going to be a huge adjustment. I'm confident we can make it work."

"Shit, I know we can make it work."

"Spirit! Watch your mouth." I couldn't help but chuckle. It's official she's mine.

"Sorry, it slipped."

"Don't let it happen again, young lady."

"Mom," she asked in her most humble voice, "I know you are getting ready to go, but can you tell me something about my dad?"

"Gianni loved you *passionately*," I responded. "When you were in my belly cooking, he would read you stories. He made sure he read them in Italian. He wanted you to be fluent in the language. He didn't want to ruin your chances of getting a job at the United Nations or anything." She giggled.

"He sang to you day and night. He thought he was the next Teddy Pendergrass, such a nut he was. He dreamed of walking you down the aisle to Teddy's song *"My Latest Greatest Inspiration."* He sang that song the most along with Sade's love songs. He made sure he read the sports section to you. He was determined to take you to all sporting events. He told the world about you. And when you were born, the whole of Brooklyn knew about it." I paused, reflecting back. Smiling I said, "He called you..." In unison we said, "My Italian Mocha Chocolate Flower." She knew this story all too well.

She said softly, "I wish I knew him, Mommy."

"You do baby, you do, and Gianni lives in your heart." We were both silent for a moment before I said, "Okay, baby, I have to speak to your grandparents again and by the summer, you'll be in New York. I promise you that."

We said our goodbyes, and I love you's and promised to speak

again soon.

I was so inspired by my conversation with my daughter; I pulled out my fluorescent journal and began:

Here I am, Here I am
Am I really here?
I don't think so
With all that is going on in my life
I am not sure where or who I am
Here I am, here I am
Moving two steps forward on Wednesday
And taking two steps backward on Thursday
I am scared this may be a constant battle
I would forever have to fight
Here I am, here I am
Weak from all of the inner wars I had to fight
Physically and mentally weak from the bullets I dodged
I pray everyday the troops will come
And put an end to my Inner War
Here I am, here I am
A daughter who would or could live up
To her mother's high expectations
A child so desperately looking for her mother's love

But knowing that may not be possible

Here I am, here I am

Trying everyday to find new ways for her to love me

But coming up empty every time

Do one and one really equal two?

This hurt, this anger doesn't really add up

Here I am, here I am

Will I forever be a motherless child?

Am I motherless even though she is very much alive?

I am very much motherless

She died when she allowed her husband to abuse me

Here I am, Here I am

Wondering why she turned her head, and closed her eyes

Wondering why she consoled him, and disgraced me

Dictating my life with his rod

Choosing a man over her offspring

Here I am, Here I am

Here I am praying and seeking strength

Choosing love and life, ignoring death

Trying everyday to gain harmony, life and passion

Here I am, I am here I've arrived.

The fucking funny thing was that I wrote I had arrived, but I hadn't arrived a damn place. I hadn't spoken to Veronica or Taylor in years, Dupri gave up on us, and Spirit, my sweet Spirit, wanted to come home to a mother who wasn't sure she could be a mother. I even had issues figuring out the right mask to wear. Me being fucked up was an understatement.

I crumbled to the floor and gave into my emotions. I allowed myself to surrender and let go of all my prejudices. I let down my wall and took off my mask. I stood there naked, with my soul uncovered and my inner face exposed. I granted myself the permission to feel those emotions and set them free.

With a soft whimper, I began to peacefully unravel. Soon my soft whimper turned into a burning wail. I exhaled and started bawling, crying like a newborn baby in search of its mother's breast. Fervent tears poured from my being and caused me to slump over. I cried for every day of my childhood that was lost; cried for the motherless and fatherless child I was; and cried for the daughter I gave away.

I wept away my old life and the abuse I had no choice but to embrace for the past thirty-four years. As I wiped my nose, I held my head and allowed myself to feel each pain, each disappointment. I didn't once try to stop what was happening to me. I stayed in the moment of the pain, knowing that this was the only way to heal.

Weak, I was unable to move from the bed. I looked up at the ceiling and screamed, unsure of how to handle all these emotions, which had reared their ugly heads. I beat my mattress with my fists, hammering away my tortured soul until I fell asleep.

Chapter 29

"I've been here damn near two hours waiting for you." We hugged as she firmly held on to her glass of wine. Her eyes were glazed from the drinks she had consumed. Huge triangle shaped gold earrings, and a bright orange oversized cowl neck sweater adorned her lithe body. Matched closely to her once ocher colored hair now auburn loosely pulled off her face.

"Of course you would, chick. It's a wine tasting." We both giggled like schoolgirls.

"There is a hottie I have had my eyes on from the moment I walked in. I'm trying to work up the courage to say something to him." I grabbed a napkin off the table she had sectioned off for us. I smiled at the other wine tasters seated.

"So how are the wines so far?"

"They are all good." I shook my head. I didn't expect any other answer. She pushed the tray of cheese my way as her gold necklace dangled in the air.

"Here try these cheeses. They are all good." I tasted the white one with the green specks in it first. She was right it was good.

"There he goes." Her eyes followed a medium built white man with a baldhead. He had a construction worker look that belonged on Wall Street about him.

"You kill me. You want to marry your boyfriend, but you are always looking." I took a sip of the latest wine they placed on the table. "By the way, whatever happened to the Mediterranean guy at Café Noir?"

"Oh him, great lay. No, I'm lying a fucking superb lay." Her raspy voice roared loudly. I couldn't help but join her.

"Back to serious business, I do want to marry Cho, but we aren't married yet. So I can still have a little fun. Besides I'm not going to sleep with any of them." Her eyes peered mischievously over her drinking glass.

"Tober you slept with the other dude?" I raised an eyebrow.

"That may be true, however I will not sleep with this one." I shrugged and laughed.

"Going to the bathroom."

"Do not attack that man in the bathroom, October." My glossy lips widened.

"I can't make any promises." Her gym toned behind bounced seductively as she made her way to the restroom.

I sat listening to the woman at the front of the room describe the latest wine that was placed on the table. An Italian wine, served best with meat dishes with a prevalent hazelnut taste.

"His name is Frank." I tuned out the woman and focused on Tober. "That was quick." I sipped the hazelnut wine.

"His office is in Chelsea. I hit it big gurl he's a chiropractor! We made plans for this weekend. He owns a townhouse in Forest Hills on Austin Street. No kids, no dogs, loves music, dancing and last but not least he is a Scorpio also." I couldn't help but laugh.

"It's a done deal. You are leaving Cho for real."

"Never, let's get out of here." She picked up her bag as I followed suit. He waved at her from his table.

"You are too much." I pulled me gloves out of my coat pockets, fastening my hat tighter. We vigorously walked toward downtown.

"I haven't slept with a Scorpio in years. The last one had a penis size of a new born, but rhythm like a salsa dancer. I'm telling you size

doesn't always matter." Her deep throaty laugh filled the air.

"You think?"

"Yep, I've been with big guys and they weren't saying anything."

"You are sick woman."

"Anna?" Her voice got serious. I placed a dollar in the beggars' hand as we crossed the street.

"What's up?" I looked at her quickly.

"I don't have the money."

I laughed. "If I said I wasn't surprised I would be lying. Why don't you have my money October?"

"It's been difficult keeping up with the mortgage payments and all. I even had to take on a new job." I stopped in my tracks; I no longer felt the cold outside.

"I'm a waitress at the diner on Ninth Avenue."

"I honestly don't give a shit what you are doing now. Or what you have to do to pay me back. I gave you the loan with the notion that it had to be paid back within the time limit that was set, no fucking exceptions."

" "I know Anna, but..."

"No Tober, this shit was expected. You are so careless and irresponsible. If I was a bank and you didn't pay back the loan, your shit would have been foreclosed yesterday."

"Damn, Anna, I'm going to pay it back. I just need a little bit more time."

"Let's go into this coffee shop."

"I'm going to have the money back in about three months."

I pulled off my hat shaking out my hair. "You will not pay me back in three months. Your ass will pay me back in two weeks."

"How the heck can I pay you back when I don't have the money." She tapped her feet.

"You'll find the money. I need my money. Ask your fucking father for it or some shit, but make sure I have my money."

"Keep your voice down. The whole shop doesn't have to know I owe you money."

"Whatever! You always bring me out to these places to ask me

shit, yet you have the nerve to tell me keep my voice down. I'll raise it where I damn well please."

"What is your problem? Every time some shit happens between us, you always mention my dad. I'm not my father, damn it."

"You are just as irresponsible and fucked up as he is." Tears replaced the usual zest in October's voice.

"Anna, how can you say that?"

"Simply. Neither one of you have taken responsibility for the way you bitches have fucked up my life."

"Do not call me a bitch. I did not fuck up your life. All I did was love you."

"Did you really Tober?"

"Yes Anna, I did. Why are you so angry, with me? All I ever tried to be was the best sister I knew how. I'm sorry he beat you Anna." She allowed the tears to escape wildly not trying to hide them.

"He didn't just beat me chick. How can you not know what he did? Huh? Do you not know how he took my innocence away?"

"Yes Anna, tell me. Tell me why you hate me so much and how my daddy took your innocence."

"He molested me October. Your fucking wonderful father used me as his late night madam. He treated me like the whores that were on the movies he watched. When you and Mother weren't home, he would make me watch them and tell me to do everything they did." She began to tremble violently.

"He raped me of my youth, my esteem, every God-damn thing. I hated being left in the house by myself with him, or going to sleep for that matter. Everyday for two years he raped me. I prayed you and mom would have stayed up all night long so he wouldn't touch me. Or one of you guys came back early. I tried to tell Mother but she wouldn't believe me. I mean she never did anything about the beatings so what the fuck was she going to do about the other stuff."

"My dad, my daddy did this? Are you sure you don't have him confused with someone else?"

"Why would I lie? What the fuck will I gain from that shit? It's like he knew when you went off to sleep. As soon as you did, he came knocking. I would pretend to be sleeping but that never stopped him."

"Tell me he didn't do that? My daddy isn't the monster you are describing?"

"Remember I would talk to you until you would fall asleep?" She shook her head sluggishly.

"Sleeping was the worse. I figured the longer I kept talking the longer he would stay out. But he would come in and beat us for talking, well not us me. When you where sound asleep he would come back in and touch me. He use to put his finger in me." She closed her hands over her ears.

"I was so mad at Mother. If only she slept with him, then he wouldn't have wanted me. She was so fucking lazy."

October popped out of her seat and came to hug me. We hugged each other tightly crying in each other's shoulders. "I'm so sorry Anna. I never knew, I swear I never knew. If I was awake I would have beaten him up."

I cupped her face in my hands. "Did he touch you October? Be honest."

"No, Anna he never touched me. How could he do this to you? I wonder if mother knew."

"I'm pretty sure she knew. The look she gave me every morning told me she knew."

"Nah, I can't believe that she is that evil. I refuse to believe."

"I promised myself I was never going to tell anyone. But I lost it when you said you didn't have the money. It sort of reminded me of when I would tell him to stop, but he never did. I felt you weren't listening. Like you didn't understand that I really wanted my money back by the time I gave you. Like Mother and him, you didn't hear me. No one hears me"

"I did hear you, I truly have been struggling. I want you to be proud of me Anna. I want you, of all people to know I can handle being an home owner."

"I was always proud of you Tober. You were the one thing that meant anything to me. You made living there bearable. I want to go home now." I wiped my tears with the back of my palm pushing my thick hair out of my face.

"No, stay Anna. We have to talk about this."

"I have to leave." I stood up leaving October crying into her palms.

Chapter 30

Exhausted from the previous night's emotional purge, I called my job and took a couple of days off. I hated to do that to my students, but I needed some time. Mary-Ann, the secretary, was very sympathetic when I told her someone died in my family. It wasn't really a lie; I was mourning the lost of my old self.

I stayed in bed all day long, feeling sorry for myself and blaming myself for everything that had ever gone wrong in my life. My room was stocked with ginger ale, Herr's cheese doodles, applesauce, and Mrs. Field's chocolate chip cookies.

There was no reason for me to leave the room except to use the bathroom. If I had it my way, I would have a toilet in there with me also. Mary J., Jaguar Wright, Anita Baker, and Onyx were in the stereo for motivation. This was going to be the best all-day pity party.

I snuggled in my bed and grabbed my childhood pillow. Only my pillow knew my true self. Shit, the damn thing had a better sense of who I was than I did. Grabbing my journal, I looked forward to sharing my thoughts with it again.

Help me Lord to overcome my continual battle

Help me Lord to be the victor, not the victim

Help me Lord to control the doorway of my mind

Help me Lord to lose these demons and live

Help me Lord to fly, soar, and shine

Help me Lord to love not a man or an object

Help me Lord to love me the great, beautiful me

Help me Lord to embrace me, divine, beautiful me

Help me Lord, Help me Lord, Help me.

That damn phone! I put the pen down and prayed it was Dupri calling. *Of course I'm going to forgive you baby*, I thought.

"Hell-o-o?"

"Why the hell are you home?" She ain't Dupri. "I knew your black ass was in the darn house."

"Hey O., how the heck did you know I was home?" I asked through breathless quivers of emotion. I hoped she was not calling to talk about last night. This is what I get for not having caller-id.

"No, the question is *why* you home? Don't you have students who need your assistance? And don't ask me how I know anything, I have my resources," October teased. "Anyway, I called to talk about last night and to give you a message Mother left on my voicemail."

"I don't want to talk about last night."

"We have to talk about last night." My chest immediately started heaving in and out wildly like dancing marionettes. "But first Ma, is having a party for Grandpa, and she would love it if you were in attendance. You are his first grand, you know. I know you don't want to go, can't say that I blame you. I don't want to go neither, but I think you should go." October paused. "It's been two years since you spoke to Ma; she doesn't even have a clue as to why you stopped speaking to her."

"You and I both know she knows darn well why I've been distant. She just chooses to ignore the truth." I slammed my hand on the bed.

"It's like no one wants to acknowledge what happened. Don't they understand what they did to me?"

"Here we go again feeling sorry for yourself," October snapped. "I'm so sorry for what happened to you Anna, believe me, I am. I use to pray that they would file for divorce or that he would die in a horrific car accident or something. You know more than anything else that I'm just as scarred as you are. Shit, Anna, it was *my* dad that beat you. It was my dad that raped you. How the fuck do you think *I* feel! My dad is a child molester!" She cried into the phone.

"And you're right; no one wants to acknowledge what happened. They have decided to sweep the shit under the rug and move on. There isn't a fucking thing you can do about that, but deal with it." October was on a roll now.

"Yeah, it sucks, and it is wrong as hell, but you can't hate them forever, Anna. It will kill you in the end; shit, it's killing you now! You are spending countless hours in therapy, you lost the man of your dreams, and you took days off to stay home and eat cookies. They are living and you are dying, so you tell me, who is losing this battle? You, Anna, you." October stopped to come up for air. "I have my own fucking pain to deal with. Again it was my father that abused you." Her voice started to shake.

"You're so selfish and caught up in your own shit, you don't even know how affected I am. Last night when you left me in the coffee shop, I didn't leave. I stayed and cried for hours. That man you described in the coffee shop last night was not my father. I cried for everyday of my childhood I lost. The owner had to hail me a cab. He saw how distraught I was. Do you know what it was like for me to see my father beat you, while I sat there and got affection? I saw when he stared at you with his hateful eyes. I hated every minute of it. But all I kept thinking to myself, if I sit real still I wouldn't get what you got. Then I realized that you were sitting still, but you still got beat."

She caught a breath before starting up again. "Now there is another layer added, rape. Not only the beatings I have to deal with, I have to deal with rape now. I don't know how much more of this shit I can take. My dad is the guy your parents try to protect you from." She paused. "I remember every time he called my name I would jump. I thought I was next. I hated Mommy also, for not having the balls to

stand up to him. She was such a punk."

"You don't understand!" I yelled at the top of my lungs. "You don't understand the pain!"

"You're right, Anna, I don't understand. I don't understand your exact pain."

"I've spent my whole life hoping she would see I was just as good as him, but it never worked. I spent my life ignoring those horrific moments ever took place. Blocking it with things and people that didn't truly matter. Never ever fully able to love, thinking any minute someone was going to abuse me, so I did everything to ruin the relationship. The only man that authentically loved me was taken from me, the only fucking man, October, the only man." I was trying to hold the tears back.

"Anna, Gianni is gone, and yes, he was beautiful. In fact he was gorgeous as fuck. I still remember how he looked at you with so much love, but he left a gift in Spirit. Be thankful. You had a new Gianni in Dupri, but you chased his ass away, Anna. All he wanted to do was love you and you fought that." October paused again. "Look, the beatings, the name callings, the vicious stares, the rapes, that life ended for you at seventeen. Don't carry the shit to thirty-five. Make a choice. Make a choice to live and you will, one day at a time. I'm your rock and we'll get through this together," October stated. "I've decided to go to therapy with you. In light of these recent events I need help. My world as I know it has just been pulled from underneath me. I need my foundation back. That's if you don't mind me joining you?"

"I love you Tober. I don't have a problem with you joining me. I'll speak to Sapna, to make sure it wouldn't be too much."

"Good, I think it's the only way for us Anna. Now, I'm telling your mother that you'll be at the party in three weeks. We'll attack the mall in search of a sexy outfit for me and a Classic Anna outfit for you, the weekend before that."

Laughing half-heartedly I asked, "What the heck is a classic Anna outfit? That sounds like a freaking insult."

"It just means that I'm Anna Nicole Smith and you're Oprah, boring!" She chuckled.

"Oprah is sexy and classy, not boring."

"If that is so, why Stedman didn't marry her, answer that, smarty pants? If that's sexy then I don't want it." She laughed. "I got to go

now; I bought a new book I must finish reading. Dealing with your pathetic ass is keeping me from the great sex scene. Love ya!" With that, she was gone.

"Good-bye, crazy lady, I love you too," I said after October hung up.

O. was right; I had to get it together. I had to start from the beginning in order to put the past behind me.

Chapter 31

I still remembered the blank look on Beatrice's face that fateful day I invaded her privacy.

At the rate I'm going I may lose Tober also. I was so wrapped up in my dysfunctional childhood and feeling sorry for myself that I hadn't realized how much life I hadn't allowed myself to live. I was going to start living again, taking more responsibility for my actions instead of blaming the world. But I had to see Beatrice first. I couldn't fully begin to live until I put that chapter to rest.

I had been standing on this porch for approximately ten minutes. I couldn't seem to muster up the courage to ring the doorbell. How much smaller the house seemed now. When I was little it was a mansion; now it looked like a Barbie dollhouse.

They replaced the brick with aluminum siding, added a white metal fence, repainted the red awning, and hung three potted plants. A satellite dish hung outside the front window of the second floor. I guess they got rid of the old thirteen- inch TV.

The door opened and a gingerly looking old man with salt-and-pepper hair and beard, stood behind the screen door scratching his

scraggly gray beard. I smoothed down my ponytail and adjusted my pants before I smiled back at him. I opened my mouth to say something, but nothing came out.

He smiled back, showing his dentures. "Yes, can I help you?" he asked sweetly.

I stood, wearing the same smile, at a loss for words, which was something that rarely happened to me.

The man spoke again, this time a little edgier. "Yes, can I help you?"

This time I responded, "Oh, yes, is Mrs. Hawkins in?"

"Who may I say is calling?" He gave me the once-over.

"Umm, you can tell her its Anna Story Harper." I adjusted my handbag. "I umm, umm, use to live on the first floor."

He closed the door a bit and screamed up the stairs, "Violet, dear, there is a Ms. Harper down here; she said she use to live on the first floor."

I chuckled; after all these years, I never knew what Mrs. Hawkins' first name was. I heard her gasp in the distance and instruct the salt-and-pepper man to let me in.

I walked into the house with a brief glanced at the door to the first-floor apartment where I once lived. Everyone had to start some place. The aroma of cinnamon, vanilla and coconut, Mrs. Hawkins' sweet bread must be in the oven. I ran up the stairs as I had done many times before, except this time I ran in my three-inch stiletto heels.

As in the past, I ran straight into the kitchen and it was as if I never left. Mrs. Hawkins was in the kitchen, watching her black-and-white television. She still resembled Della Reese, just a little slimmer, and her smile still warmed my insides. She got out of her favorite chair and gave me one of her famous hugs. I hugged her back tightly, not wanting to let go, relaxing into her warm embrace. As if on cue, the tears began to stream down both our faces. Thank God, I made the decision to come home.

We untangled ourselves from our mutual embrace.

Mrs. Hawkins gave me the once-over look and said, "Anna, you are so beautiful, I always knew you would grow up to be a beauty queen."

"Thank you, Mrs. Hawkins, you're not looking so bad yourself,

kind of sexy, I may add," I said, being silly.

"Yeah, them little young video-things have nothing on me." She chuckled. "I can bump and grind with the best of them." A throat cleared and we turned around.

The salt-and-pepper man was standing at the entryway to the kitchen. "Oh, Anna, you know how men can be, needs to get all of the attention. Anyway, dear, that sexy old man over there is Fredrick, but I call him Freddie. He's my new husband." Mrs. Hawkins cast an affectionate look at the handsome man.

I looked at her with surprise; I never thought that Mrs. Hawkins ever needed anyone. She always seemed so strong.

Freddie reached out his hand to me. "You can call me Freddie also. Shucks, being you're so beautiful you can call me anything. Just call me."

"Oh, Freddie, get out of here, what is she going to do with an old man like you? You know you can only work with rechargeable batteries and Viagra," Mrs. Hawkins said with a loud laugh.

"Humph, I know when I'm not wanted. I'm going to leave you girls now to go watch the fish in the tank." Freddie looked at me and said, "Call me if you want to take me up on that offer." He winked and walked out of the kitchen.

"Sit, sit, I'm so happy to see you," Mrs. Hawkins said as she patted my hand. "It's been so long! I've spoken to your mother over the years, but I haven't heard from her in the past five years."

My ears perked up at that one. She spoke to Mom? I didn't know Mom kept in contact with Mrs. Hawkins. What did Mrs. Hawkins know?

"You knew I loved you and your mother, Anna. You guys could have lived with me forever. It was that George; I told your mother he would be the death of her or the death of you." Mrs. Hawkins rose.

"Would you like some sweet bread and tea?" Before I could answer she was walking back to the aluminum kitchen table with my treats.

"So, baby, how is that beautiful daughter of yours, Giovanni Spirit?" Mrs. Hawkins peeked at me over her glasses as I almost choked on my tea. I guess Mom really had been speaking with her over the years.

"Giovanni Spirit is wonderful. I spoke to her a couple of days ago.

It's soon college time and she wants to go to school here in the States. She wants to be with her mother now, and I want to be with her also." I dug in my purse for her picture.

Mrs. Hawkins studied Spirit's picture. "My Lord, this girl is striking, simply striking," she said placing her right hand over her heart smiling from one wrinkle cheek to another. "Yes, you need to get her. She needs her mother now. What is she, sixteen? Seventeen? Very awkward age; they need to be around courageous woman and you are that, Anna. Courageous."

"She needs her mother and I needed mine also. Mrs. Hawkins, did my mother really want me, like she said she did? Wait, don't answer that," I said hastily. "I'm scared of the answer. I wish we never left. The day we moved out of here was the worst day. Do you know how much I loved her, Mrs. Hawkins? All I wanted was for her to protect me." I sighed. "I don't feel courageous, Mrs. Hawkins; I feel like a failure. The funny thing is, I always thought Spirit would hate me when she got older, but she doesn't. She loves me."

"Why should she hate you?" Mrs. Hawkins sat up. "You gave her a great life. How many young women can say that they were raised in Italy with wonderful grandparents? Anna, honey, we all makes sacrifices in life and you made yours. Trust me, she understands that." She bit into a piece of the sweet bread. "Your mother told me that you went to Italy every year Spirit has lived there, that the two of you took trips together, you sent her clothes and toys. Don't beat yourself up; George has already done that for you."

I felt the runaway of my beating heart. "What did you say?"

"You heard me, child. I may have stayed in this kitchen, but I knew everything that was going on in my house. And I didn't like it, nope, I didn't like it one bit. I told your mother every day, if she didn't do something about it then I would. That's why you stopped coming upstairs. She got very mad at me, said I was interfering. She was right; I *was* interfering. I was scared for your life," She paused to take a sip of her tea.

"She thought by you not coming up here, I was going to leave the subject alone, but that isn't me. I nagged her everyday, every day I told her to protect you. She chose to take you away from me instead. I loved you like you were mine."

Her gray eyes never left my gaze. "I was mad at Veronica for years, after Mr. Hawkins died. You guys were my next-of-kin. And she took

that from me. I didn't think I was going to be able to forgive her. But I said to myself, 'Violet, God uses faith and the enemy uses fear. Keep the faith and things will turn out fine,' and as I sit here looking into your beautiful eyes, I was right."

I blushed. "Thank you, Mrs. Hawkins, but there were many days I didn't think I was going to make it. I've cried so much, then and now, it's shameful."

"Crying, girl, is good for the soul," Mrs. Hawkins stated. "You have to cry the pain away so you can laugh when the joy comes and my dear, joy is right around the corner for you." She patted her chest over her heart and continued, "I can feel it. You, my love, have great things coming your way. So how are the men treating you? That left hand looks kind of empty. Don't tell me an intelligent woman like yourself is man-less?" Mrs. Hawkins laughed. "All you business women are man-less. I'm glad I was never into business, otherwise I would be man-less like you young girls."

"I had a boyfriend for a couple of years, but he broke up with me," I said slowly.

"Why would a handsome man—I take it he was handsome?" I nodded. "Why would a handsome man break up with a gorgeous woman such as you?" She shook her immensely thick gray hair. "You have to make time for these men, you know. They are like babies. As soon as they cry, shove a breast in their mouths and shut them up. It's that simple. You young girls make loving a man harder than what it needs to be." She sipped her tea. "Just love them. Don't try to train them. Don't do anything. Men just want to feel loved and appreciated. Once you have that under control, they are like mush." She laughed out loud. "So tell me, what did you do to run this man away? I can't see him just breaking up with you for any old thing."

"Where do I begin?" I exhaled loudly.

"From the top. That's the only place I know how to begin." Mrs. Hawkins chuckled again. She was getting a kick out of my lost love life.

"I've been in therapy for the past couple of months and Dupri, that's his name, had been very supportive, but something weird in me started happening. I started feeling distant and scared."

"That's another thing," Mrs. Hawkins said. "Not only are you business women man-less, you're also throwing your money away,

sitting on a couch. Come sit in my kitchen, drink some tea, and leave that same money on the counter on your way out." She shook her head again. "I really am getting old. Continue, my love."

"Mrs. Hawkins, I never told Dupri about Spirit. I didn't know how to. What was I supposed to say? 'Hey, my name is Anna and I had a daughter at age seventeen and gave her away to earn my bachelor's and master's degrees'."

"Yes, darling, that was all you had to say. You young things are really dumb." Mrs. Hawkins rose to pour us more tea. "It's called honesty. He would have been elated if you were able to do that, be honest. Let me ask you this." She didn't wait for me to answer. "Did you tell him to always be honest with you?" She paused glaring at me over her too small reading glasses. "Of course you did. Look, sweetie, whatever it is you want, you have to give that to them. He knew in his heart you were keeping something from him; that's why he left. The man was unable to trust you. Can't say I blame him." She picked up her teacup. "Do you love him?"

"Yes, Mrs. Hawkins, I love him. I miss him something terrible." I fought back my tears.

"Good, because even though I haven't met him, I can tell he still loves you. But before you run home to declare your love to him, take some time for Anna."

"Well, damn! Sapna said the same thing." I rolled my eyes, smacking my teeth. Maybe Mrs. Hawkins was right about therapy being a waste of money.

"Who is this Sapna?" Mrs. Hawkins demanded. "What happened to names like Tracy, Jill, and Beth? All these new fancy names." She laughed.

I couldn't help but laugh with her. "She's my therapist."

"Like I said, I can be a therapist. All that wasted money. Girl, cancel any further appointments and come back to the kitchen!" This time she laughed even louder. Her laughter faded as she got back to the matter at hand. "If he is for you, then you should have him; besides, absence makes the heart grow fonder." She sipped her tea. "And I can't see any man in his right mind not wanting to come back to such a wonderful woman such as you."

For the first time in a long time, I felt like everything was going to be okay. All the worry and stress seeped from my being as I sat in the

apple-wallpapered kitchen. This was indeed a good decision to come home. "Mrs. Hawkins how is Daniel, Shelly, Joshua, and Beatrice?"

"Well, my dear, Shelly and Joshua made me a grandmother, but were evil and moved away." She sighed. "One moved to California and the other went to Florida. The long-distance bill is high; I call them every chance I get." Mrs. Hawkins pushed her glasses up. "Daniel is doing well. He still lives here, but only when he and his girlfriend get into an argument. She wants to get married, but he is not making her an honest woman. Why should he? He gets free meals and sex all the time." Disappointment was in her tone. "I said be good to them, but don't be anybody's fool, neither."

She went back to the stove for yet another cup of tea. Mrs. Hawkins refilled my teacup also. "So, Mrs. Hawkins how is Beatrice? Does she still go to the day school? Is she here? It's been awfully quiet."

After taking a sip of her tea Mrs. Hawkins finally spoke. "Beatrice is dead, Anna. She died about two years ago. She is in a better place now; she lived a long life." Mrs. Hawkins searched my face for a reaction but I sat there motionless. "I was always amazed at how well you played with her. The most excited she ever got was when you guys sat in that living room." She turned in the direction of the living room. "I loved her same as I did my other children, but raising her was a lot of work." She paused regretfully. "Her passing has allowed me to live. I'm not sure you can remember, being that you were so young, but Beatrice really needed me. I had to feed her, bathe her, and even change her diaper. I never wanted to burden anyone with her. I also wasn't ashamed of her. I walked everywhere with her, for she was mine, so you can imagine how distraught I was when I finally had to admit her to a nursing home." She sighed deeply. "I was trying to hold onto her for as long as I could, but I was doing her an extreme injustice. It's funny how life is, as hard as it is to admit, is that the day I committed her to a home is the day I began to live my life. I met Freddie that day, on the bus ride back from the nursing home. Mr. Hawkins told me that we needed to do that a long time ago, but I was being stubborn. Now I see what he was trying to tell me."

I wanted to ask her how Beatrice died, but didn't think she would have heard me. Talking to me was Mrs. Hawkins' own form of therapy.

Mrs. Hawkins must have heard my unasked question. "She died in her sleep, you know. Her heart failed her, just like her daddy's. Sometimes I think it was because I failed her. I knew it was for the

best, but after the death I had such a hard time. But they say someone has to die before someone can be born, and I got my first grandbaby the day after her funeral." Another sigh. "But anyway, babe, Beatrice is happy now. She is with her daddy now and they are both at peace. The others are fine, and Freddie and me are doing great, especially since we have Viagra." She laughed out loud. "And you, my love, will be great. The next time I see you, you will be at your wedding, with Spirit at your side. Don't worry about Veronica; she is kicking herself every day for what she has allowed to happen. You don't have to do that for her." She paused. "What you have to do is win back that man of yours, but make sure you fix yourself first."

I took that as my cue to leave. I could have stayed all day long, but got what I had been searching for. "Mrs. Hawkins, thank you for always loving me."

"Of course I will always love you, girl! Now get out of here." She smiled wickedly. "Me and Freddie got to get our groove on." She smiled. "And leave that picture of your beautiful daughter for me. Next time you come, make sure she is with you."

"Good-bye, Mr. Freddie!" I yelled.

"Good-bye, gorgeous, come visit us again." Mr. Freddie came out of the bedroom and followed me downstairs. "This time I'll make sure Violet is out, so we can chat," he said, cracking up to himself. I just smiled and walked out into the evening air.

Chapter 32

"Beatrice was dead. Since hearing that news, the visit didn't go exactly as I had planned. I was supposed to walk in there and see Beatrice watching *Tom and Jerry*, just like when we were kids. I expected to see Beatrice, happy like a pig in mud when she saw me. Didn't look as though I would be able to get the closure I need from Beatrice; it was just something that I would have to do on my own.

"Okay, Anna, I'm ready," Sapna said.

Her voice woke me from my thoughts as I sat in her holistic styled waiting room. Sapna had rearranged the chairs so that the recliner and the armchair were both positioned directly in front of each other.

"I kept telling you that we were going to start playing soon, and that time has now come", Sapna hazel eyes danced. "We have been delving a lot into your past and getting your history. We even had the pleasure of doing a little play session the other evening. How do you feel, since then? Did you write, like I suggested?"

"Yes I did."

"Good. Well, the time has come for us to put that information we've gathered to use. So, our first full play session is going to be the

empty-chair technique." *That would explain the set up.* "It's simply a way to deal with your inner demons and exploring your feelings." She moved to the side and took another seat. "This form of thinking should stimulate your thoughts and spark your emotions and attitude. She took a sip of water.

"I figured we can start here, and progress further into other drama-therapy techniques," she explained as I nodded. "The way we will start is that you'll pick a chair, any chair, and sit in it. You would imagine someone in the empty chair. For example, it can be Mr. George, your mom, October, Dupri, any one of those or someone that I may not have mentioned. And then speak to that person as if they were really there. Tell them how you feel, what's on your mind. Then switch chairs and speak from that person's or thing's point of view." Sapna cocked her head at an angle.

"Do you understand?"

"So, in essence, you want me to speak to myself?" A slight frown marred my forehead. "Sapna, no disrespect, but I could have done this all by myself. Why did I pay you all this money, being that my insurance doesn't pay for this type of therapy, to talk to an empty chair? Or why did I come here for the past eight weeks to end up talking to an empty chair? I understood play was involved in this form of therapy, but this isn't what I signed up for."

"You're one hundred percent correct, Anna. It is a simple exercise but the stuff that comes up is difficult. That's why you need a trained professional to push you in the direction you need to go. And on that note, let's begin, if you feel safe in doing so. If not, Anna, then we can do something else; it is your call."

I stood there, pouting and indecisive. Did I sit and talk to an empty chair, or did I walk out, never to see Sapna again? Walking didn't seem like a bad idea. I mean what was the point? Beatrice was dead, Dupri wasn't going to reap the benefits, and Mother couldn't give a shit. But I came too far to turn back now. How hard could talking to an empty chair really be? Besides, Sapna wasn't going to make anything happen that I didn't want to happen. Dealing with all the other crap in my life should make this a walk in the park. Resigned, I took a seat in my usual chair that was now faced a vacant red armchair.

Sapna patted my shoulder as I took my place. "All right, Anna, you have to decide who you want to speak to in the chair. Imagine that he or she is sitting there. Imagine what they are wearing, what

they smell like, allow yourself to fully focus on that individual. When you have chosen your person then let me know." Sapna paused. "I should also inform you that it doesn't necessarily have to be a person, it can be a thing, also. You can visualize a dog, a belt, a heart, whatever or whomever you want to speak with. Do you understand?"

"Yes, I understand." I cleared my throat.

"Have you decided on whom or what you would like to explore your feelings with?"

I nodded. "Yes. My Mother."

"Good. Now see her vividly," she said, taking a moment. "Envision what she could be wearing, her facial expressions, and her hairstyle. Clearly see your mother in the chair before you."

I shut my eyes tightly and took deep, cleansing breaths. I searched my memory bank for a clear vision of my mother. The first memory that came to mind was of her wearing the wedding dress she wore when she married Taylor. I saw her sitting at the reception table with a glass of champagne in her hand, wearing a stark white chiffon lace A-line dress. The smile plastered on her face was just a diversion to hide the nervousness in her eyes.

"Anna, have you captured the memory of your mother?" Sapna asked from behind me. "Not only do I want you to think of a memory, or see her physically, but I want you to feel her aura, her smell. Get in touch with your mother's spirit; capture her essence." I heard her move around a bit. "Now, once you can visualize your mother in front of you, I want you to prepare yourself to talk to her. Tell her all the things you have always wanted to say to her. Speak to your mother from the deepest part of yourself. We want you to create a long, detailed emotional interaction, a conversation." She paused.

"The goal for this conversation is to clarify your feelings and reactions to your mother and give you a better understanding of why she made the decisions that she made. Are you clear on what it is that we are doing this afternoon?"

I again nodded.

"Good. I will guide you through this session by asking you key lead questions. I will also nod my head or gently pat your shoulder, signaling that it is time to switch chairs." Sapna settled down with her notepad in her lap, ready for the session to begin. "When you are ready, begin speaking to your mother. Remember to speak from your

heart."

I digested Sapna's instructions and searched for the right words to say. After sitting in silence for a few minutes, the words began to leave my lips.

"Mommy, when I was younger I was so jealous of Beatrice. In my young eyes, she had it made. There was constantly someone fussing over her. Whether it was feeding her, combing her hair, taking her to the bathroom, just plain ol loving her, she was loved. My perception was if I were more like Beatrice, I would have a better chance of being loved. I can recall you saying how sorry you felt for Beatrice, calling her mentally challenged, whereas I saw her as mentally capable. She was capable of having her family love unconditionally. There was a direct correlation between the two of us; we both had muted words inside of us that couldn't come out."

My voice became more intense. "Ma, I told you once before that I love you; in fact, I've told you that many times through the years, and those words I spoke are indeed the truth. But along with that deep love that I have for you is also hate running neck and neck." Was I doing this exercise correctly? I decided not to think about it too much. "I can't, for the life of me, figure out why you have abandoned me. Why did you allow your husband to take control of my life? No, why the fuck did you allow him to take control of *your* life?" Rage and helplessness rose within me. "I loved you, Mommy, when you neither deserved to be loved by me nor appreciated my love for you. I often thought I was crazy or something when I was younger. Here I'm thirty-four years old, still dwelling on the events of my childhood, know what I mean?" My voice rose an octave higher. "Then I realized that I'm not the crazy one; you and your Satan husband are."

Sapna patted my left shoulder and whispered, "I want you now to change seats and, as your mother, answer the questions that you just asked her. As you sit in the chair as your mother, feel the vision of her that you created in your head and speak from that being."

I switched seats. "You can't possibly understand how long and hard I'd prayed for a daughter like you, Anna. The years leading up to your conception, I prayed earnestly every day for your arrival. February 27, 1970, was the day the heavens opened and sent me an angel. You were the prettiest little thing to me. As I lay in that hospital room, I kept thinking how blessed and proud I was, all at the same time, to be your mother. You weren't abandoned, Anna, you were loved."

Sapna patted my left shoulder again; time to change seats once more. I switched back to my original seat and sunk deeply into the chair cushion. "Sapna, I want to stop. This is harder than I imagined it would be."

Sapna twisted her naked lips. "Are you sure you want to stop? You are doing great, and I'm proud of you, but if you want to stop, then we shall." She paused. "But like I said many times before, it has to get hard before it can get good again. This stuff you have to deal with is some hard stuff, I know this, but believe me when I tell you that you'll walk out of this office much freer today. Just stay with me, stay with this, and it will all be over soon. Trust me on this."

For what seemed like an eternity I sat frozen in my seat and thought about Sapna's words. Freer, she said. I couldn't possibly understand what the fuck being free would feel like. It was weird—, for as I sat there devouring the concept of being free, I wasn't sure if I were ready to be free. I'd been enslaved by my demons for so long; living without them never seemed like an option. How could I survive without them? They had been my comfort for so long. Linus, from the *Peanuts* cartoons never got rid of his blanket; at least I didn't think so. So why should I?

I ignored the devil on my right shoulder that told me to stop the exercise and went with the angel on my left one. By sitting there I was just stalling and wasting time, time that I could no longer afford to waste. For years I held on to fears that did nothing but destroyed the relationships, and myself, I had developed.

I smiled at Sapna to let her know that I was fit to finish what I came here to do. I promised myself to make this the last attempt in interrupting this session with my fears. I had to endure to the end; no matter how difficult and painful...

I recaptured the memory of my mom in the wedding dress and picked right up where I left off.

"Every relationship I've been blessed with has failed. Whether it was my relationship with men or women, Mommy, it has failed. I constantly beat myself up about it. Always wondering what it was that they did wrong; why didn't the men love me and the women no longer wanted to be in my circle." I searched for the right words to continue. "The blame always fell back on them, never myself. Then one day I began to understand that I blamed everyone who crossed my path for the abuse I sustained. Ironically, the women became my weak,

pathetic mother and the men became my controlling, abusive stepfather. But because that was the only life I knew and was used to, I put up with the mechanics of the relationships but didn't really benefit from them. I wanted out, but believed I needed to stay and fall victim to the trash they would throw my way. Looking back now, I thought they loved me; fuck, I wanted them to love me. They were only microcosms of the real problem, which was your apparent denial of the horrors that took place in that house."

The rage spilled over. "*Why*, Mother? Why the *fuck* did you allow that bullshit to go on? Why did you not stand up and protect your daughter? Why did you not stand up and love your daughter? I did everything I was supposed to. I got good grades, I cleaned my room, and ate all of my food!" I cried to the empty chair. "Make me understand, dammit! Make me understand why you chose him over me. Let me into that head of yours, because I don't fucking get it. I don't get how the child that you claimed for years you wanted, you allowed to go unloved and unprotected." I was still inflamed even as I felt Sapna's tap on my shoulder.

I changed seats for what I hoped to be the last time. Now playing my mother, I had to let go of the emotions that just plagued me. I took on my mother's calming, emotionally detached spirit. For what I hoped to be the last time, I would speak from her voice.

"Anna, I'm sorry that you have felt this great pain throughout the years, but I did the best that I could," she said slowly. "I have two girls and I tried to give them both all the love that I have. I knew going into this marriage that I would make some mistakes, but I never believed that my girls would be affected by any of it. Why didn't you share any of this with me? I could have helped you sooner." I schooled my features into the same expression she would have had, had she been sitting in the chair for real.

"Mr. George was good for us. He kept a roof over our head, and food on the table. He was a good man. He made sure that you girls went to the best school and had the best life possible. After I left Taylor, I had no idea how I was going to make it. I couldn't possibly stay at my father's forever; I had to one-day move on. So when Mr. George called and said he was still willing to marry me, even though I had you, I jumped at the opportunity. I wasn't getting younger, you know, I was rapidly approaching my thirties. It wasn't a good thing for a woman to be divorced during that time. Your likelihood for someone to marry you was slim, so when he said he would take me with you, I

went. There is no book out there that tells you how to be a mother and I did the absolute best that I could do. I clothed you, I fed you, and made sure you had a great education. What more did you want from me?" I questioned the chair, as my mother would have.

"Regretfully, I lost my mother at an early age, so I didn't even have her to lean on for guidance. "Do you know what it is like to be raised without a mother? You may think I was awful, but at least you had me there. My grandmother and father did the best they could, but they were not my Mother. I appreciate all they did. I craved my mother during those important times in my life. Like when I gave birth to you, when you gave birth to your own daughter, at your graduations, I needed her. I needed my mother." I took a pause like my mother would have.

"I tried, Anna; I tried with all that I had. Don't hate me just try to understand. You're a mother, too; we make mistakes that we can't change but it doesn't mean that we love our children any less. It just means that we are human." I took a deep breath, rose and changed seats.

I didn't need Sapna to tell me it was time to do so; I knew it in my heart. My mother said all that she had to say to me; now it was time for me to get closure.

Right before I opened my mouth to say my final words to my invisible mother, a strong feeling of connection to her came over me. For the first time, I saw her for who she really was. She was a woman, like many women I knew, who sought love and acceptance. She was insecure, weak, and scared. I was slowly getting the concept; my mother couldn't be the mother I wanted her to be. Her emotional state didn't leave her with the proper capacity to play that role effectively. Whatever "effectively" meant.

The anger slowly left me and I began to feel sorry for her. When I gazed at the empty chair my frown leisurely released it's tightly formed scowl. I pitied her for never having the courage to stand up and be the confident woman I knew lay somewhere in her being.

As if Sapna was reading my mind, she said, "You have really done a complete job with the empty-chair technique. Let's put a close to the session and then we will discuss it in full detail."

I stared at the empty chair with a new confidence. "Mother, you are right. I'm a mother, and the thought of being remotely like you has terrified me. As much as I thought I was running away from being

similar to you, the more I ran straight into the woman you are. For years I beat myself up for abandoning Spirit the way you abandoned me. I've concluded that I have no way in hell put her through what you allowed me to suffer through. I at least made sure that Spirit was loved. You, on the other hand, made sure you were the only one that was loved.

"Do I hate you? Not anymore. It hurts too much to hate you. I feel sorry for you. Hating you has stunted my emotional growth, barring me from what could have been fruitful relationships. Shit, hating you made me push Dupri away, the only man besides Gianni that loved me with no strings attached. Yeah, I've stopped hating you. It isn't worth it. With all that being said, you, Mother, are who you are and I am who I'm because of it. Your passiveness has made me aggressive. Your weakness has been my strength. Thank you."

Chapter 33

"Okay, Anna," Sapna began as she took a seat in the chair once occupied by my mother. "I want you to close your eyes, inhale and exhale slowly." I did so. "Now, take a moment and focus on the session that we just had, before we discuss it."

I sat with my eyes closed and congratulated myself for completing the task and not running away from it. Lord knew I wanted to get up and get the fuck out of this place, but I stuck with it. *Go, Anna! It's your birthday! Get busy! You did it!* My brain party came to an end when I heard Sapna's voice.

"All right, Anna, open your eyes. I must say you have guts like a burglar. You were exceptional throughout the exercise. How do you feel about the exchange that just took place?"

"For one," I started, "I was a little nervous that I wasn't doing it correctly. I felt very foolish looking at the empty chair while holding on to the image of my mother. That got to be a bit tedious at times, but once I relaxed, there were times when I did feel that she was sitting before me. Somewhere in the middle I figured that there was no correct way to do it, I just had to do it. Does that make sense?"

"Yes, Anna, that makes plenty of sense," Sapna said bobbing her head wildly. "This form of therapy is not like conventional talk therapy, as you have experienced first hand. In order to fully grasp the full concept, you have to sort of have an out-of-body experience. Think outside of the box, some would say." She beamed at me. "You did extremely well, Anna. I can't say that enough. In the beginning of the session I said I would ask you key lead questions, but I didn't have to. You took the ball and ran with it, and achieved your slam dunk." Sapna smile sparkled emphasizing her rosy cheeks.

"By placing your mother in that chair, an individual that gives you great difficulty, it showed that she is really a part of you right now. The things said and felt by you in both chairs are parts of your being in the here and now. Your emotions, memories, and expectations about your mother are yours, not hers. I'm not saying that your feelings aren't valid, but they are emotions that you created and that you'll have to deal with."

"You are so right," I said nodding. "After listening to myself as my mother, I realized that she just doesn't get it, she did not once hear what I was saying. She never acknowledged the abuse. She made me feel like those beatings never took place, like they were a figment of my imagination. But those beatings were real. They were just not her problem to deal with. So I hear you when you say it was something that I created and had to deal with on my own."

"I'm so glad that you see it. This animosity you have toward her festers in you, and that makes it yours to deal with. She is never going to take you in her arms and murmur that you are her darling. That nurturing that you are looking for, you'll have to find in yourself." She made some notations on her notepad. "If you believe that your other relationship issues are your mother's fault, you'll do nothing to change it. It would just become a constant cycle that you would forever repeat, never assuming responsibility for your own actions. Through this exercise you begin to see that it's you that harbors these feelings, as I'm sure you have noticed.

"You have always been connected to one side of your internal conflict. Once you got in touch with both sides, and saw both views, you could begin the healing process. Your mother wasn't the mother you needed her to be. She was more concerned with her own emotional needs to meet yours, but you can't allow that to seep into every other relationship in your life. Now you have started to deal with the repressed feelings that still mess up your life. I again applaud you for

completing the session and moving forward in your healing work."

"I ain't cured," I joked, "but I do feel a lot less stress and ready to move on, like you suggested."

"Anna, people are flawed. But the flaws are what makes us beautiful. The flaws and the cracks are how the light gets in. The light is getting in Anna the light is getting in! Nurture yourself Anna, like you wanted your mother too. You have already begun that process by coming to see me, writing and now becoming the mother you always wanted to be to your daughter," I smiled deeply as my eyes held her gaze. "This one little exercise doesn't mean we are done. There are still things to explore, but we are heading in the right direction."

"Sapna, I told October about the rapes." Her head rose from her notepad.

"You did? What did she say?" She crossed her legs.

"She was in shock. Destroyed obviously because it was her Father. But she wants to start seeing someone with me and by herself. I realized how much hate I've been directing towards her." Sapna's hazel eyes beamed. "She doesn't deserve that. Sapna she is as much a victim as I am."

"You are so right Anna. That poor girl is definitely a victim also. But that October is a good person. You are so lucky to have her in your corner. I'll be happy to see the both you two." She patted my knee.

I nodded "So, next week, same time, same place?"

Sapna shook her head. "Actually, I will be on vacation starting the day after tomorrow and won't be back for two weeks." She frowned. "I thought I told you this before?"

I tried not to panic. "No, you didn't tell me."

"Well, I do apologize. We can make our appointment for two weeks from today." Sapna scribbled a date on the back of one of her ever-so-popular appointment cards. "Though I'll be on vacation, I don't want you to stop healing. Continue writing your poetry; do some reading, anything that will be centered on yourself. This time will be excellent; it will allow you to thoroughly process this experience without running to me. But if you really need to see someone, my colleague, Mr. Shawn Wright, will be seeing my clients on an emergency basis."

I took the card from her. "I think I'll be fine, but if anything comes up I will be sure to contact Mr. Wright." We both walked in silence to the front door.

Chapter 34

I hurried to my car. The husky wind molested my exposed neck. I wrapped my colorful wooly scarf around it to protect myself—the same scarf that Dupri had purchased for me during our first winter together. The one I had prior to this one I had had since high school. My scarf was an odd bright neon green color, so old and tattered that much of the fabric had unraveled. October tried for years to burn it, but I wore it as though it were the latest Hollywood fashion.

Not until Dupri and I went to Nordstrom at the Garden State Mall in New Jersey did I put my dying scarf to rest. Or should I say, he put it to rest for me. In the accessory department I went straight to the handbags, but he managed to find his way over to the scarves. After mulling through the racks for some time I noticed that he was at the register. I ran over to meet him and spotted the package in his hand. I circled my arms around his neck leaving a lipstick imprint. I knew that whatever he bought was for me. I snatched the bag out of his hand and opened it. It was the most exquisite scarf I'd ever seen. Beautiful colors, perfectly woven together, creating the most luscious accessory that had been created. I don't know if I felt that way because he bought it or because that was the truth; either way I loved it. I was so happy

about my new scarf that I threw my high school one in the department store trashcan. I sucked on Dupri's lips to demonstrate my love and appreciation.

How much I missed him. I really wanted that man back in my life. I just wasn't sure how to go about regaining his love again. He never even got a chance to meet Spirit. My intuition told me that they would have gotten along perfectly.

Our little family could have been like the three bears. I would have been Mama Bear, Dupri would have been Step-Daddy Bear, and Spirit would have been Baby Bear. All of us would have been sitting at the kitchen table, eating our porridge. Instead I was In Therapy Bear, Dupri was Anna-Has-Issues Bear, and Spirit was Mommy-Can-You-Bring-Me-Home Bear. *Now ain't that a functional family*, I thought as I placed the key in the ignition.

A commercial on the car radio advertised a newly opened lounge in the Clinton Hill section of Brooklyn, not too far from home. The commercial went on to entice the listeners by describing a dimly lit, candle-adorned, lush space that offered great food, erotic music, and an open-mic feature every Thursday night.

I couldn't plug my headset into my cell phone fast enough. October and I were always looking for a place new to hang. This was something she would love to get into.

"Hey, O!"

"Hey, Crackhead, why do you sound like that? Did you just get laid? Please tell me you finally got some dick?"

"Do you always have sex on your mind? Nothing, I'm up to nothing. I'm actually on my way home from Sapna."

October's voice was filled with concern. "Oh, really? How was your session today?"

"Gurl, it was the best ever. I can't even put into words the feeling I got from today's session. I'm ready to get out there and do the damn thing."

"Thank goodness for small miracles! I was tired of your dumb behind lying around the place. You were making me depressed."

"Thanks for the support, sister dearest," I said with sarcasm. "I'll tell you all the gory details some other time. I actually called to tell you about this commercial I heard on the radio, about this new spot around the corner from me."

"There was a new spot, recently opened around the corner from you, and you had to be in your car driving back from Jersey to hear about it. Your pathetic ass was really living under a rock, I see."

I couldn't help but laugh. October was right; how silly had I been? I must've been wearing blinders or something since the darn spot was located right next to my Laundromat. "Anyway, like I was saying before you rudely interrupted me, they have an open mic night and I was thinking—"

"No, Anna, don't think! Once you start doing that, bad things begin to happen." My crazy-ass sister laughed.

"Whatever, chick, like I was saying, I was thinking we can round the girls up and I could possibly go by this coming Thursday and read one of my poems."

"You, read your *poetry*?" October quizzed, practically choking from laughing so hard.

My overly sensitive nature went into overdrive. I held my composure and waited for her to contain herself. "Yes, chick, me, Anna, read my poetry. What is so freaking funny about that? No, don't answer me. Do you want to do it or not? It sounds like fun."

October stopped laughing. "Of course I want to go! Are you stupid? I wouldn't miss this if my life depended on it. I will do anything to see the girl who had to take speech three times in college before she passed it, get up in front of a large crowd and read her innermost feelings." She smacked her teeth. "Gurl, I'll be there way before the doors open, making sure I get a seat way up front. You can count on your sister to support you in this new venture."

I wasn't sure if October was sincere or not, but wasn't about to question her. She said she was going to do it and I was going to leave it at that. "All right, lady, it's confirmed. Put the date in your Blackberry so you don't forget," I ordered with my older-sister voice.

"I'm putting it in my Blackberry, on my fridge, shit; I'm placing sticky notes all over. I'll be there, you can believe that." October paused. "Do you want me to call the others or are you going to do that?"

"Nah, you can call everyone, I need to work on my writing. I'll just tell Zoe when I go to work."

"Gotcha, this is going to be a blast! I know I was cracking up, but I'm thrilled you are going to do this. Almost feels like I'm going to be the one on stage instead of you! Let's run to the mall and get a new

pair of stilettos before you go on?"

"Sounds like fun. Any reason to hit the mall, I'm there. But I'm going to get off this phone. I'm crossing over the Brooklyn Bridge now and I think I wasted enough cell-phone minutes on you."

"No problem. I've to get ready for a hot date anyway. Aye, have you spoken to Lady Spirit lately?"

"It's funny you should mention her, because I was going to call her when I got in. I miss her, October, and can't wait for her to come home. It's going to be energizing having her around."

"Yeah, it will be funky having someone around that I can poison with my crazy antics," October said with fondness.

I chuckled. "Enough of the mushy stuff, this was supposed to only be a two-minute conversation. I'm getting off the phone."

"You love me," October shot back, "that's why." She tittered before continuing, "I'll see you Wednesday. I'll even drive out to the mall."

"Wow, you must really want to see me make a jackass of myself on stage." I laughed. "No problem. Love you much."

Chapter 35

"*Buon giorno*, Mrs. Contadino, *come sta lei?*" I said in my broken Italian as she answered the phone.

"*Buon giorno,* Anna, how are you dear?" Mrs. Contadino asked brightly.

"I'm doing great. Life is going good on this side of the world."

"I'm delighted to hear that. We haven't heard from you too much lately and I was beginning to worry. Spirit said she spoke with you the other day, but I was saddened that I didn't get the opportunity to speak to my son's greatest love." Mrs. C. had always been so gracious toward me.

"I'm sorry, Mrs. C., I've been very busy lately with work and stuff."

"Life does get busy, but sometimes you have to make time for the special people," Mrs. Contadino preached.

"I know, I know. I will do better. Mrs. C., I'm glad you answered the phone. I've been meaning to speak to you for some time now." I was nervous not really sure which direction this conversation would take. A sigh came through the phone line before I spoke again. "Mrs. C., Spirit has shared with me on several occasions her desire to come

and live with me in the States. And I can't say that I don't want that, either."

"I knew this day was soon going to come," Mrs. C said with some sadness in her voice. "Once a young girl reaches her formative years, she begins to seek out her mother's love."

"I need her love also." I breathed.

"Of course you do. Every mother wants the admiration of her daughter; I wouldn't expect anything less."

"I love her, Mrs. Contadino, and want a few years with her before she goes off to college. Is that so much to ask?"

"No, my love, that isn't much to ask at all, I would want the same myself."

"Your understanding is refreshing and I thank you for it."

Mrs. Contadino sighed. "Mr. Contadino is going to be lost without his shining Spirit around, but we both knew this day was inevitable. Thank you for allowing us to raise Gianni all over again."

My eyes began to tear. "No, thank you, Mrs.Contadino, for allowing me to obtain my degree, build a decent life for myself and Spirit. For that I'm forever grateful. I love you guys."

"Mothers never think that the women their sons choose would ever live up to their mothers. We always have a way of thinking that we are better than their wives, girlfriends, and so forth. Such a tender, vulnerable age you guys were when you fell in love; I never thought it would last. I had to stop thinking negatively and put my feelings aside and be happy for my son, for he was happy. After all, I did have to deal with my own prejudices within my own relationship. I'm saying all of this to say, Anna, that I see why my son fell in love with you. You are smart, gorgeous, and courageous, reminding me every bit of myself. I now know that you were the right woman for him and the right woman to bear my first grandchild. You are blessed, my dear." Her tone turned cheerful.

"Enough of all this talk, you're going to make me cry, you know I hate to cry. Let me go get Spirit for you. I also have to go tell that husband of mine that Spirit is leaving us soon."

"Thank you, Mrs. C., for those sentiments. It means everything to me. Bringing her home during the summer was my first option, but I think I want her with me for Christmas. Is that okay?" I asked, knowing

what the answer would be.

"Sure, my dear, that will be fine. Now let me go get that girl so that I can go off and cry. Hold on." Mrs. C and Mrs. Hawkins loved me like I wanted Mother to.

I fought back the tears while waiting for Spirit to answer. It never dawned on me how difficult this decision would be for everyone involved. My heart told me that this was for the best. Spirit and I needed to be together now. I just wish the Contadinos didn't have to hurt in the process.

Spirit's gushing teenage voice interrupted my thoughts. "Hey, Mom, how are you? I miss you! I love you."

"Hey, lovely, I miss you too." I tried to keep the tears from my voice. "I just spoke with your grandmother and told her about you coming to live in the States."

"I know. She didn't tell me but her tears did."

"I know, baby. I feel so bad. They did a marvelous job raising and loving you. I hope I can do half as good a job as they did."

"Are you kidding me? You'll be superb, just a bit strict. I can tell from the way you handle your students."

"You've got to be kidding me," I said in mock annoyance. "My students are treated like precious jewels." I giggled, knowing darn well that Spirit was right. I continued, "The catch, love, is that you'll come to the States way before next year. I want to bring you home for Christmas."

The phone dropped and a squeal came from the other end.

"Are you serious?" Spirit squealed after finally getting herself together.

"Of course I'm serious. I've been without you for too long and it's time. No need to wait damn near another year to be together when we can be together now."

"Mommy, I love you! I really love you and I can't wait until I can live with you. But do you know the coolest part?"

"What, silly? What is the coolest part?" I was enthralled by her delight.

"The coolest part is that I will still be close to my grandparents and Daddy, even in Brooklyn, since we'll be living in their house."

"You are one hundred percent right. You are a Contadino. Forever will you be surrounded with their likeness in some form or fashion. But you should know that you would be attending school in the middle of the school year. I will call some of my administrative friends to get you placed in a good school." I paused for breath. "You'll also have chores," I added. I didn't want to forget anything.

"I'll do whatever. My friends are going to be so jealous! Can they come stay with us in the summer?"

"Child, you are getting ahead of yourself," I said with some exasperation. "We will work all of that out at a later date." Hearing her depressed sigh I reassured her. "All things are possible and can happen. Let's just get you where you belong first. Over the next several days I'm going to work on getting the airline tickets. I'll call you in a couple of days with the itinerary. I'm going to bed now; I have a long day tomorrow."

"Mommy, thank you for bringing me home, I'm going to start packing now. I love you."

"I love you also, precious. But I almost forgot one more thing before you go. I thought about what you said the other day. You know about this being a weird situation and all. You know the both of us having to get use to each other. So I decided we will see a friend of mine. You know, a therapist."

"A therapist, Mom, I don't think it's even that serious."

"Well, I think it is. This is a new beginning for both of us and I want us to have a nice adjustment period."

"I guess, whatever works for you, Mom."

"No lady, whatever works for us?"

"Love you, Mom. Talk to you soon."

"See you soon and speak to you even sooner."

Chapter 36

The next few days went by smoothly. I managed to purchase my airline ticket to Italy and tickets for Spirit and me back to the States. They were bought earlier than our Christmas confirmed date, but it didn't matter. I hope the Contadino's weren't going to be too mad, but I thought it would be fabulous to do some Christmas shopping together.

While scurrying around for Spirit's bedroom accents, I imagined her next to me, pestering me for the latest fashionable teenage item. Thinking of those soon-to-be new memories added new excitement to my shopping experience. We were going to have tons of mother-and-daughter shopping trips, I was pretty sure.

October and I hadn't mentioned the molestation since we last spoke about it. I assumed she needed more time to deal with it. We just continued along as usual.

October's voice carried from the other end of the department store floor. "Anna, what about some purple pumps?" My sister was officially crazy; did everyone need to hear about her purple pumps?

I walked closer to her so that I didn't appear to be just as ghetto as

she was. I gave her the attention she so desperately needed. "Turn your feet around; let me see the side of them."

October turned her feet so I could get a better look. "So, what do you think?" she asked, again losing patience.

"I think they look fine. Just don't wear a purple shirt or it will be way too much."

"Oh, no, I had no desire to do that," She stopped abruptly glaring at me. "I was actually going to borrow your purple fuchsia-printed Furla clutch bag," she checked her reflection.

I stopped dead in my tracks and stared at her. I wanted to curse her out at assuming she would be wearing one of my favorite purses, but said nothing. All I could do was shake my head. There was no need fighting over it because she would use her spare key and take the bag anyway.

"Grandpa's party is still next week, right?"

"Yep, it's still on. While we are here we should try and grab something to wear to that, too."

As much as I didn't want to, I knew I had to. After not speaking to my mother for two years I couldn't show up at the party looking like trash. She wouldn't let me hear the end of it. Not only had I not spoken to her in a couple of years, in her eyes I would be sabotaging the party if I weren't dressed to her liking. I waited for October to pay for her shoes before we headed off to the eveningwear department.

"Do you think I should get the traditional black?" I asked as I sifted through the dress rack.

"Sure." October shrugged. "You can never go wrong with black."

"I was thinking the same thing. I'm going to the fitting room; see you in a few." It took me all of seven minutes in the fitting room. Those three-way mirrors were enough to make you slit your wrists. Choosing the lesser of the evil dresses, I took my merchandise to the register. My mother would just have to appreciate the outfit; if she didn't, then that was her business.

The car ride home was filled with October's constant prattle about what poetry I was going to read. I didn't know what language I should use on her, because it didn't seem like she understood me when I said "no" in English. She kept going on and on, not once getting the clue that I wasn't paying her any attention. She had no choice but to get it

after I turned the car radio up to maximum volume.

As we neared my block we noticed the lounge. "Thesaurus." The gates were pulled down, not allowing us the glimpse we were looking for.

"Anna, what a name, huh?" October asked, already infatuated.

"Yeah, Gurl, that name is brilliant. I hope I can do it justice tomorrow."

Chapter 37

"Thesaurus" was dimly lit, candle-adorned, and very lush, just as the commercial stated. It had been decorated with Ikea light fixtures, round gold-toned leather stools, earth-toned multi-colored velvet armchairs, tables lavished with plush burnt-orange tablecloths. Fresh flower petals had been sprinkled on each table to add an inviting feel. Bohemians, yuppie African-Americans, dirty backpackers, and Wall Street cats filled this enchanting new lounge.

October and the others were more than likely already part of the mixed crowd. They wanted to come by my brownstone for a pre-evening cocktail but I needed a few moments by myself. My sister was right; I couldn't even get through speech class, now I was going to stand in front of an intoxicated crowd. My empty chair session with Sapna must have really motivated me. Like a fish out of water, this was way out of my element.

I stood on my tippy toes until I saw October and the others at a table smack dab in the front of the stage, just where she said she would be. Before heading over to meet them I went to the bar.

"Can I get a Long Island Iced Tea?" I asked the green-eyed bartender.

"No problem," he responded.

While waiting for my drink, I checked out his ample ass. I'd never been with a white boy before, nor had I ever approached a man first. Since tonight was a night of firsts then why the heck not? Dupri didn't look as though he'd be coming back to me any time soon, so I might as well go on and live. When the bartender brought me my drink, I slipped my number with his tip. I was looking pretty sharp tonight, so he should bite.

"Are you always so bold?' he asked after I slipped him my number.

"Only when I see something I like." I smirked.

"A woman who knows what she wants, not bad, not bad at all." He paused placing a napkin in front a new patron. "I'm Jonathan."

"I'm Anna."

"Anna, that's a very classic name."

"What you thought my name was going to be Shaquita or something." I laughed.

"No I thought it was going to be Beautiful." He laughed also.

"That was so corny. Couldn't you come up with a better line?"

"That was the best I had. Is this your first time here?"

"Yes. Are you here every night?"

"No, I work here part-time. I'm actually a full-time cop. This is just for some side cash."

"A cop, interesting, I'm a teacher."

"Umm, I never dated a teacher. I'll give you a call so I can change that." He confidently handed me his business card.

"I'm looking forward to hearing from you. By the way, how old are you?"

"Twenty-seven why? Is that going to be a problem?"

"Not at all, just curious, my friends are waiting." I walked away, feeling very sexy. I never had a youngster, guess I was going to get my groove back after all. Hopefully he wasn't gay.

I pushed through the crowd and made my way to the front where my people were saving a seat for me. "Hey ladies!"

"Hey, Anna," Zoe said first. She highlighted and spiked her pixie cut more than usual tonight. "You look magnificent. I'm really loving

those boots; they look great with your skirt." Her voice was filled with fondness. "You out did yourself tonight."

"I tried, but it wasn't easy, Gurl. You should check out my bedroom; clothes are all over the place. I thought I was going to wear one thing, but changed it before I walked out the front door."

"Good choice. You look great."

"She looks aight," October chimed in. She got up to give me a hug.

"Shut up," I said, hugging my sister back. I turned to give smooches to my other girlfriends who came out to support me tonight.

Samantha was there. Since we last saw each other on the Westside Highway, she hadn't call or e-mailed me. She allowed me the space I needed. Moving my newly relaxed hair out of the way, I gave her a huge kiss and tugged on her fiery red ponytail. Kerri and Priscilla, friends from college, were all in attendance. Having my girls there to support me was just what the doctor ordered.

"So, are you ready?" October asked crossing her legs.

"As ready as I'll ever be. I got a Long Island Ice Tea to calm my nerves." I raised my glass.

"'I see," she retorted with a puckered brow.

"What?" I feigned innocence.

October shrugged biting on her bottom lip. "Nothing, but you and I both know you can't hold your liquor. I don't want you going up there and making a jackass of yourself, better yet a fool of me. Maybe I should sit someplace else so people don't realize I'm with the drunk poet."

"I'll be fine," I retorted.

"Enough, you two," Zoe ordered. "Can't we ever go anywhere without you two going at it? Anyway, let's give a toast to Anna, for having the guts to bare her soul to us tonight." My four friends and my sister raised their glasses. Zoe began, "Anna, you are dynamite. Break a leg when you get up there. We love you. Cheers!" A chorus of cheers echoed around the table. Each one of us put a glass to our lips and drank down our relaxation. We soon began a chorus of the latest gossip while waiting for my theatrical performance to start.

Will Downing's deep voice sang "Daydreaming," which was piped through the lounge's various amplified speakers. The song was

interrupted by the tiny voice of the MC for the night.

"Ladies and gentlemen, I would like to welcome you to our first open-mic night here at Thesaurus." Thunderous applause erupted throughout the lounge. "We are so elated to be a new addition to the neighborhood. We hope to be here for many years to come." She smiled surveying the crowd.

"My name is Ella and I'll be your MC for the night. We have a fantastic show lined up for you guys," Ella assured us. "Sit back, eat up, drink up, and prepare to be enlightened."

The first poet was introduced and shared his heart. I was up third and seeing him made me a bit nervous. My stomach got an automatic Boy Scout knot. Zoe patted my arm. I smiled back my thanks for her support. But that wasn't enough to calm my nerves.

I shot a glance over to the front door. I could probably make a run for it. But a herd of people was standing up in the back, blocking the path to the door. I looked to the right and figured that the bathroom was a better option.

As the poet left the stage I made a beeline for the bathroom before act number two began. I was feeling really nauseated. The bathroom attendant's head spun like Carrie's as I crashed into her space. I almost knocked over the toiletries. I braced my hands on the counter to catch myself. My head was spinning. What the fuck had I gotten myself into? Me and my bright ideas; I did this to myself all the time. I walked into an empty stall and began to pray. Only the Lord could help me now.

"Dear Jesus, give me the clarity and strength to go out there and speak to the crowd. Give me the courage and understanding to speak from the heart. I also ask that you make sure I don't fall as I make my way to the stage. That would not be a good look, especially since I look sexy as heck in these three-and-a-half-inch stilettos knee-high boots. These things I pray. Amen."

I walked out of the stall and gave the Mexican attendant a tip in her cup. I strutted out of the bathroom and returned to my seat. The second artist was still performing the end of her story.

The girls turned around and smiled at me with love as Ella made her way to the stage to introduce the next act, me. I was calmer after my prayer and more prepared to share my voice. I heard the applause as Ella announced my name and I walked the circular stage.

It's now or never, I thought as I looked out at the crowd. Blue eyes, green eyes, and brown eyes stared at me. Some faces held smiles, while others had looks that questioned if I were going to do a good job. I could see Jonathan, the young bartender. He almost spilled the drink he was making, when our gaze interlocked. Next to him was another man in a red-ribbed turtleneck.

The glare from the light didn't allow me a good glimpse of his face. My gaze darted back to the girls. Their loving smiles gave me the encouragement I needed to begin.

"Hey, everyone, I'm Anna and this is my first time at an open-mic. So please forgive me if I make any mistakes and I hope you enjoy my little poem as much as I do." I took a breath. "It's called *My Chocolate Dreams*." I exhaled again, and then began:

Why do I dream of chocolate?

Sweet little Hershey kisses

Beautiful dark chocolate truffles

Thick German chocolate cake

And smooth chocolate liqueur.

I didn't always dream of chocolate

I use to dream of yellow pound cake with white icing

Lemon sherbet ice cream

And creamy vanilla milkshakes.

I was told don't dream of chocolate

It can be bitter and sometimes stale

Processed food loaded with calories

Evil substance stacked with sugar.

I was told if I dreamed of chocolate

To add substances, to change it up a bit

Like half-n-half, milk, whipped cream or marshmallows

Never eat it pure, for it can make you sick.

My dreams never changed, they always contained chocolate

Regardless of how hard I tried to make love to the lemon sherbet

Or idolize the creamy vanilla milkshakes

My dreams embodied chocolate, exploded chocolate.

My dreams teach me all about the beauty in chocolate

No two flavors are ever the made the same

Each piece of chocolate is made authentic, pure and divine

Every cocoa bean made with its own special blend

Why do I dream of chocolate?

I dream of chocolate because I am chocolate

Sweet, smooth, authentic, dark chocolate

Pure, divine, made from a special-blend chocolate

In my euphoric state I stood there and watched as my sister popped up immediately after my last word. The other sitting patrons followed suit. The entire place burst into a roaring applause. They gave me more love than they gave the others before me. Overwhelmed, I thanked everyone and walked off the stage to join my crew.

Chapter 38

After my Tony-nominated performance the girls and I gathered at my brownstone for a much-needed *Waiting to Exhale* moment. How much I missed our days of hanging out together! I was so caught up in my own real-life movie; I pushed those days into a corner of my mind. Getting tipsy and talking trash was what I needed.

"Make sure you guys leave your shoes at the front door," I said. "I don't need ugly shoe prints in my off-white carpet."

October mocked me in the background. "Shut up, O. I can hear you."

"Good, I'm glad you can hear me, hear this also. Who the heck buys off-white carpet? You ain't royalty you know."

I was going to knock this chick out.

"Would you two give it up already? What do you have to drink Anna?" Zoe didn't wait for an answer but instead went toward the bar.

"I don't know. Check. I did buy a bottle of red wine the other day; it should be there." Over at the stereo system, I settled on Donny Hathaway and Teena Marie as our musical entertainment for the

evening. After playing disc jockey I went into the kitchen and looked for some grub for us to munch on. I removed a liter of water, some crackers, cheese, and a cake I picked up from the bakery.

October noticed my struggle to carry the food and ran over to help me, all while running her mouth a mile a minute. "So, Anna, tell us, how does it feel? You were fabulous, by the way."

"I got nervous for a minute when I saw you run to the bathroom," Zoe added. "I was like, uh-oh, this chick isn't going to make it."

"I don't know what happened," I replied. "I was fine when I walked in, even flirted with the bartender, but during the first act, I lost it."

"The bartender?" Zoe asked with narrowing eyes.

"Yep, he was kind of cute and I was kind of horny." Oh God, I forgot that she was Dupri's sister. The minute I finished the statement I tried to clean it up. "I don't know it just sort of happened." I hoped Zoe wasn't offended. It had only been about seven weeks or so since Dupri and I broke up. I didn't think she wanted me to sit around pining over her brother forever.

"Sounds good to me," October piped in. "You with a white guy, me and my Korean dream boat, it will be like going to the United Nations for Christmas." October had us all in stitches.

"Okay everyone, I have some good news!" Zoe bounced on the couch, about to burst. We all got comfortable in our seats while she stood up to share her good news. "My adorable husband and I decided, are you guys ready to hear this?" Zoe giggled.

I threw one of my many plush velvet throw pillows at her. "Woman, would you just spit it out already?"

"Gosh, you guys are so impatient," Zoe managed to say through her own laughter. "Anyway, like I was saying before I was rudely interrupted," she was still laughing, "We are adopting a baby boy. The birth mother is going into labor in a week, so we are flying out to Colorado the day after next."

October and my other girlfriends immediately jumped out of their seats to hug Zoe.

I stayed put in my spot on the sofa and cried. This time, my tears were of joy and a bit of sadness. Sad because by being so self-absorbed, I forgot about my girlfriends and their life issues. Joy because after

Zoe survived cancer she was told she would never have children, which crushed her. She felt less than a woman but with her supportive husband, every day she began to feel more and more like the woman she was. They talked about adopting for quite some time, but I never knew they'd made a final decision.

"Zo, congrats! You are going to be the world's greatest mother." I rose from the sofa to add my own hug.

"Thanks, Anna. That means a lot to me."

"So when did you get the good news?" Samantha chimed in.

"Well, we searched the Web for women who were looking for adoptive parents for their unborn children. On the weekends we flew out to interview with different women. On, like, our third trip, we found this young lady we fell totally in love with," Zoe sang with pride. "She is a student, getting her master's, about to embark on a trip to Africa to study abroad. Having a baby at this time was not a good thing for her. She wants to be a distant parent and of course, I told her that wouldn't be a problem. I want Zurich Hamilton to know both of his mothers."

"Oh, my God, you named him already! That is so wonderful!" October shouted. "Zoe I'm so happy for you, along with the fact that I'm going to be a godmother also." October shouted as if she were the one adopting the child.

"Everyone let's grab a glass and make a toast to Zurich Hamilton," Samantha said. Everyone was poured a glass of red wine.

"I'll give the toast," October commanded. "First, to my sister Anna, for her award-winning performance tonight, you were fabulous. They should've given you the Academy award. Halle Berry, watch out."

"Cheers," we all said in unison as we clicked glasses.

"To Zoe, for her new addition, Zurich Hamilton, you'll be the best mother ever. We wish you guys the best. Can't wait until you bring him home, we are going to have a party."

"Cheers," we said again in unison after October's speech.

"Now to me, for being extremely gorgeous, sexy, and for accepting my Korean boyfriend's proposal, I'm getting married!" She waved her ring finger at us.

My wine glass dropped as I noticed the shiny diamond on my sister's left hand. Now I was the one who messed up my carpet, guess I couldn't

complain about that anymore. Tears ran down my cheeks and my heart started racing. I could not believe that I'd missed so much in the lives of these important women in my life.

"Anna, are you happy for me?" October's bright wide-set eyes begged for my approval.

"Are you crazy? I'm ecstatic, October. I love you. Congratulations!" I screeched through my flow of tears. "This is wonderful, I'm going to run out and buy every bride magazine on the newsstand. Why didn't you tell me?" I already knew the answer. October knew I didn't need an answer as well. Instead, we gave each other the deepest sisterly hug ever.

We talked and talked until the early hours of the morning about everything and anything. We all played catch up since we all led such busy lives. It was comforting to spend time with my sister friends. When I told them Spirit was coming home, they were excited also. And, as expected, October did another toast.

Everyone but Zoe, who was a bit hurt that I never told her about Spirit. When I met Zoe four years ago, I never thought she and I would become as close as we were now. I tried to keep her at arm's length but she made her way into my heart. When Dupri and I broke up, I thought we would definitely go our separate ways and just remain teacher friends, but that was not the case. Our friendship was bigger than him.

She had no clue that I was a mother. That night I told her everything, from the abuse, leaving home, birth of Spirit and the death of Gianni, and my low self-esteem. We hugged and cried that night. She said she was mad with me for not opening up to her brother, but understood my fears. She also confided that Dupri would have loved me more if he knew and that he was still hurting from our breakup. As glad as I was to hear that, I couldn't worry about that now. Dupri's decision to break up with me was a good thing. I was forced to get my act together. Our relationship's demise was the fire I needed under my butt.

I showed Zoe all of Spirit's pictures. She marveled at how beautiful Spirit was. Like the proud mother, I rattled on about her cute little baby stories, including our trips together to exotic places. Zoe and I both shared our nervousness about being new mothers and how to fit our new lifestyles into our demanding careers. I'm petrified I'll fail.

Dear Book,

It's almost over. Whew! It took long enough. I thought I would never see the Easter Parade. I am so excited Book, I am speaking foolishly. My latest session with Sapna was good. I made a lot of progress. Oh and I almost forgot to tell you about poetry night. I was the best darn thing there. It felt exhilarating. Just reading that one little poem made me feel like I can conquer the world now.

In a few more weeks Spirit would be home. I'm a little nervous but quite happy. Everything is going along smoothly, for the first time in a long time. Lawd knows I can't handle any more drama.

Bye Book

Chapter 39

My nerves were really kicking my ass as I lay in bed. I tried several times to get out of the bed, but my body and mind weren't making the connection. Why did I tell October I would go to Grandpa's birthday bash? The idea seemed good on paper, but realistically... Suppose my mother and I got into a huge fight? If she pissed me off bad enough I could seriously see that happening.

My newly engaged sister would be here in about an hour. I wasn't going anywhere. This was one family affair that this member wasn't going to be a part of. I picked up the receiver and dialed the memorized number.

"Hey, O., what's up?" I hoped she didn't realize I was calling to cancel.

"Hey, Anna, listen, I'm going to be about twenty minutes late. So you don't have to rush."

"Well, that's why I was calling you," I managed to get out while taking a breath. "I'm not feeling that well; it's that time of the month, so I'm not going tonight."

"You're joking, right?" October wasn't laughing. "Look, I told

Mom you're coming, so take two Advil's and I'll see you in an hour and twenty minutes." She hung up.

If I could've reached through the phone, I would've slapped that Bobbi Brown makeup off my sister. But instead, I crawled out of bed and went into the bathroom. Under the steamy hot pulsating shower stream, I thought about Spirit coming home soon. I furnished her dad's old room with all of the new stuff I bought for her. Her entire room was decorated in purple accents lined with books, cd's, furry bears and love.

I had lived in Gianni's family home for over sixteen years but always managed to avoid that room like the plague. I kept the door closed in order to keep his memory out. With Spirit coming home, I understood that Gianni's spirit needed to live. It was a part of my healing, just like this party today. I had to put the past behind me in order to have a prosperous future.

I sprayed myself one last time with my favorite perfume and surveyed my reflection before walking out to meet October. October was right in suggesting I wear black. The black silk halter dress, with my black sequined shawl and matching three-inch heels, was the perfect outfit to face my mother.

"Hey, O." I kissed my sister on the cheek.

"Hey, lady, you look great," October, said flashing an exuberant smile.

"You don't look too bad yourself. Mom is going to be proud of her girls." I fiddled with the car radio. How much time we spent in the car, bonding? We didn't always need to talk, but just being in each other's company was enough. We were the new-age Thelma and Louise.

My sister took a wrong turn.

"October, the banquet hall is toward our left. Where are you going?" I hoped she didn't get us lost.

"Ma said we should go this way because there might be traffic if we followed the other directions," October stated as she looked directly at the road ahead of her.

I shrugged and deferred to her directions until I noticed a familiar truck up ahead of us.

My sneaky-ass sister pulled up behind Dupri's royal blue SUV. I sat there, stunned, not believing what the fuck was going on. Through

breathless quivers of emotion I took in every new detail of him. He allowed his trimmed goatee to grow into a full beard. His pierced ear that was always adorned with a diamond stud now lay naked.

He allowed his hair to grow in sporting a dark caesar instead of his normal baldhead. Dupri wore an outfit Tyson Beckford had probably worn on the catwalk. He looked as exquisite as an Armani suit. My heart fluttered. All the feelings I felt when I saw him in Zoe's classroom for the first time came back. I flipped the passenger side mirror down to check my makeup.

October said in a lighthearted tone, "I hope you don't hate me, but I want you to be happy. You deserve it."

Dupri opened my door and said, "You look beautiful, Miss Lady."

"Thank you," I mouthed, but no sound came out.

October rolled her eyes. "You guys are killing me. What's up, D.? I'm glad to see you, now you can take her pathetic ass off of my hands." She cracked up, laughing at her *Mo-Nique* wannabe pathetic joke.

"Hey, Lady O., thanks for bringing my lady back to me," my Pumpkin said with a huge smile. "And congratulations, by the way, on your engagement. See you at the banquet." Dupri took my hand and held it as we walked to his car.

Chapter 40

"So, you're into white guys now?" Dupri asked with an impish grin. Instead of following the arrow that said Flatbush Ave, Dupri went to the left following the arrow that said Eastern Parkway. He opted for the service lane instead of the main street. So much time had passed since I'd been this close to him.

I've missed driving next to him. He was totally sexy leaning to one side, his seat pulled all the way back and steering the wheel with his knee at times switching to his pointer finger. He had this mole on the pointer that was just the cutest. I wished I could be as relaxed as he was, but my palms dripped with sweat.

"Huh? What are you talking about?"

He smirked. "White guys, the opposite of black guys. Some are blonds, redheads, need I say more?" He gave a hearty laugh.

I rolled my eyes, smacking my teeth together. I wanted to punch him for his slickness, but I held my temper. The goal was too stay in the car. We approached the Bedford and Eastern Parkway intersection, stopping at the stop sign.

"I know what a white guy is, fool, don't be so darn sarcastic. What

I'm asking is what does a white boy hafta do with me?"

"No, Anna, that isn't what you asked." he laughed. "You specifically said, 'What are you talking about,' and I told you, white guys. You didn't ask anything else." He was laughing louder now.

"Dupri, don't piss me off."

Mocking me in a mock high-pitched voice he repeated, "Dupri, don't piss me off." I rolled my eyes, and folded my arms under my chest.

Dupri pinched my thigh playfully. "You are still so sensitive and slow I see." He glanced in my direction.

I wasn't annoyed anymore, but continued to act as though I was.

"White boy, as in the one you gave your number to in Thesaurus the other night." He took his gaze off the road for a millisecond and looked at me.

I unfolded my arms. My mouth was agape, but nothing escaped it. How the heck did he know about Thesaurus? Don't tell me Zoe told him. She swore my secret was safe with her. I guessed blood was thicker than water. Did she tell him about Spirit also? We came up to another stop sign.

He stretched his hands over and turned my chin to meet his eyes. "Tell me you're not really into white boys. Tell me I have a chance to get my lady back." His penetrating eyes crinkled in a smile. He bent my head down and kissed my forehead. I was still stuck on the fact he knew about Thesaurus.

A horn blew. A voice yelled, "Take that shit home!" Dupri stuck his finger up at the rearview mirror. He kissed my forehead again, before placing his foot on the gas and taking off.

"Did Zoe tell you about Thesaurus?"

He grabbed my left hand with his right one. He traced the cocoa-colored lines in my palm with his thumb. "No she didn't." He kept his gaze straight, his thumb still stroking.

She didn't tell him. She had to have told him. How else would he have known? I had to ask.

"If Zoe didn't tell you, then how the heck do you know about Thesaurus?" Another stop sign.

"Zoe did tell me."

"But you said—"

"Shhh woman, let me finish." He placed his index finger on my lips. We crossed the stop sign. "I own Thesaurus. I was there the night you took the stage."

"Oh," was all I managed to say. I took my hand from his and started rubbing both of mine together.

"I told you I wanted to open my own lounge once I left Goldman Sachs," Dupri began.

"You did mention that."

"I looked around at several spots in the city. I came up empty every time. I was getting pretty frustrated. One day I got a call from one of my frat brothers. He heard what I was trying to do, said he could possibly help." He paused, checking traffic before finishing his explanation.

"He bought some property, out here in BK and would rent it to me for cheap if I liked it. Of course, you know me: I can never pass up a good deal, so I decided to check it out. He told me the address. I was like 'oh, man, that place is right next-door to Anna!' For that reason I almost didn't take it. I kept thinking I would run into you and that awkward moment between us that would occur. You know that moment when you are not sure whether to speak or to run the fuck in the other direction. My mom convinced me otherwise. She said I couldn't run forever." He paused again, this time searching my face for emotion. Then continued. "Mom came with me to check it out. We fell in love with it immediately. It was roomy, classy, and in an up-and-coming neighborhood. Everything I wanted and more...just like you." He tried to make eye contact, but I averted my gaze. "I paid him the down payment and the rest, like they say, was history."

"You weren't going to take the place because I lived around the area?" My heart sank.

"No, I wasn't, but let me finish, okay?"

"Okay."

"My mom's friend, who is an interior designer, helped me decorate the place. My cousin is an intern over at the radio station, got me a commercial spot. Everything happened so fast, I was excited and still am."

"You should be very excited, but I don't know what to say, I guess

congratulations are in order." I had a hard time believing everything.

"I know you're in shock, but I was so excited to see you that night. Don't get mad at Zo. I begged her not to tell you. She was so confused. She wanted to tell you, but knew what the truth would do. She knew you wouldn't have performed that night."

"She was right about that." I giggled nervously.

"Are you upset?"

"No, not really, I just feel a bit weird. I feel exposed. Sort of like you seeing me naked for the first time. It was fine to have my girlfriends there, but knowing you were there puts a different spin on things."

"It shouldn't. It's just little ol' me, Dupri." He grinned in my direction. Then made a right turn onto Buffalo Ave off of Eastern Parkway.

I touched the side of his face. I was yearning to do that from the moment I stepped in the car. "So where were you positioned in the club, the night I was there?"

He rubbed his face on my caressing hand. "I was in the office, which is hidden behind the bar. I stood there behind the plexi-glass window, walking in circles, awaiting your arrival. I started cheesing as I saw you walk through those doors. You had that look on your face. The one you always have when you are in new surroundings. That half smile which shows no teeth but plenty of vulnerability."

We pulled into the BP gas station. I relaxed, knowing I would soon have a few moments to steal for myself.

"Don't go anywhere, I'll be right back."

I exhaled the breath I was holding from the moment I got in the truck. I tapped my feet, checked my reflection, and straightened my dress. I peeped out the driver's side back window. He was almost finished pumping the gas.

"I'm back." He slammed the truck door and glanced down at his watch. "We have a few more minutes before the festivities get started. I want us to talk for a few minutes. Is that okay?" He pulled into a corner of the gas station's parking lot.

"Sure, what do you want to talk about?"

"Us! What else, silly?" He pinched my nose. "You looked great on Thursday. You looked like you owned that stage." He smoothed my updo.

I closed my eyes, exhaling at his soothing touch. "Thank you."

"Oh, those boots were so sexy. I just kept imagining you sauntering around the bedroom with those boots and a black teddy." His hands were still in my hair.

"You *would* envision that," I teased.

"No, I'm serious and not let me forget the poem. That poem was amazing. Watch out, Nikki Giovanni, here comes Anna Story Harper. I was very proud of you. I swear I never knew you had it in you. The texture of the poem, the rhythm, and play on words were too much."

I couldn't help but laugh hysterically. This fool was really laying it on thick.

"What's so funny?" Dupri demanded. "I've been practicing forever what I was going to say to you this evening." His breath got heavy.

I took my hand and rubbed the side of his face again, hoping it would show him I understood.

"You didn't answer me— are you into white guys now?"

"I was having fun, Dupri."

"So, is that the answer?"

"Yes."

"Are you sure now?" His eyes darted wildly from one corner of my face to the other.

"Yes, Dupri, that is my answer."

"Alrighty then, but I took the liberty of taking your number from him. So the answer is no, you are not into white guys. You're my woman."

I raised my eyebrow. But I wouldn't have expected anything less from him.

"I dream of chocolate also. I missed having chocolate snuggled close to me at night."

"Do you really now?" I couldn't help but giggle like a young girl, being kissed by her boyfriend on a train ride home from school.

"Yes Anna, I do. I missed you something terrible. I've been lonely without you. I had Janet Jackson's, 'I Get So Lonely', on repeat."

"You are so corny." I couldn't help but laugh.

"I had to cook my own meals. Zo was getting tired of me showing

up every night with my empty Pyrex dish. I had to tie my own tie in the morning also."

I chuckled.

"I even went as far as buying a carton of soy milk. I didn't drink any of that shit though."

"You are pathetic," I joked.

"No, I was lonely. Now I know how a child feels when they lose their parent in a mall."

"I see. But remember the parent always tells the child to stay close. Don't go walking off by yourself. You didn't hear me, Dupri, you went off by yourself, running from me when I needed you to stay close by my side."

"You didn't need me. You needed something bigger than me, that I couldn't give you."

"You are not me, Mister Haynes. You can't sit there and tell me what I need and don't need."

"Yes, I can, woman. All I was doing was hurting you. I had no idea how to fix your internal pain. I thought if I stayed close that would work. Support your therapeutic sessions that would work. Nothing worked. It wasn't as easy as screwing a screw with a screwdriver. The funny shit is that everything I did seem to do more harm than good."

Tears formed in both of our eyes. We each bit our lower lips to hold them back. We looked away so not to let the other see each other's pain. No one said anything for a moment. We listened to each other's heartbeat. I tuned into that ol' familiar sound of his beating heart. After two minutes of our needed silence, I spoke first.

"You were not supposed to leave me Dupri. That wasn't part of the plan!" I cried.

"No, you're right, that wasn't part of the plan, but neither were your issues. I didn't make plans for that shit, Anna." He tried to look directly into my eyes that couldn't meet his.

"Do you want to know what I planned on?" Sniffling he didn't wait for me to respond. "I planned on asking you to be my wife. I planned that the moment I laid eyes on you. I planned on us having a wedding party of ten. Silver would have been our wedding color of choice. I could watch you walk down the aisle in a tight strapless white wedding dress. Our first dance would have been to Marvin and

Diana, "Special Part of Me." A cruise around tropical islands for our honeymoon was my plan. We would come back to our new house in the Catskills. Later on, after two to three years of marriage, we would have two point five children, with decent college savings. I planned on loving you, sharing everything with you, not the bullshit you forced upon me. None of what I planned happened, none of it. You got consumed with yourself and left me out in the dark. So don't sit there and tell me about plans. I had many." The tear came loose from his right eye and made its way across his straight nose with the slight hump, down his chiseled cheek kissing his shivering lip.

I kissed his salty teardrop lip. "Do you think I wanted that to happen? Do you really think I planned on allowing my craziness to take over our relationship?" I cupped his face in my hand and kissed him again.

"I don't want to sit here and fight any longer, Anna. I'm tired of fighting. Playing the blame game wasn't my intention for this evening."

"I don't want that either."

"I want you back. I want our old life back. The life where we saw every movie and laughed at every joke, I want *that* life back."

"I want that, also Dupri." I kissed him again this time longer. Our lips made soft tender taps unsure of which direction they should go next, but happy with where they were at the moment. We separated in love with each other again. This time it felt different.

"We should get going."

"Yeah we should." I flattened out my dress and reapplied my lipgloss.

Dupri grabbed my hand when I was finished. With my left hand held by his right, he put the car in reverse. He checked the mirrors, backed out and took off out of the gas station. "I think our little break from each other, was good for us. We are no longer the same people."

Was he serious? The distance almost drove me crazy. "I'm not going to say it was good, I will not admit to that." I pouted.

"Come on, Miss Lady, you have to admit we both grew because of it. You became a poet and I became an entrepreneur. That wouldn't have happened if we were still together. We would have been too busy fucking and crying." He let out a boisterous laugh and squeezed my hand. I punched him with my free hand.

"Ouch!"

"Whatever."

"I missed this." This time he kissed my cheek as we approached Kings Highway and Utica Ave. He made the left onto Utica Ave.

I decided it was time to share the truth with Dupri. If we were going to start anew, everything needed to be on the table. No more secrets.

"Dupri, I've something important to tell you." My stomach muscles contracted as my hearts thumping became noticeably louder.

"Go ahead, shoot," he answered with a huge smile.

Without hesitation I said "Dupri, I have a teenage daughter who lives in Italy with her paternal grandparents. She's coming to the States to live with me in a few weeks." Dupri swerved as not to hit the dollar van in front of him.

"Pull over to the spot up ahead and I'll tell you everything," I instructed.

When the car was safely parked his look of heartbreak lingered in the depth of his gaze. I touched his arm but he pulled away. My tears started to fall. Through blurred eyes I looked at his. With profaned eyes, he clenched his teeth tight enough to make his jaw ache running a hand over his face.

I continued despite his chilling look. "I was abused by my stepfather both sexually and physically from the age of five until about sixteen years old, when I finally left home. I met a man, Gianni, we fell in love, and I got pregnant and had a baby girl. Her name is Giovanni Spirit Contadino." I removed the picture I always carried of Spirit and tried to hand it to Dupri. He refused to take it.

I continued anyway. "Her father died and his parents felt it was best that they raise her, being that I was so young. I agreed. It hurt like hell to let her go, but I felt it was good for every party involved." I stopped and wiped my nose with the back of my hand, sniffling twice. Another crease affixed his forehead.

"I made it my business to see Spirit every year. We speak every other day. When I met you I was going to tell you, but you thought I was perfect. I was your precious Anna. I was terrified to show you my insecurities, like giving my daughter away. I didn't want you to think I was any less of a woman." My tears came harder. Instead of wiping

mine away, I reached my hand to wipe his tears, but he pulled away from me. He never once removed his gaze from mine.

"Dupri say something, just don't sit there staring at me." He remained silent. "Dupri, please say something, please say anything."

"Who are you? Who the fuck, are you? All of this time and you are nothing but a fucking lie." His words veered between rage and sadness.

"I was scared, Pumpkin."

"I ain't your Pumpkin, don't ever use that to address me again. I'm Mr. Haynes to you. If you can't call me that, then don't fucking call me. Do you *hear me*?" I nodded scared of his next move.

"You are one sick ass woman. You ain't scared of shit. That shit right there, is another fucking lie."

"I'm not lying. I was scared of what you would think of me."

"You don't really want to know what I think. I think you aren't anything but a coward, a selfish-ass coward. There you have it— my feelings laid out on the table. Are you happy now? Huh, are you fucking happy?"

"I'm not happy Dupri, don't do this. Hear me out; there was a reason for my actions."

"Like I said, please refrain from using my name, it's Mr. Haynes to you. I'm not going to say it again. There is no reason for your stupid actions. If you told me the truth in the beginning, I would have dealt with it, it wouldn't have changed a thing. I would have still loved you. Now I have no respect for you, none, two years, two years thrown down the damn drain because of your stupid insecurities. Two years of nothing but fucking lies. Get out of my car!"

"What?" I was shaking from the force his voice evoked.

"You heard me, get out of my fucking car!" He screamed at the top of his lungs. "Get your shit and get the fuck out. I can't be with a liar." He started sobbing uncontrollably.

"I can't get out: we just found our way back to each other. I can't go now." My cries became heavier. My chest heaved in and out with quick erratic movements.

He let out a loud scream, banging his fists on the steering wheel and on the dashboard. His tears and snot were everywhere. He made no attempt to wipe either away.

"Together? Nothing about this relationship was about togetherness. The entire thing was built on lies. You were too selfish to think about us being together. You were too consumed by your own damn thing. Anna and her insecurities, fuck Dupri and what he needed out of this relationship. This shit right here was and is all you. You have been the driver in this relationship from jump. You have fucked with my head too many times over and I'm putting an end to it. I refuse to have any more sleepless, lonely nights over your dumb ass. You have broken the straw on this camel's back for the last damn time. I want you out of my car."

He gave a sidelong glance. I pulled the mirror down to check my reflection. I didn't want the passerby's to see my tears.

He pushed it back up. "You don't understand I'm not fucking with you. I want you out of my car. I don't want you in here a second longer. You are a bold woman, first a concession of lies, now you want to check out how you look. I'll tell you how you look, you look like shit."

"Please don't—"

"*Please get the fuck out my car!*" He jumped out the car ran around my side and practically ripped the door off the hinges opening it for me.

"GET OUT!" he bellowed.

There we were on the corner of Utica Ave and Ave N. five minutes away from my grandfather's party, with Dupri's face stricken with tears, holding the door open for me. A redhead pushing a twin stroller looked in our direction. I tried to touch him again and he flinched.

"Please just leave me alone, I'm begging you," he said in a whisper

I stopped fighting him and got out of the truck. He slammed the door behind me, got in the car, threw the car in drive, and made a U-turn going back the direction we came. I stood there for a moment hoping, he would come back for me. Apologize for the harsh things he said. It never happened. I walked the few blocks left to the party, dropping a tear with each step I took.

Chapter 41

I walked in my grandpa's birthday bash, wishing Dupri were by my side. I found the bathroom quickly, rushing in to reapply my eye-makeup. I had to be as strong as possible to deal with my mother. No way in hell could she realize that I was crying.

My mother spotted me as I walked out of the bathroom. She smiled, waving me in her direction. She wore a spaghetti-strapped silk dress. The top part was beaded with the finest crystals. She wore open-toed two-inch maroon sandals that matched the dress exactly. My mother looked classy and sophisticated.

Her raccoon-like eyes beamed. She stopped speaking with the partygoers, to greet me. "Anna! I'm glad you could make it," she said as she hugged me.

I hugged her back. I didn't realize how much I had missed my mother. I tried real hard to hold back the tears and she did the same.

"Where is Dupri? I thought October said he was bringing you?" she asked, looking over my shoulder for him.

"He had an emergency at the club. He said he would try to make it. He sends his blessings."

"That's a shame, he's such a fine man. Give him a hug for me next time you see him. Come, come, I told everyone you were coming. Your grandfather has been waiting all evening to see you. You know his health is failing. You should call him, you know? Remember when we had no place to go, he let us into his home? He was your father for a while, don't disrespect him, you hear?" My mother was still giving orders and asking a billion questions.

We walked into the banquet hall, which was dressed in gold and silver accents. Each table was garnished with huge centerpieces of lily of the valley and white gardenias. Gold and silver balloons were splashed throughout the hall. My mother hired a calypso band, which was playing in the corner. The lead singer, light skinned, with medium-length blond dreads and a gold tooth, sang the smooth songs of Allison Hinds, a bajan calypso songstress. A huge banner over her head read: "HAPPY 90TH BIRTHDAY GRANDPA."

My family and friends greeted me as I entered the main dining area. My Aunt Vivian and Auntie Cookie waved at me from their seats. I spotted October and Cho, her fiancée, at a table snacking on hors d'oeuvres. Leave it to my sister to be the first one eating. She raised her eyebrow mouthing, "Where is Dupri?" As she got up to come in my direction, I proceeded over to grandfather.

I kissed my grandpa on the cheek pulling up a chair next to him. "Hi, Grandpa."

"Anna dear! What took you so long?" he said with his failing voice.

"I'm sorry, but I got stuck in traffic."

He patted my knee. "Well, you are here now. How are things? Where is that boyfriend of yours?"

Was everyone going to ask about Dupri? Damn. "He got stuck at work." "He seems like a nice guy, I hope you marry." He whispered.

Well that idea was thrown out the window. I sat with my grandpa a little longer, shooting the breeze and listening to him tell stories of his childhood, until October came and snatched me up. She dragged me back to the bathroom I recently escaped.

"Where's Dupri, Anna?"

I looked at my sister and she instinctively knew the answer.

She grabbed me in her arms and I cried in her shoulder. "You told

him about Spirit?"

"Yes"

"He had a hard time with it?"

"You should've heard him, O. He was so nasty. It was like he hated me. I've pissed him off before and he said some things, but I've never seen him like this. If he could, he would have hit me today." Her jeweled tone lips dropped open. "You can't be serious?"

"I'm serious, October. It was ugly."

"Anna, I'm so sorry. When he called me, I thought everything would be cool. I told him you had something very important to share with him and he said he loved you so much; he was willing to hear anything. I never thought he would react like this."

"Neither did I. He was so pissed he threw me out the car. There were people around and the whole nine yards." My sister stood there with her mouth open. "But as much as I would love to stress over it, I just can't. I'm not going to worry about that. I have to deal with Mother. I'm hurting, yes, but he left me before and I got through it, I'm pretty sure I can do it again."

"You can. Anna?" She opened her evening bag and took out a white legal envelope. "Thank you so much for helping me purchase my first home. I told you I would give it back to you."

I'm shedding entirely too many tears for one woman. But I couldn't help it. The money meant nothing at that moment.

"Keep it. Look at it as a housewarming gift. October I love you and value you. Through all of this you've been right by my side. I'll yell at you on Monday and your calling me Tuesday asking me out. I call you ugly and you call me beautiful. I couldn't have asked for a more enchanting woman to be my sister."

"You are too emotional sometimes. Couldn't you have just sent me an hallmark card." Her huge smile told me she felt what I was saying. I snatched the envelope out of her hand.

"I said you were the emotional one, not me. Give me back that envelope." I smacked her thigh with my purse laughing heartedly.

My sister gave me a strong embrace and kissed me on the cheek. I checked my face and went back out to face my mother again.

Surprisingly with all that happened, the rest of the evening went smoothly. We ate and danced all night long. I was warning Cho about

what his life was going to be like, married to my crazy sister. I even chatted for a minute with Mr. George. I thought that was going to be difficult, but I just looked at him for the pitiful man he really was. My aunt Vivian told me earlier that evening that prostate cancer was eating his insides.

You would think that after all he had put me through that I would be overjoyed. However, that was not the case; I was sick when she told me. No one, regardless of how evil they were, should have to suffer like that. I felt sorry for him, sorry for my mother, and sorry for October; all those people had to live with the effects of his cancer. So when I spoke to him that night at the banquet, I spoke from my heart. I put those years of turmoil where they needed to be, in the past. Both he and I needed a fresh new start.

"How's Spirit?" Mr. George asked.

"She's doing well. She will be coming to New York soon."

"Wow, that's great, for how long?"

"Permanently," I responded, beaming.

"That's good. I was hoping one day she would. Anna I want to say"

"No need to say anything, George."

He smiled at me, reaching out his hand to shake mine. I looked at his hand, but did nothing. I'm trying to forgive, but I can never forget. His once hateful eyes were now laced with desperation, told me he understood.

We continued to talk longer. Excited Spirit was coming home, he offered to take me to the airport the day I was to depart for Italy. I took him up on his offer to give myself peace. We discussed me going back to school to get my PhD and he was all for that. Our conversation was the best we'd had ever.

My Mother, on the other hand, was a different story. She greeted me with warmth when I first walked in but before the night was over she tried her hardest to get under my skin. She criticized my dress, saying I should've worn red instead of black. She asked if I were going to a funeral instead of a party. I sucked it up and ignored her. When I told her that Spirit was coming home, she told me it was about time. I had waited long enough. That was when I lost it and told her I needed to see her annoying Virgo behind in the back.

"Ma, what is your problem?" I snapped. "This is supposed to be a

festive occasion. Why are you trying to get under my skin?"

She wailed in her West-Indian accent still prominent. Her words sang as if she was climbing up a mountain only to be dragged down in a haste "You are still overly sensitive, I see, can't say anything to you with out you getting upset."

"Sensitive? Sensitive? I'll show you sensitive! Since I walked into the place you have been ragging on me. I could have stayed home, for that shit. I told you Spirit was coming home and you tell me crap. What is your *problem*?"

"Spirit should've been with her mother a long time ago. No good mother gives her daughter way."

I wrinkled my arms under my cleavage swaying on the tip of my heels. "What are *you talking* about? You act like since Spirit has been in Italy, that I've been running the streets having more babies. I got my degrees, I'm the best teacher in my school, and I have a hefty savings account. If I may say so myself, I'm pretty all right."

My mother continued with her bullshit, "I'll repeat myself, no good mother leaves her daughter."

"Okay, this must be your shit," I snarled. "You must see yourself in me."

"I have no idea what you're talking about. I never left you." She'd obviously forgotten my early years.

"Do I really have to stand here and go over my childhood with you? You're behind left me, so you could tend to your husband. Don't forget how you locked me in October's closet when I was younger." I sighed and made a conscious decision to release my anger. "Look, I'm not here to fight with you. That was not my goal for coming here today. I came to put the past behind us." She took her handkerchief out her purse and patted her wrinkled brow.

"If I close my eyes today," she began, "I would feel proud of the way I raised my girls. I gave you a roof over your head, a father to replace Taylor, and I clothed you. I did the best I could and I have no regrets."

I shook my head. My mother would never get it. Still saying the same shit she said when I was twelve. She hadn't changed at all. In her eyes she did the best she could, and I wasn't going to try and change her vision any longer. "I love you, Ma," I told her before I walked back in the banquet hall, to say my goodbyes.

Chapter 42

I exhaled deeply staring out the window of the black Lincoln Town owned by Quality Car Service. The moon lurked dazzling bright amongst the stars. It seemed to be given the driver the directions home. I took my hair down from its loosely formed bun and fingered combed it. Cho and October offered to drive me home, but I declined. Too emotionally drained from dealing with Dupri and my mother, I opted to be by myself.

Mother's behavior tonight was so predictable. It couldn't have gone any different if I'd written the script myself. I told October that was the precise reason as to why I didn't want to attend the party. There was not a moment that she didn't try to destroy my spirit with her idle mess. Didn't she want peace? I may not have liked her behavior, but was prepared for it a whole lot more, than Dupri's. I never expected him to react like that to the news of Spirit.

"That's twenty dollars, Miss," the cab driver informed as he pulled up to my home.

"Damn, twenty dollars! That's a whole lot of money." I searched through my purse for my wallet.

He said with an unfamiliar West-Indian accent. "Well, my dear, blame the TLC commission. They raised the fees, so we hafta raise the fares."

I stopped being annoyed over something I couldn't control and handed him the twenty along with a three-dollar tip. Hopefully the little extra would help him with his fees. I double-checked to make sure I hadn't left anything behind, thanked the driver for a safe ride, before slamming the car door behind me. Good thing October wasn't around to witness that. She would never let me hear the end of it.

I kicked off my shoes, unsnapped my bra, and put the key in the door. Exhausted as shit, I couldn't wait to go to sleep and put this dreadful night behind me. Dumping my purse by the television, I flipped on the lights and walked into the kitchen for my nightly tea.

"What in the world are you doing here?" Dupri sat in my kitchen.

"I used my spare key," he answered, his deep voice barely audible.

"For what? What do you want?" I asked with my hand on my hip, annoyed as shit.

"I had to see you before I went to bed tonight. I knew if I called you, you probably would not have answered the phone, and I was too ashamed to come back to the banquet after what happened."

"What do you want, Dupri? Oh, wait I forgot, it's Mr. Haynes."

"Anna, I'm really sorry for they way I acted earlier. I was so caught up in my own emotions, that I lost it."

"Losing it is an understatement. Dupri, you called me some nasty things and then you kicked me out of your truck in the middle of the street. You were acting like I was some stranger on the street. I wish I had a tape recorder so I can play back your audio."

He started in my direction. I raised my hand and stopped him in his tracks, glaring.

"Anna, I wish I can take back everything I said earlier. I was driving around all night beating myself up about what went down. I even came back to the banquet hall. I was going to come inside, but I chickened out and came here, sat in my truck for a minute. After about an hour I said, fuck it, used my key, and came on up. I knew you would head straight into the kitchen, so I just hung out here. I'm truly sorry for everything, I really am." He took off his dark shades revealing his tear filled brown eyes.

I shook my head. "I don't know what to make of this. You kicked me out of your life twice and then you come back, once you realized you made a mistake and feel all should be well. I'll give you the first one. I was not myself, caught up in my own stuff. Like I explained earlier, I was going through it, Dupri. Tonight when I saw you I was nervous yet excited. I was like okay; the Man upstairs is giving us a second chance at this thing called love. I knew I was going to be completely honest with you, no matter what the risk. However, with that being said, I was not prepared for your reaction. It said a lot, Dupri. It said that you and I still need time apart. We are not ready for this. I'm sick and tired of fighting. I've been fighting my whole life. Those fights I couldn't control, but I can control this and I'll be damned if the man I'm with is going to drive me crazy. I have a daughter, Dupri, which I kept from you, I'm totally sorry. If I could do it all over again, I would have told you from the first night when we met. But I didn't, shoot me." I stopped, coming up for air.

"Anna, listen—"

"No, you listen, Dupri, you said enough earlier. I love you, there is no denying that, but our relationship is going to need some revamping. There is so much we have to deal with. I haven't been well for years, but I'm trying to get there. Everyone I keep in my circle has to be supportive of my journey or they can't be around. I want you around, Dupri, but we cannot have another episode of what happened tonight, take place. Also we are going to tackle couple therapy should we get back together." I came to a halt.

"Anna, when I was driving around tonight I realized how wrong I was. But when you told me you had a child, I felt so mislead. It also pained me to know about the abuse you endured. I felt like I had no idea who you truly are. It's a whole part of yourself that you didn't let me into. It made me furious. I work so hard to be a good partner, that I failed somewhere. I truly do love you. I want to revamp our relationship also. I'll do anything to make this right again. If that means going to couple therapy, I'm there." He rubbed his hands together exposing that oh so sexy mole.

"Don't you see, Dupri, when I met you I had no idea who I truly was? I was so busy shucking and jiving from the truth of who I truly was I lied. It was nerve racking keeping up with the lies and such. October use to beg me to tell you, but I just couldn't. But that doesn't dismiss your attitude this evening. But even with that, I love you so fucking much, that's why I'm willing to work at this. Truly work."

"I love you, and I'll work at this also."

I smiled. We had a long road ahead of us, but Dupri was a good man. We spent the rest of the night talking, I mean really talking. I told him all about the abuse. I was honest about the sexual and physical abuse. He allowed me to cry on his chest. He had a hard time hearing the truth about the sexual abuse. But he held it together.

I told him about Gianni and Spirit. I showed him her birth certificate, her baby footprints, her grades, and her pictures.

That night he began to understand why I would rather the lights off when we were making love or shun from him when I was in the shower. I was hiding my stretch marks. We talked about our future. We wrote down what we wanted and what we didn't want. This time I truly opened up and invited Dupri into my heart.

Chapter 43

During the next few weeks, Dupri sold his loft and moved into my brownstone. We both felt it would be better economically to pay one set of bills. Also it would be closer to the lounge and Dupri would no longer have to pay for Manhattan parking.

We grew closer than we ever were during those weeks. We worked together, preparing for Spirit's arrival. I called Spirit one day and they had a lovely conversation. I came in once and caught him on the phone with her, while I was out. I was a little taken aback, but happy that they were bonding.

Couple's therapy was going well also. Sapna recommended a great therapist. She was allowing both of us to see where we helped and hindered each other.

October and I also got closer. I never imagined that our relationship, which I thought, was powerful enough, could possibly go beyond that. It did. We have managed to gain a higher respect for one another. I stopped blaming her for the sins of her father and started counting my blessings we had each other.

We did start therapy. Seeing Sapna with me was not an option. All

three parties involved felt we should see someone else. I released my need to control and allowed October to pick the therapist. Of course since it was October choosing the person, our therapist was a fine brother. She choose Sapna's colleague Shawn Wright. He was an average height brotha with a baldhead and salt and pepper beard. Tober tried to bed him after our first session. I had to remind her that she was now an engaged woman. Something's just don't change.

On the day of the big trip to Italy, as promised Mr. George drove us to the JFK International Airport. We heard the plane's descend and take off all around us as we pulled into the Alitalia Airlines Terminal. As he took my luggage out and placed them on the curb he slipped a hundred-dollar bill in my pocket. I mouthed thank you and waved at him as Dupri and I walked into the terminal.

We checked in at the ticket counter before Dupri ran to the bathroom. I sat on a nearby chair, tapping my feet, with my hands tucked between my legs looking around at no one in particular. I couldn't believe I was bringing my baby home. This was a day I had thought about for so long. I was snapped out of my thoughts by the sound of my sister's and Zoe's idle chatter; I would know those voices anywhere. I turned and was shocked as hell to see them walking toward me, with Dupri bringing up the rear.

"What are you crazy ladies doing here?" I exclaimed.

Before either could chime in, Dupri spoke up. "I invited them to come. I wanted the two people we love more than anything in the world to be with us on this special day." I looked at Zoe, then October, but both women simply, stared at me.

Dupri walked forward and that's when I noticed he was carrying a single white gardenia. He got down on his knee and in the middle of the airport terminal.

"Anna, we've been through the good and bad times, and we are about to embark on a huge journey. But before we leave, I want to know if you'll be my wife." Of course my friendly neighborhood tears showed up. He opened a box with a round solitaire engagement ring, set in platinum.

I looked at Zoe, then October. "Of course, I'll marry you. But first I have to call my dad, Taylor, so he can walk me down the aisle."

Epilogue – Father's Day

I touched my father today, today on Father's Day.

After decades of not feeling his touch

I touched my father today, today on Father's Day

We didn't shake hands nor hug, our souls touched, today on Father's Day

Looking into daddy's eyes I saw the love only a father would have for his little girl

He said, "Anna, you want some chocolate?" I said, "Yes daddy."

I smiled he smiled His eyes danced. His stare touched me. His smile touched me

I never knew so much passion could be felt between father and daughter.

When I got the call a week ago, saying he had a massive stroke

I never thought I would touch him again.

I tucked my pride in my pocket and touched my father.

His touch was still so soothing, still so strong; I was still daddy's little girl

So many years lost between us, so much time passed

I am mad at him for not being there

For not loving me the way I needed

For not being there for the Father and Daughter dance

He missed the birth of his first granddaughter

Now we have touched he'll be there for the birth of his first grandson

He'll meet his grandson right before I marry

We'll play catch up and discuss the plans for walking me down the aisle.

He'll get to know my fiancé Dupri

And spoil is granddaughter Spirit, rotten with candy and treats

He'll get to know me all over again, his daughter he hasn't seen since she was little

My daddy is back!

My daddy is back!

I touched my father today, today on Father's Day